THE
TRUTH

RENDER WILDE

Copyright © 2021 Render Wilde.

The characters, events, and places in this book are fictitious. Any similarity to real persons, living or dead is coincidental and not intended by the author.

All rights reserved. No part of this book may be reproduced, stored, or transmitted by any means—whether auditory, graphic, mechanical, or electronic—without written permission of both publisher and author, except in the case of brief excerpts used in critical articles and reviews. Unauthorized reproduction of any part of this work is illegal and is punishable by law.

ISBN: 978-1-948928-50-2 (sc)
ISBN: 978-1-948928-53-3 (hc)
ISBN: 978-1-948928-75-5 (e)

Because of the dynamic nature of the Internet, any web addresses or links contained in this book may have changed since publication and may no longer be valid. The views expressed in this work are solely those of the author and do not necessarily reflect the views of the publisher, and the publisher hereby disclaims any responsibility for them.

Before we get started, we need to limber up and stretch. Work up a little perspiration and get the heart rate elevated, then you will be ready to read a Wilde book. A song by Jonathan and Melissa Helser called, "I Will Not Be Silent" should do the trick. Just keep moving to the beat. Okay – ready, set, go!

CHAPTER 1

I was sitting behind a desk nervously chomping on a wad of gum. It had lost its flavor some time ago, yet I still nervously chewed on it. I stared down at my hands and noticed I had chewed my nails down to the quick. I was feeling very apprehensive about doing these interviews. If I told them the full and truthful story, well let's say nobody in their right mind was going to believe a thing I told them. I think that is why Joey had a hard time trying to get me to believe all the nonsense I thought he was throwing at me. Once I lived out that nonsense, I no longer can say he's full of shit. Now, they say that about me.

Bob was the first to walk in. He looked more nervous than I did, and with good reason. If I told the full story, he would probably be behind bars before the day was through. He looked over at me before he sat down and mouthed to me that everything was going to be okay. Just relax. I could see his hands were shaking as he looked over some of his notes. I didn't know what I was going to do. I started to have a panic attack and had to do some deep breathing exercises to calm me down.

The next person who walked in with a couple of staffers was the man that would be doing the interviews. He gave me a stern look like he was trying to intimidate me. It was working. If I wasn't nervous enough, I took it to a whole new level. I started to flush. It sure was getting hot in here. I reached down and grabbed the cup of water they had provided me and drank it all. I asked for another. My hands were shaking so badly that I nearly spilled it when the staffer came back with another full cup of water. I had to get my act together, but what was I going to tell them? I looked over at Bob and mouthed to him that I was sorry. I had no choice.

The last man who walked in that would be sitting in on the panel was the one person I didn't think I would ever see again. Why was he here? He was my husband's right-hand man, the man some say drove Urstin to do all the evil things he had done. I heard he got into politics after he and Urstin went their separate ways. How was I going to tell the whole story now that two of the three people sitting on the panel were a great part it?

He looked over at me, gave me a big toothy smile, and said, "Good to see you again, Anna."

I sat in disbelief that this could be happening to me. I just nodded at Ivan and let it go at that.

The man in charge of these classified closed-door meetings was a powerful politician from the great state of California, the place where a lot of the story had taken place. He introduced himself as Walter Bennings, Senator from the State of California. He said we will now proceed in a fact-finding investigation in which we would all be under oath to tell the truth, the whole truth, so help me God. We were all sworn in and it was now time to begin.

Senator Bennings began.

"Anna, I would like to thank you for coming today. I know this won't be easy for you, but I must insist that you give us as much of the story as you can remember without holding anything back. This is a matter of national security. We must find out what happened to the President and why it happened to him."

I stood up and asked him if the President was still alive.

"Yes, he is, but his mind is just not right. I have a picture taken of him just this morning."

He held it up for me to see. Our President, who was nearly seventy years old, looked to be in his late forties. He had a huge smile on his face and looked just great. I let out a fake gasp. The formula had worked on three of the people that I knew of that had taken it – the formula that Maria had stumbled upon. The one thing I was told by my Lord

Himself that could destroy our world as we knew it. The Lord had said that it must be contained and destroyed before it got back out.

The first time it was widely used in the world, it ended up with Noah floating around the world in an ark for a very long time. I sure didn't want that to happen again. I regained my composure, sat back down, and tried to focus.

Bennings said, "You now see why it's so important that we find out what happened." He finished that statement with, "Right, Anna?"

I had known the President had been given a dose of the same stuff that had all begun with Joey, poor Joey. He never knew what hit him. I was the first to see him after the formula had started to work on him. We had been apart for a couple of hours and when I next saw him, I thought I had gone back in time. I looked up at Senator Bennings and stated I was ready to begin.

The staff all took their places and began to record all that I was about to say. I gathered my thoughts and was about to begin when I had an urgent need to go to the bathroom. I had been drinking a lot of water and now it wanted out, and I mean right now.

"I must use the restroom room before we begin."

I stood and headed for the exit and was followed to make sure that I didn't make a run for it. As I sat on the commode, I had a realization that this wasn't going to turn out so well. I wasn't going to be able to tell them everything. My daughter needed to be protected. The Queen Bees had grabbed her in the middle of the night a week after she was born. I was told that she needed to be protected and that if she stayed with me, that wasn't going to happen – she would be dead before her first birthday. The fact that I had given birth in the first place was a miracle all by itself. I asked if I would ever see her again, was shocked when they said probably not. I started to fight them and was quickly brought down and secured. I was told that once Sophia was out of the picture, I would once again be able to have the man of my dreams. All these thoughts ran through my head as I finished up and flushed. I had a story to tell that wasn't going to be believed and surely would be taken as me trying to deceive them. I wondered if my day would end with me being charged for contempt and tossed into a jail cell. I was about to find out.

* * *

The story begins.

I sat down and began my story. "Let me begin where this story has its roots. I was in the director's office talking to Bob, who is sitting to your right."

Everyone immediately turned to stare at Bob.

He spoke now, "That's right, I had an assignment that needed an agent. Anna volunteered for it."

I thought to myself, well I did kind of, but I felt I didn't have a choice. I was a walking dead lady anyway. I was looking at witness protection and I knew it wouldn't be long before they found me – they always find you.

"I've got this, Bob. Please let me speak."

He nodded for me to continue. I wondered if he was going to keep interjecting when he thought he was going to look bad. Which I was sure was going to be quite a bit.

"He was on the phone with someone, I didn't know who he was talking to, but I could see he was upset and concerned. When he hung up the phone, he asked me to take the mission."

Immediately Bob stood and protested. Walter started to bang his gavel and called for order.

"If this kind of behavior occurs again, I will have you removed from this hearing and hold you in contempt. Are we clear?"

Bob sat back down and glared at me. We had a few issues along this very bumpy road and I sure as hell wasn't going to soft ball him.

"Sir, I apologize. Let me start over." I was such a fool.

"I wasn't ordered to take this mission, but I didn't volunteer for it. My husband is Urstin Trevosky. I married him while working undercover trying to expose his group of criminals, one of them sits to your left as I speak."

Ivan stood up to protest, but quickly sat back down when Walter reached for his gavel. Walter looked at Ivan and mumbled, "You will have your chance. Please let her tell it, and then we can sort through all the lies and distortions."

I looked at Ivan to see how he would react. He seemed calm and full of himself. He must have the goods on a lot of people in this town. My bet is he could take down half this town with his stories. Helen Harrison was bad enough, but when Urstin and Ivan teamed up with her, they were formidable. We came very close to the country falling into their hands. I was sure their plan wasn't finalized. I could tell something was in the works. I just didn't know what it was. I was out of the loop for over a year having my baby. It was what happened leading up to that event that had us all here at this time.

"Well, as I was saying, my husband was very mad at me for foiling a plan of his and now wanted me dead. I knew with all his contacts and friends that even if I went into witness protection that they would find me, so when the opportunity arose to save the President from an assassination attempt, I jumped at it. I was told only the area where it would take place and to watch for Joey Hopkins. If I found him, I would find the assassin."

Walter jumped in and spoke now. "So, you say that Joey Hopkins, the movie star, was the assassin."

"No, I'm not saying that at all, I said, find him and you will find the assassin."

I watched Walter Bennings throw his hands in the air.

"Please clarify for us, Anna. You're making it sound like Mr. Hopkins is the assassin."

"Sorry, no. Joey knew where he would be, I just had to find him and then I knew I would be able to find the person I was looking for."

"Sounds like Joey was in on it then."

"Let me begin again. I can see this isn't going to be easy."

CHAPTER 2

Joey's place in the story.

I was playing with Jackson when he came into the room. Another emergency in the world that only we could prevent from becoming a national disaster. Scarlett was in the kitchen cleaning the breakfast mess I had made making pancakes and bacon for all of us. I admit I might have caused a little of a mess, but she was carrying on like I had trashed the place. I heard her cussing me out more than once.

"How does he get grease on the ceiling?!" she was shouting now. Lucky me when Jacob came into the room, I saw it as a possible way to escape her fury.

"Old dude, we are needed in LA. Book a flight right now. We have to be there before the sun comes up tomorrow."

He still can't resist giving me a hard time. I make one small mistake, he makes me pay for it for the rest of my life. I wish I hadn't hit him in the head with that bat, but I couldn't take it back now. My luck being what it is, I ended up getting him as my guardian angel, the seventh one, he so frequently liked to add. As for his wife, well I still don't think that is entirely my fault, I did try to resist. I must admit I did get a very wonderful daughter out of that one.

Scarlett popped her head around the corner. She had Katrina in her arms.

"Clean her up. She is covered in syrup."

I was handed a very sticky little girl. Jackson laughed at me. I noticed he needed to be cleaned up as well, so I dragged them into the bathroom. Jacob followed us in complaining all the way.

"Joey, I know you have a lot to do here, but we are needed in LA right now. We have got to be on our way."

"Okay, just let me take care of things here for the time being."

I washed the children up and got them all squeaky clean. I was just about to walk out when Scarlett pushed us all out of the way and dove for the toilet. I didn't think my cooking was that bad. Concerned, I asked if she was alright. She raised her head from the toilet and exclaimed that she better be, turned back, and heaved some more. Confused, I exited the bathroom with the children and waited for her in the living room. When she came out, I told her I needed to head to LA on some business and had to leave right away.

She gave me a look and stated, "I need to head out and switch back with Maria next week. Will you still be out there?"

I knew she had the biggest film of her life coming up. They were about to begin filming and no way was she going to allow Maria to do this one like she did the last one. All I heard lately from everyone was how good she was in that last film and that it was like she had taken it to the next level. When you're already one of the best in the industry and they start heaping compliments on you like that, it's hard to swallow when you know your mirror image did the film for you. I also had a film coming up, but no face time. It was voiceover work. An animated film where I would be playing this cute little panda bear and Maria was going to be playing a squirrel with an attitude. It was the perfect part for her.

I called my friend Billy and asked if he could get me to LA tonight. He didn't have anything for a few days. I knew I had free airline tickets any time I wanted to fly, but because of all the mishaps every time I got on a plane, people would see me and start getting off the flight in fear for their lives. It was so bad that the airlines started removing me from the flight so that they still had passengers to fly. I started to use Billy. He had private jets and cargo planes. It was nice when he would pick me up in one of the private jets, but lately, it had been cargo planes. I froze my ass off every time I flew that way. The nice private jet he had was still on top of the mountain, crashed beside the lake. I remember that flight fondly. I joined the mile-high club on that one, and no, that's not what made the plane crash. That was Scarlett's fault. She looks so much like Maria that the assassins mixed her up and thought they were killing Maria, and I was just a bonus prize for them. Our fuel lines were tampered with and when we were crashing, Scarlett decided she wanted to go out with a bang. I was just along for the ride. Fortunately, Billy is a great pilot and it was wintertime. The lake was frozen, so we had a place to crash land.

I looked at Jacob when I got off the phone and told him it wasn't going to happen. I couldn't get us a ride to LA in time.

"Bullshit. Say goodbye to Scarlett. We leave in another minute."

I wasn't sure what he had going through his mind. I went to find Scarlett and found her rubbing her breast like they were sore or something.

"Are you okay? You seem to be very moody and that episode in the bathroom this morning has me concerned."

She looked up at me with a look that might have been able to kill me if she had those superpowers.

"You best hope I'm okay. Call me when you get in so that I know you made it safe."

I promised that I would, kissed her, and walked outside to find my spirit friend and inquire what our mode of travel was going to be. He grabbed me by my hand, and we walked straight into a flash of bright light. I absolutely hate traveling this way. Not only does he break my watch every time we do this, but sometimes I lose time doing it this way. I looked around to see where he had taken me. Right away I recognized Scarlett's house. The problem was the sun was about to make its appearance. I had lost close to a whole day on this little trip through time and space. I yelled at him for doing this to me. At least the last few times, they were life and death situations.

"Why must you do these things to me, Jacob?"

He laughed. "I got you here, didn't I?"

I stormed off beating on my watch to see if I could get it going again. Looked like another one was headed for the dumpster. I was frustrated when I entered the house. I thought maybe I would find Maria fast asleep in bed. If that was only the case. I walked into a nightmare of Maria's making. The place looked like a mad scientist lived there. I must admit, she was something of a mad scientist. When she discovered the cure for cancer that almost got us all killed, I didn't know if I hated or loved her. When it ended up saving Jackson's life, I could only thank her for everything she had done. Now it looked like she was up to her old tricks. I could only hope this wouldn't get us all killed this time.

CHAPTER 3

Maria gets curious. Time to experiment.

I was bored between scenes and was sitting in my dressing room. They were doing the action scenes where I came in and fought all these stupid bad guys. Right now, they were putting the set back together to do a retake because I accidentally kicked one of the stuntmen in the nuts and he fell out and ruined the scene. I thought he should have worn a cup. Accidents do happen you know. They told me I would have about fifteen to thirty minutes to kill, go grab some lunch. I couldn't eat, way too much tension. I grabbed a Gideons Bible and started to read. Those folks leave these bibles everywhere.

I started at the beginning and began to read. I was fascinated by the fact that some of the people from early times lived so long. The circuits in my brain started firing off and I began to formulate an idea. What if there was a formula that they took that enabled them to live so long? A formula that had long been lost but still existed. I had a degree in chemistry and started to think about all the ways chemicals react to one another and how some elements could be deadly by themselves; combined they were necessary for life.

I had an idea and as soon as I finish up today, I'm going to refine that idea. The last idea I had almost got us all killed. I thought the world would welcome the cure for cancer. I didn't realize that the powers that be would frown on that discovery. They crushed it like a bug and denounced it as way too dangerous. The Viagra half of the formula they just loved. I noticed they were trying mighty hard to reproduce that part of the formula. I was sure that was the most dangerous part of the mixture I had concocted.

I did some research on the way home. The traffic sucks here in LA, and I had plenty of time to use my phone to do the research. I had almost gotten home when I found it. I turned my car around and headed for my favorite college. UCLA here I come. I sure hope the last student I used there was going to recover from all his injuries. The powerful bad guys roughed the boy up pretty good trying to get information on what he had supplied me. Even after he told them, they still beat him to an inch of his life. I thought maybe I should take a different approach this time, but I figured who would care about a drug that could make you live a few extra years? Sometimes smart people can be so stupid.

The student who finally agreed to help me was a bit of a jerk. He had demands. A movie star that gave him good time demands. No way was I going to go to bed with this idiot, but there were other services I knew I could get him to agree to. So, If I wanted the Pharaoh Cicadas, I had to put my big mouth and ideas to work. When we exited the utility closet, he had a big smile on his face, and I had to wash my mouth out with soap. I swore as soon as I got out of there, I was going to stop and get some nacho chips and the hottest salsa I could find to wash the taste from my mouth.

The student came out with my prize and I rewarded him with a big kiss full on the lips. Even gave him a little tongue. It didn't seem to bother him in the slightest. I spun and left the college in a huff. I had to get to the supermarket fast. I needed the rest of the items I would be using. A lot of foods with antioxidants. The wheels were spinning fast in my head. I knew without a doubt this was going to be a sleepless night.

When I got to the supermarket, I noticed some homeless people.

I needed guinea pigs. These people needed shelter and food. It would be a nice trade-off. When I left with all the items I would need, I had very little room left in my car. I had plenty of volunteers that wanted to hang with Scarlett Davis for the evening. I didn't have the heart to tell them I wasn't her, but they would never know the difference anyway. I laughed. I did more as her than she did lately. I couldn't believe all the job offers she got from my performance at the Academy Awards. The headlines said that it was a true Academy Award experience. I was kind of drunk and just a little pissed off, well maybe I was really pissed off – a lot of pent-up aggravation escaped from me that night. I was trying to ruin her career, and instead made her a bigger star than she already was, go figure.

When we got to Scarlett's house, I put everyone in a room and treated them like kings. I fired up the big screen TV and made sure they were well fed. I wanted happy and willing folks to work with. I hoped I didn't hurt anyone, but I knew that nothing I would be giving them had anything that might hurt them. I would use the blender to make sure the cicadas wouldn't be noticed in the drink I was going to give them.

The kitchen was full of all the stuff I was mixing all together, and I decided I would make it into a nice smoothie. I was also furiously working on some very spiced-up nachos. They were flaming hot and my lips were numb from the burn. Sweat poured off my brow and made it hard to see. I ate a lot more. I had to get that taste out of my mouth. The things I did to get the stuff I needed. I could have waited another sixteen years and got all the cicadas I would ever need. I'm not sure what happened that morning when Joey walked in. I gave him the same stuff that I gave to the homeless folks. The results were quite different. It didn't work at all on them, and Joey – well, that was another story. The next time I saw him, he was twenty years younger and looking terrific. He wasn't very happy about it. No appreciation at all. I would have to find out what he ate after he left my place. All I knew for sure was, he had done something different and I needed to find out what that was.

CHAPTER 4

Joey arrives to save the day.

I walked into Scarlett's place to find that Maria had set up the kitchen to look like a scientific lab. She had Bunsen burners going with stuff heating up inside. Piles of food items cut and tossed all about. A blender full of ice and other items whirling away. Test tubes and chemicals lay about on the counters and table. I was about to yell at her and ask her what in the world was she up to now when she came out of nowhere and planted a huge tongue-filled kiss on my unsuspecting lips. I felt them burn immediately and was in desperate need to cool my mouth and lips. She handed me a fresh smoothie and I gulped it down in need of its cooling pleasures. What had she been eating that would have set my whole mouth on fire? She giggled and said that she had been eating fire nachos.

"I bought this pepper called the Carolina Reaper. I'm having trouble feeling my lips, but I love it."

I hadn't even eaten any and I was having trouble as well. I just shook my head and looked around the house. There were about five people that were obviously without lodging, camping out on Scarlett's living room floor.

"Maria, what are you up to?" I asked this tentatively because I knew she was always up to something that usually turned into a lot of pain and suffering on my part as I got caught up in her little schemes.

She shrugged, "I had an idea and I needed some test subjects. They are my volunteers."

"Do they know what they are volunteering for?"

"Yeah, I had this idea for this great new smoothie, and they are my taste testers. By the way, did you like yours?"

Great! I was part of her test subjects. God only knew what would happen to me. By the end of the day, I would know, but I didn't know that at the time.

I asked her if I could borrow her car as I had a very important meeting that I couldn't miss, and I had no way of getting there. She never bothered to ask me how I got to the house, just tossed me the keys, and said she needed gas.

"I have got to be back to the studio by noon. We are finishing up my scenes and then Scarlett will have another movie under her belt. Good thing she only had a few small parts in this one."

I told her I would do my best to have her car back in time. I never realized it would be over a week before I saw her again. When I did see her again, I wouldn't quite look the same. I really hate her and her mad ideas and formulas.

I got in the car and fired it up only to be greeted by the low fuel light. If I made it to the gas station, I figured it would be a miracle. Jacob was whining and complaining about how long it was taking, and I was having a hard time tuning him out.

I snapped at him and said, "You want me to push the car all the way to our destination?"

That shut him up, but only for a few minutes. I pulled up to the pumps and started to get some fuel into the tank when a canteen truck pulled up beside me. He had something cooking in there that smelled terrific and I couldn't help myself because my stomach was growling so much.

"Something sure does smell great." I was making small talk while the gas was filling up Maria's car. The driver smiled at me and told me he had just got a shipment of these wonderful clams from Iceland.

"You have got to try these," he said as he handed me a quart of them with a side of butter. "The best you have ever tasted," he exclaimed to me. I was very hungry, so how could I refuse?

"What do I owe you?" I asked him as I was fishing in my pocket for my wallet.

"On the house my friend. You have a great day."

He smiled, got in his truck, and drove away. Funny I never saw him put any gas into his vehicle. I had bigger fish to fry, or rather to devour. I got back into the car and dove into those clams. I heard Jacob warning me, but I just shut him out. I was tired of all his whining and complaining all morning. Those clams didn't stand a chance and I made good use of the butter. I made a small mess, but fortunately, Maria had plenty of napkins in the glove box.

We finally made it to our destination. I asked Jacob if he knew what the emergency was and where we were heading. He said that he did, but we had to find the spot. He wasn't exactly sure, so we would have to search for it. I parked and we headed down this street that looked like an urban campground. Tents were set up in every spot you could find. I had to watch my step so that I didn't step into any feces. The smell was the worst, I felt like I was in an outdoor outhouse. I used my fingers to block my nose and walked down the street with Jacob searching for the spot where it would all go down. We stopped about halfway down the street. A tent with red and white stripes was to our left and Jacob stood and stared at it. The way he was looking at it convinced me we had arrived.

"What now Jacob?" I asked him as somebody reached over and put their hand on my shoulder. I whirled and was about to throw a punch when I recognized the person under the hoodie. You can never miss those lovely green eyes. They just pop out at you and are unforgettable.

"Anna. What are you doing here?"

"I'm saving you, Joey, like you have done for me so many times. Get out of here. It's going to get ugly very fast and I don't want to see you get hurt."

"Anna, I got this. I just don't know what I got. Do you know?"

She stared at me and shook her head.

"There is an assassin in that tent. The President of the United States is going to stick his fat head in that tent, and he is going to die a quick death unless I stop it. You can't do this. I must be the one. Now please let me do my job, Joey," she pleaded with me, gave me those pretty green eyes to stare into. I melted like butter in the summer heat.

I gave in to her and let her do her thing. Jacob was pitching a fit. I walked away and headed back to the car. When I got back into the car, I noticed that I had lost Jacob somewhere. I sat there and tried to figure out what just happened. I came to the sudden realization that I might have screwed up. I wondered if I didn't just let the real assassin go into that tent to wait for the President. I began to become worried. My stomach started to mix with that smoothie and those clams, and I thought I was going to be sick. I opened the door to retch, but nothing happened. I broke out in a cold sweat and felt slightly lightheaded. I thought I might pass out. My breathing started to increase, and my body began to ache. Suddenly I was hot all over and thought I might be having an allergic reaction to the clams.

I exited the car and walked around it for a few minutes until the feeling subsided. Within a few minutes, I was feeling much better and returned to the car. I turned on the radio and felt like I was going to be sick all over again. The President had been taken hostage and was in a life-or-death situation as we speak. The news described what Anna had been wearing as the person who had taken the President hostage. I was so screwed. How could I have messed everything up so badly? I thought it was very easy for me to mess things up. It was what I was good at, seems like I had done it again. That feeling disappeared when Anna dropped out of nowhere and into my lap. She took one look at me and nearly passed out. I was sitting inside the car by myself one second, and the next I had this beautiful woman sitting in my lap barely conscious.

This could have only been the work of Jacob. What the hell did he do now?

CHAPTER 5

Anna explains.

Walter Bennings stood up and asked for a break. We would be taking a short break, so I sprinted for the restroom as all the water I had drunk was now asking to be released. When I came out, he was waiting for me. I knew who he was, had sat in the car with him on the night of the second assassination attempt. This time it wouldn't have just been the President. It was going to be more than half of all the political players in Washington. The only survivors were going to be the ones that had been vaccinated from the deadly virus that was going to be released. Those that had been vaccinated were all bought and paid for and this country was going to be taken over by the most corrupt and vile people that we had ever encountered. It was his plan that had foiled it all. At least that was what he said. He held Maria's manuscript in his hands and read what was going to happen. He just wanted to watch from the parking garage and see if it all came out as she had written. Thankfully for Joey, it had. I think R.J. Ted might have had a hand in the outcome as well, but that's another story for later.

"Anna, I must warn you. We need to tell them the complete story. It would make me very happy if you left my part out of it. I know what Bob and Ivan have done in the past, so feel free to get that all transcribed. Please, Anna, don't let them know I was involved. This country depends on it. The few of us that remain hidden in the shadows are all that keep us from going down the tubes. Do you understand?"

I told him I did and would do my best to keep from shining a light on him. I watched him walk away as I stood there and tried to gather my composure. Every time I thought I knew who the bad guys were and who the good guys were, I got it wrong. The only two that I knew for sure that were on my side were Joey and R.J. I loved them both, but R.J. will always be the love of my life. I ended up having Joey's child, but I would have rather had R.J.'s.

I put these thoughts back where they belong and began to focus on what I was going to reveal next. They weren't going to believe what I was going to tell them, I knew this, but I knew no other way. I sat down and stared up at Bob. He had not aged a day since he had taken the formula. He said there were others in that group, but they never turned up. It was only him, Joey, and now the President. That was it that I knew for certain had changed. My guess is that my story was going to sound so unbelievable that he was going to be able to get away with his part in all of this. My problem, how to make it sound like a perfectly sane person was telling a totally insane tale and make it sound believable.

I looked up and watched Walter take his seat and bang on his gavel. Ivan slipped back in and quickly sat down. He had a huge smile on his face. If he was smiling, then something was about to take place. I still can't believe he was an undercover CIA. He did way too many evil things to possibly be playing for the good guys. I would have to watch my back closely.

I began, "Let me tell you what happened when I entered the tent and I will take you through the rest of that day."

Here we go. I remembered that day well as I told the story.

I entered the tent to find a man dressed the same as I was, sitting in the back of the tent. I squeezed in beside him like I belonged there and listened to his protests and how he wanted me to leave right now. I straddled him and looked him right in the eyes. He remained transfixed on my stare as I pumped him full of a sedative that would keep him quiet for a little while. It would give me enough time to save the President. I was still working the plan out in my head when I felt someone sit down beside me. It must have been hard for him to reveal himself to me, him being a spirit and all. I knew him from when I was working in Richmond. He was a rookie agent that just got his first undercover assignment. It was his job to infiltrate the Gambella family using Rocco's daughter, Maria. I went to his funeral about a year later. Now, many years since he died, he was sitting beside me and I was sure I had lost my mind. I couldn't remember his name, just his face.

He laughed at me and said, "I guess you can see me. I noticed you even recognize me."

I just sat with my mouth open, I had no idea what to say.

"My name is Jacob by the way, just in case you forgot. I'm here to help you live through this day. If you listen to what I tell you to do, you might see another sunset." That sure was reassuring. "Joey thought you might need my help, so he devised a plan. You must tell the President that this is Joey's plan to save his sorry ass."

I laughed. "You want me to tell the President that Joey came up with a plan to save him?"

"That's right, and make sure you use the phrase about his ass."

I was skeptical. I didn't know at the time how much mischief Jacob was always getting Joey into.

We went through the plan and he told me it had to be done with precision timing. If we didn't get the timing down just right, the wrong person was going to die today. That person would be me, and I thought he was right, get the timing perfect.

I waited for him to show up. Right on cue, he sticks his head in the tent and I leaped up and held the syringe I had brought which contained pure heroin to his throat. Enough to send any full-sized man to his death within a short time from a massive overdose. I held it to his throat with just the tip of the needle slightly poking into his skin. I whispered in his ear the only choices that remained for him and if he wanted to live, he had best listen to everything I instructed him to do. I told him to give the order to his secret service agents to stand down and retrieve his SUV that he came in here today. He complied, but as he was doing so gave a snide remark to the head of his secret service.

I heard him say, "Gary, if I live through this day, you're fired."

I told him to stick with the plan and jabbed him just a little harder.

The SUV arrived and just as Jacob had said, there were two agents in the front seat. He had told me one was good and the other was bad, he just didn't know which was which. We had to put on a show for the two of them as they would be our witnesses to what was going to happen in the SUV.

I had the President sitting below me while I straddled his body, my head in close to his so I could give him instructions and information that his men in the front seat would be unable to hear. I was in so close I could feel his whiskers against my face and smell his aftershave. He had the same feelings, as he could feel my soft body and smooth face against his. No way was he going to confuse me with a man sitting before him. He also got a good look into my eyes and I think they were burned into his memory banks. I gave him the information Jacob had instructed me to give him, and what was about to happen.

"You've been set up by your own secret service. This was an assassination attempt, and it would have worked if I didn't interfere. Joey Hopkins came up with this plan to save your sorry ass. I hope you thank him someday. In about a minute, you're going to take the knife in my pocket and stab me to death. If you hesitate, it will cost you your life. As soon as you hear the flashbang go off, reach for the knife and kill me. Do you understand?"

"Why do you want me to kill you?"

"If you don't, I kill you – isn't that enough incentive for you?"

"I guess since you put it that way, I have no choice."

"That's right, and neither do I. Remember that, and don't hesitate."

I was very forceful with that last statement. Now, all we had to do was wait. It seemed like an eternity. I heard the flashbang hit the floor, where it came from, I couldn't tell you for sure. The President's hand was in my pocket holding onto the knife and the next thing I knew, I had gone back in time about twenty years, at least that was what I thought. I was sitting on Joey's lap in a car. Joey looked to be about twenty years younger than when I last saw him a couple hours ago. I must have gone back in time right, wrong. I was so overwhelmed with what had taken place that I might have passed out for a moment or two.

When I did come to my senses, I was sure I had finally gone insane. I was going to need therapy for years to come after this day.

Joey got me back into the here and now. He tried to explain how everything that I told him could happen. He even showed me his watch, which was still broken but that he was still wearing for some strange reason. When I told him why I thought I had gone back in time, he grabbed the rearview mirror and stared at his reflection. I heard him mumble something about how he was going to kill her. I didn't know who he was talking about then, but now it's easy to see he was referring to Maria and her magic potion.

I thought I had explained what I thought they might believe. The rest of that day I wasn't even going to attempt to tell them about, but I just might let you in on a little secret. That secret being that there was a disturbance in the universe that day. The battle between good and evil had taken a turn, and it wasn't a turn for the best. Joey and I had started up the car and had just begun to get back into city traffic when it happened.

One minute we're driving down a busy city street, the next we're trying to recover from a blinding flash of light. Joey slams on the brakes practically putting me through the windshield. I look out the side window and ask Joey, "Where are we?"

He replies, "Not in LA anymore, that's for sure."

I was staring at what looked like a rural area out in the Midwest. Not a paved road to be found, not a building or person in sight. We were just in a busy city and now we were someplace else. Maybe I did go insane and this was all part of my new mental illness. If so, then Joey was sharing my mental state of mind. We got out of the car and looked around. In the distance, I saw a man on a white horse heading in our direction. He had on a Stetson hat, dungarees, and a Western shirt. I noticed his feet were encased in an old-style riding boot, minus the spurs. He had a beard and long hair.

He rode up and greeted us both by name, as if he had known us for years and we were his best friends. Joey knew who he was, but I never recalled meeting the man. He invited us for ice cream, pointed out a trail that would take us to the meeting spot, and said he would meet us there shortly. He had another guest that needed to be at the meeting. He smiled at us and rode away in a cloud of dust.

"Joey, who was that?"

"That man, Anna, was your savior, Christ our Lord. Jesus in the flesh."

Had we died in a vicious car accident and I was just finding out I was dead? Was I in heaven and just didn't know it? All this and a lot more I would find out shortly.

We found the ice cream shop and took a seat. The first person that walked in was Jacob. I quickly stood up as I could tell he was no spirit anymore. He was solid flesh and blood. He gave me a hug and told me I had done a wonderful job and our plan worked out perfectly. He turned and introduced me to a young lady that was just entering.

"This is Mrs. B. She helped us today. Without her, I wouldn't have been able to pull it all off by myself."

I shook her hand and we all sat down. Two riders approached at a very fast gallop. One rider was dressed all in black while the other was the man on the white horse – the one that Joey said was Jesus. They entered and sat down with us. We were all at the same table. It was the only one in the place and we were served the best ice cream I had ever tasted. Once we finished, the meeting began.

Jesus stood.

"A very dangerous thing has been released upon the earth that could destroy all life as we know it down below. Once, this formula was widely used by the masses down below. It proved to be much too dangerous to remain in existence and Father decided to do a reset and remove it from the world. You might have heard of the story of Noah and the ark. What you might not have known was that the reason the world had to be destroyed was because of that formula. Noah and his family were the last to use it to help repopulate the earth, but it died with him. Now, because of the mischief that Lucifer has done, it is once again upon the earth, ready to be found and used by the many innocent people that will be corrupted by this sinister concoction. It is easy to be bad, but it is very hard to be good. The longer you exist in that environment, the easier it is to be corrupted."

The man in black said, "I had nothing to do with this. How can you stand there and say this is all my fault?"

That is when it happened. I saw something that day I hope I never see again. Jesus and Lucifer were standing nose to nose in an argument that you might have seen before on a baseball field with an umpire and manager going at it. I wasn't sure if this meeting was going to come to fisticuffs or not. As quickly as it started, it was over with Lucifer sitting back in his seat and apologizing for his misbehavior. I was dumbfounded. I wasn't sure what I had just witnessed but was glad that it was over. The meeting broke up and Jesus asked me to stay for a private conversation.

"Anna, I have to ask you to stay away from R.J., at least for a few years. I have a very important mission for him, and you will distract him from it. I won't have the best and only man that can do the job if you're in the picture."

I started to cry. I really wanted to be with him. Jesus hugged me and told me he knew how difficult this was going to be.

"I also have a very important mission for you. Now that the formula has been released back to the earth, I need you to find it and destroy it. Lucifer will be doing everything in his power to make sure it gets back into use. It must not, or the end is imminent. You have seen what it has done to Joey, but you don't know all of it. He will not age again for fifteen years, then if he takes the formula again, he will not age for another fifteen years. The formula becomes available every seventeen years. It only works on men. It will kill a female within hours if she takes it. That's all the information I can give you on it."

He patted me on the shoulder and told me he would help me along the way as much as he could. When he touched me, I felt different, like he had healed my soul and I felt very good inside. I thanked him and went to find Joey. I told Joey what Jesus had told me as we made our way back to the car.

"Joey, how are we going to get back?"

"Get in. I'll show you."

He fired up the car and got us going down the dirt road at breakneck speed. He hit the brake and that caused the car to be engulfed in a cloud of dust and smoke.

"I thought for sure that would work," I heard him say.

As the dust subsided, our view of the outside world came back into focus.

"I guess it did work," he said with a big smile.

We were back in LA right where we started from. The only difference was, we had lost a whole week in the few hours we were gone.

CHAPTER 6

The Presidential view of things.

I lay in bed dreaming of the day's events. It was a nightmare come true of a day. I wasn't concerned that they had tried to kill me. I had been wondering when they would make their first move. I wasn't very much liked in this town, so an attempt on my life was what I was expecting. My head of security, being the one person I thought I could trust, had let me down. I knew for certain he was the one that had orchestrated the whole event today. The smirk on his face as that woman led me to my SUV with the syringe poking into my neck containing deadly heroin that would take my life rather quickly was a dead giveaway. I had to let him know I knew, so I told him if I lived, he would be fired right in front of all those cameras that were recording the whole scene.

Something went wrong, something that wasn't part of their plan. This woman that had taken me hostage wasn't the one that was supposed to do it. I could see it in his eyes once he realized what was going on. When I got into the SUV with the crazy lady, that's when things started to become slightly weird. Let me try to explain. I have a weakness for dominant women. This lady was doing her best impression of a very dominant person. She took control right from the start and I was butter in her hands. I was also in fear for my life and hard as a rock. I told you it was weird.

Let me start from my days as a representative of the great state of Georgia. I had the Twelfth District and my lovely wife had the Fourth District. She also had the whole state eating out of her hand. She was just the kind of woman I had always desired and I was just the kind of husband she needed. One that she could order around, but strong enough that people could take seriously. I was good at playing the con game and we were both very serious players in the state. She had White House aspirations. I had my doubts. As a man, I didn't want to be labeled as the First Gentleman of the United States. It was a matter of pride to me. I thought I was only going to put a wrench in her plans. It was supposed to be an accident. One that would force her to give up her run for president and let me go back to my nice quiet life. If only it had happened that way.

Helen Harrison wanted to be the first female president. I was fine with that, so we formulated a plan together. She had people that could make accidents happen; I was a fool and let her know exactly where and when they could make their accident happen. It turned out to be a disaster for me and Helen. My wife ran into a very large white oak tree with one of her assistants by her side. They were traveling over eighty miles per hour and stopped rather abruptly when they hit the tree. My wife was DOA, and her assistant lived a few hours more before succumbing to his injuries. Rumors of her having an affair with the man circulated and other rumors followed. Never once did any attention to her death fall on me. That was a relief. I was guilty as sin. I wasn't the only one, Helen had played her part as well.

I was grief-stricken. She was only supposed to be injured, not murdered. Helen contacted me and told me I had best keep my big mouth shut. She had plans and didn't want anything to ruin them. I was so mad at her I picked up the torch and ran with it. My wife, her name was Stacey, my first name is Stanley. All the posters and paraphernalia read Adams for President. In my grief and sorrow, I decided to play the con game and picked up where my wife had stopped. I was now running in her place. I played it up for the country, and it was working. Helen and I were neck and neck all through the primaries. She already had a plan in place to take down the top candidate from the other party.

Whoever won our primary was going to be the next president, she had made sure of it.

A few days before super Tuesday, the video was released to the world. A video of Helen rolling around in a pile of dung raging like a madwoman sealed her fate. It went viral and showed the whole world just what type of a person they would be getting. I won in a landslide. The other candidate was disgraced just like Helen had laid out and the next thing I knew, I was sworn in as the President of the United States. Funny how things work out like that.

I had no business being anywhere near this office, yet here I was. I had done so much bad stuff on my way to this post, yet it was all buried. All I had to do was tote the line. Give the fat cats that hide behind the curtain just what they want, and all would be good. It made me sick. I started to stray away from what they wanted, and wouldn't you know, suddenly I was a target. The trip to LA to try to reform all the homelessness was a start to my plan. I stepped on a lot of toes, but thought it had to be done. I wanted to tour a particularly bad street and get some firsthand information from these people camping in the streets. The secret service had the job of canvassing the area and made sure it was safe for me. They did their job except for one tent. The one they led me to, where their assassin waited. Except he wasn't there – she was. This is the second part of my story, the dominant woman.

After my wife passed, I was now a single man in search of a woman who would control me and keep me in line. That person turned out to be Bethany Devlin. She ran a salon just north of Gainesville, Georgia and I had met her by accident one day in a grocery store. She was in a big hurry and I was not. I was off in my own little world just meandering around the store and she had to get her stuff and go. We crashed our carts in aisle nine. Knocked me flat on my ass. She scolded me and told me what an idiot I was. Got right in my face and was shouting at me. I was in love. I asked her if I could make it up to her and if I could help her in any way. She gave me one of those cat-got-the-mouse look in her eyes and I was given a phone number and an address. "Make sure you're not late," was the last thing she said to me.

When I got to her house, I was in for the surprise of my life. She was a dominant woman alright. It was one of her jobs you might say, and she was very good at what she did. Expensive as well, but I paid and kept right on coming back for more. I was a fool. I realized I had to stop. The stakes were too high for my little kinks to be getting in the way. I would detail more of what we did, but this is not what this story is all about. It is about how it all came about and where it all ended up, which I will get to.

In the SUV, she was straddling me and giving me instructions on what to do and when to do it. I was informed that one of the two agents in the front seat was not on my side. She didn't know which one was which, neither did I. I did my best to hide my excitement, but those green eyes just bore right through me. The fact that she had me pinned and helpless to her every move was driving me wild.

She explained what Joey Hopkins had done and how he had saved my sorry ass. Now I must repay the favor and plunge a knife that she had in her hoodie into that beautiful chest of hers. If I didn't do it, I was a dead man. I don't know if I can do this. My breath became short and I thought I might hyperventilate. I had to keep my composure. She said it had to be this way and not to worry, I was doing the right thing. I felt in her pocket and found the knife, just where she said it would be. I just had to wait for the flashbang. I heard the grenade hit the floor, one of the agents yell grenade. I tried to close my eyes to the flash but was a little late. In my fear and desperation to save my ass, I pulled the knife and plunged it into that wonderful young lady. I would have dreams of her for months afterward. It wasn't the kind of dreams you would think; they were sexual in nature. I must have rammed that knife into her at least twenty times, maybe more. I was tossed to the side as the SUV came to a screeching stop. The agents were out of the vehicle in a heartbeat and had me pulled to safety and a dead man was lying by my side. When she was whispering in my ear, I felt how soft and smooth her skin was against my face. The smell of her shampoo and her perfume still filled my nostrils. I was staring at an agent I had fired several weeks ago for being disloyal. He had at least a week's worth of beard growth on his face and he stank of a homeless person. No way could I have got the two of them confused with each other! Yet here he was, and no trace whatsoever of any female perpetrator. I was confused – I was stuttering out my confusion when the agent that had been in the passenger seat pulled his gun and said, "Fuck this!"

He was about to put a round in my head when my driver took him out. He had been looking around the scene to see if there was indeed another person around like I had been saying. He turned just in time to see the bad agent pull his gun to end my life. The man was a very good shot and he took care of the threat. I was in desperate need of someone like this, told him so, and promoted him to head of my security team. I needed someone around that would save me, not kill me.

The rest of my security detail showed up and I began to fire people right on the spot. The cameras arrived just in time to get it all on film. I told you it was all a con game, and I think I had just been conned.

How could I have one person with my life in her hands, on top of me one second, and with a flash have another person take her place? I shook my head. It was just impossible, yet it happened – or did it? That rumor was floating around Washington. How convenient that my new head of security take out the only other witness to the event in the vehicle. It was too neat, too scripted they would say. It was now time to take me out another way. I beat them to the punch. I'll get to that shortly.

CHAPTER 7

Bethany Devlin.

I got a group text message from Leon. I don't know why he kept me in the loop after everything I had done to him. I was in the middle of working on this walk-in client when the text came in. My client wanted her hair longer and blonder. She was already very girly, and this would make her even sexier. I had just completed the hair extensions that brought the length of her hair just above her butt and was about to get to the color when I read the message with the photo attachment. I gasped at the photo, looked at my client, and felt warm all over. This was going to be my way to get Leon back into my life. I knew this would be a mistake because he was my kryptonite, but since we were kids back on the beaches of California, I have craved his love and attention.

I don't know why I have such a weakness for gay men, but I do. Being a part of the Queen Bees was a little strange for me because I'm a real girl unlike a lot of those Queen Bees. Leon had a soft spot for me and let me hang around like you would a kid sister, except I wasn't his sister – I wanted to be his lover. It's hard to get a gay man to make love to you when he craves the other sex. I could put on a strap-on if that would be what it took, but he never took me up on the offer. I tried many times to change his mind.

Now here was my chance to get him back into my life again, sitting in my chair just waiting for me to make her beautiful. According to

THE TRUTH

this text message, it was a him I was dealing with. A very dangerous and deadly person. I so love a challenge. I made my way back and did some small talk. I had to be positive I had the right person before I put my plan into action. I offered her a bikini wax, which she refused. She said that she had every one of her pubic hairs removed permanently. We giggled at that. I inquired about a few other things and confirmed my suspicions. This was indeed my target. Franny was going to get the deluxe treatment. I came on to her, let her know I knew she wasn't all girl and I would love to spend some private time with such a beautiful girl as she was.

Franny never stood a chance and before the sun set, she was tied up and waiting in my little playroom. I had clients tonight, but no way was I going to give up that cash cow for this piece of trash. I made sure she was sedated and secured so she wouldn't ruin any of my fun time with all these weak and worthless men. It's funny how the clientele I have are all rich and bored men. They could have any trophy wife or gold digger they wanted with all the wealth they had, but they choose to come to me. Poor guys don't have these kinds of issues. Those poor guys only know how to get up and go to work. Come home and work some more at the house. Go to bed and wake up and do it again day after day. Rich guys didn't have that problem. They were free to do whatsoever they wanted without worry they weren't going to be able to pay their mortgage or child support. Especially these trust fund kids. I had a bunch of them on my client list. I made them pay a pretty penny. It wasn't just monetary. They paid in the amount of pain I dealt out. They kept coming back for more.

I kept taking their money. I also took their pictures. I made films from all my sessions and archived them all on a secret hard drive. I even had some film on the current President. I contemplated using it to make some big bucks, but in the end, decided I didn't want that kind of exposure. I figured he would have me killed off like he did his wife. Yes, I got him confessing it all on film. I could take him down in two seconds flat.

I finished up with my clients and woke Franny up. I told her I had sold her to a sheikh. They just love girls like her. Homosexuality will get you killed in their country, but if your man looks like Franny, who is going to ever know you're not with a woman? Yes, I told her, you're going to make me a bunch of money. I didn't want to tell her I had called Leon and told him where she was and when he could come and pick her up. He had warned me not to rough her up. He needed her for some big assignment he had and that she was critical to that assignment. I thought he was full of it.

I decided to play a few mind games with my little treasure until he arrived. Before I was done with her, I had her begging to become a real girl, pleading with me to make it happen. I got it all on film. The only manly part left of her was her penis. Her face could use a little bit of work, maybe the nose and chin. I told her she wasn't worthy to be a real girl and I made her cry some more.

Who would have thought just a short time ago that this was a macho LA homicide detective? He also did wet work on the side for some very nefarious people. Leon said Franny had been on a killing spree and had killed over ten people in just the last couple of weeks. Be very careful of her, he warned me. I looked at her and laughed. She looked anything but dangerous. I would have to keep my guard up. I secured her with a chain attached to her ankle and left her with enough length of chain to get onto the bed and over to a corner where I left her a bucket to do her business in. I was tired and looking forward to a very busy day tomorrow. I didn't know then that tomorrow was going to be the last day of my life. I should have been more careful.

CHAPTER 8

Jenna. Peter comes back.

I was on stage feeling on top of the world. The band Savage Storm had made their way over to our stage and when we finished our last song before the voting had even begun, they raised Deke's hand and proclaimed us the winner. From the sound of the crowd, they couldn't have agreed more. I was excited and knew the show had been a success. Getting Ben to set it up and put it on in just under two weeks had many people doubting this would go well. The fact that the whole show was for charity had helped with the turnout and we found that the people from Richmond were very giving and charitable people. The fact that you could walk the streets at night again didn't hurt our cause either. If the people had known that the lead singer that they so cheered for was the vigilante sniper, would they have cheered louder, or would there have been a different reaction?

Ben had come out on stage and was giving numbers to the people, thanking them for all that they had given. The numbers were staggering, and I wondered where all that money had come from. The guys were packing up and Zachery was just about to put his banjo away when I heard it. The first couple of chords from "Dueling Banjos." I looked over at Zach and yelled to him not to do it, but he succumbed and quickly answered the challenge. I looked at the guys from Savage Storm. I knew most of them. Their drummer was still back on the other stage. I asked them if they were up to playing a few songs with me. We discussed which ones and they jumped at the chance for me to lead them when they played. I had been offered a spot in their band more than once. We were close friends.

Deke looked hurt, but he was smart enough to know that we had played all the songs he knew. We had nothing new to give the crowd. I looked at Beats, he said he could play anything. I believed him. For a child of eight, I think he could do just about anything he put his mind to do. He held up his drumsticks, yelled to the guys, "Let's do this!" I couldn't agree more.

The band had to borrow our instruments since their equipment was on the other stage with Peter and Church Band. We prepared. I wasn't ready for what Peter was up to. I should have known we would fight it out with music. I hadn't seen him or my kids since the incident at his house. Deke's wife, Ellen, left with Peter and we had been staying at his house waiting for their return. Maria's potion had residual effects and Deke had paid for all the fantasies he ever had. Now he was trying to find excuses to be away from me. I had just seen the doctor the other day and finally think I have my desires under control. I hadn't thought of sex in the last two days. When I told Deke that he might be safe now, I heard him mumble, "Thank God." I felt the same way.

I loved Peter, not Deke. It was something unique with Deke, like we were meant for each other. I couldn't explain it even if I tried. I really did try to explain it to myself. Then I would jump his bones again as he tried to get some sleep, which by the time I had got done with him, he needed badly. I was totally out of control and I knew it.

Peter and Zach finished up and then Church Band played what I knew would be three songs. It was how Peter did it. He got me good with the first song. I had tears in my eyes as I listened.

"Faithful" by Finding Favour was the first salvo. He followed up with "Pride" by The New Division. I was on my knees now. If he played that one, I knew I had really hurt him. The last swing was "Redemption" by The Rising.

The last song he played me was his way of saying he was sorry when it should have been me saying that. I whispered to the guys the next song. They looked at me a little strange but started to play. They knew Peter walked out on me, but they didn't know why. Love and the Outcome has a song called, "If I Don't Have You." We followed that with "All That I'm Made For" a song by Out of the Dust. I finished with my song of true love called "Never Stop" by Mosaic MSC. The crowd was on their feet cheering and dancing. Ben had to come out again and told the crowd it was time to wrap up and he hoped they liked the encore performance.

It had been a while since I had been front and center on stage and the people seemed to really like me. I had other things to worry about, like getting through this crowd and seeing my children. I could see them on stage with Peter and Ellen just waiting for me to make my way through this crowd and come see them. It wasn't the easiest thing I have ever done, but I made it, just barely. Beats helped me out with a drum solo that had everybody staring at him in amazement. How could such a little kid have so much talent? Once I was on the other stage, I looked back at him and he raised his sticks. His way of saluting me. I threw him a kiss. I didn't see him again until the next day.

Peter greeted me and the children excitedly pounced on me.

"We had to come back. Ellen was at her wit's end. I think they deliberately tortured her the whole time we were gone. I heard her say she never wanted to have children."

I looked at little Maria and just knew she had to be behind it all. The boys would never have been able to come up with a plan like that. She gave me a big smile and a hug. I was having trouble seeing with all the tears flowing down my face. I looked around for Ellen, but she was gone. I wanted to apologize to her as well. It was her husband I was banging behind that wall when they all left in disgust. I looked Peter in the eye and tried to explain to him what happened. He knew the whole story. Somebody must have filled him in. I hope he didn't know about the last two weeks, because I'm not sure if that was me or if it was Maria's formula that made me so bad.

Peter didn't say anything about it, seemed anxious to be getting back to our normal life, so I left with him to go back to Jarratt. I hadn't been back there since the incident. If he didn't go back, then the place must still be trashed. It was. He looked at me as if to say, where have you been staying? I wasn't eager to start a fight, so I said nothing. He went in and cleaned up the children's room while I stayed in the car with them. They were all fast asleep, so I was left with my thoughts. What was I going to do? I loved him, but we seemed to be at a crossroads in our lives. I had no idea what the short-term future would bring us.

He came back out and helped me get the kids inside. I knew I couldn't leave this mess for the children to wake up to. So much glass and debris on the floor. I grabbed a broom and mop and began to clean. Peter came up to me, held me, and asked me to come to bed. I knew upstairs didn't look much better. I was tired but I had no intentions of sleeping with Peter tonight. Disappointed, he went upstairs to clean some more so he had a place to lay his head. I was busy for about fifteen minutes before I ran out of gas and sat on the sofa. It would have to be replaced. Someone had taken a knife to it looking for Maria's formula. It also had a bunch of bullet holes in it.

I looked around the house thinking what I had been doing while this was all taking place. We thought it was moonshine and were trying to take the edge off while hiding behind the wall in the secret cupboard area. Neither of us knew we were drinking the formula that could cure cancer if taken in small doses. If a larger amount was consumed, well, let's say it sure worked better than Viagra ever did. It also had the added feature of removing tattoos. I now had to do my own damn eye makeup. Funny how mad I was when I discovered Maria had first used the super henna on me. She had drugged me and done my eye makeup. It had been on long enough that it had set and was much like a tattoo, permanent. I've gotten used to it, and now I kind of want her to redo it for me. It wasn't the only thing she did to me that night. I still feel like a very young schoolgirl every time I shower. I think that was the real reason I was so furious at her.

It felt like I was only sitting for a few minutes when the kids got up and came running out. I grabbed them and brought them outside only to discover that Smokey was sitting there in his police car. He was puffing on a cigarette which he hadn't done in many years. If he was smoking, then I knew something was awfully wrong in the universe.

I had a little play yard off the side of the barn and while taking the children over to it, I noticed the empty grave.

Jake sure was a good dog. I knew he was going to be missed. When Deke had first seen the grave, he was very upset, dug it up, and found Jake. I was relieved because I thought it was one of the children. Deke wanted to take Jake to his favorite spot. Now his dog has a very nice resting place in a park beneath a tree.

Once I had the children in a safe place, I walked over to speak to Smokey. He got out of the car and said these words to me, "Jenna, we have a problem."

I could see that, but what he asked me next was not going to be an easy problem to solve.

"Where is the boy? The one they call Beats?"

CHAPTER 9

Anna has a dilemma.

"Anna, is any of this relevant to the bottom line of finding out what happened to the President?"

Walter Bennings was standing, and he seemed irritated. How could I make them believe everything I was going to tell them if I didn't give them the whole background story leading up to the day the President was given the formula?

"Yes, sir. You need to see the whole picture to be able to understand."

"All I'm seeing right now is a bunch of stalling and irrelevant information," he fumed.

"Sir, if I can't tell it my way, then I need to be somewhere else today."

I stood and made like I was preparing to leave. I had no intention of doing so. I had way too much information I needed to gather from these fools. One of these idiots was going to tell me where the formula was hidden or knew where it was hidden. Once I had that info, I was going to destroy it for good this time. It was my mission given to me by Jesus. I intended to fulfill the mission he gave me.

"Anna, please sit down. We'll do it your way," Bennings conceded. He didn't look happy doing it my way, but he had no choice now, did he? I was feeling pretty good about myself when I looked up and saw the door open and in walks the President himself. The man sure did look a lot younger. Before he took the formula, he was in his upper sixties, now he looked like he was in his mid-forties. Joey was about ten years younger when he first took the formula. It always seems to be so unreal, even when you see it with your own eyes. Somehow, something must be fake, just your imagination or something like that.

He motioned to me and asked for a private conversation. Bennings stood and protested to no avail.

"Take a recess. I must talk to the young lady immediately."

I didn't think this day could get worse. It just did. I stood and followed him out of the room. We walked in silence until we reached another meeting room. He opened the door and waved me in. As I walked past him, he grabbed a piece of my ass, and that's when I lost it. I spun and dropped him to the floor so fast he didn't know what hit him. He had no secret servicemen with him because this was supposed to be a very private conversation. It was. I laid on top of him giggling and he was happy as a lark.

"We can't be doing this, sir. You know it isn't going to happen between us, right sir?" I questioned him.

"One can only hope."

I let him up and he got down to business. I had found out that one of the side effects of the formula, its original intent, was to procreate. It made you very horny and always ready to get it on. The President was a single man and was having a very difficult time with this side effect. I wasn't going to be one of his conquests no matter how much he proclaimed his love for me.

"Anna, I know it has been very difficult for you, but I need you to find out where the formula is hidden."

"Yes sir, that is exactly what I intend to do."

I wasn't doing it for the reasons he had in mind. I knew he would want to take it again when the time came. I couldn't ever let that happen.

"Sir, you do realize how very dangerous this stuff is? It may not kill you, but a lot of others will be gunning for you if you never age."

"I know, but I feel so damn good, I want this feeling to last forever."

"Is there a reason you called me in for this private conversation?"

He smiled. "Yeah, I wanted to jump your bones."

I looked at him in disbelief and walked out. I headed straight back for the conference room. I knew they would want to find out what I had talked about with the President. I was going to have to lie my ass off some more. I headed straight for my seat. I should have headed for the bathroom to straighten out my hair and makeup. I had a disheveled look about me.

Bennings' only question for me was, "Is the President alright?" I was just a little perturbed and stated, "He's still breathing." He left it at that. I think he'd also observed the strange behavior of the President since the change.

We got back to business and my storytelling. The story was so complex, but all roads led to Bennett's estate in California. I had almost lost my life several times in the short time I was there. If it hadn't been for Beats, I surely would be dead. That little boy was incredible. Most kids would have crumbled under all the stress, not him. The more deadly the situation was, the better he handled it. I'll get to all of it soon. First, I must tell you how we all got to that lovely place in hell.

CHAPTER 10

Jenna goes to find Beats.

I had last seen him playing that drum solo so I could get across the courtyard to Peter. I didn't have a clue where he went after the show. Mrs. Perkins, the veterinarian who worked for Mr. Gould was someone that he had been staying with. I left the children with Peter and headed out in my search for Beats. When I got to the stables, I saw they were already working out another horse for another future big race. I knew Beats had a thing for a certain horse at this stable. Her name was Truly. He named Deke's band after her and they called themselves, Truly Blessed. As I figured, he was there in the stall giving her a rub down with a brush. It looked like she had just finished her daily workout.

I called to him, he ignored me. I called again. He must have known I wasn't going to leave because he answered with, "What do you want, Jenna?" He seemed to be mad about something. I couldn't think of anything I had done to him. He kept right on working with his back turned to me.

"I need you to meet with a friend of mine. He just wants to ask you some questions."

"I saw your friend last night. He arrested Deke and hauled him off to jail. I'm not going to jail Jenna. I know I did some bad things, but I only did them to save the children and you. I don't see why I have to go to jail for that."

He had a point. The shots he made from the cemetery killed two people. One in Joey's house, and one when the crazy cop came at us at my father's funeral. In his defense, two other people shot her as well. His shot just removed half of her head.

"He promised me he just wants to talk. You have no fear of being brought into custody. You have my word."

"I need to work. The stables need me to get things done. If I don't do it, who will?"

Larry, the jockey that should have ridden Truly in the Kentucky Derby, spoke up. "I would be happy to cover for you while you're gone. It would be my pleasure."

I heard Beats groan. He was running out of excuses. He gave Larry a dirty look and told me he would like to clean up.

"I'll be right back."

I stood there for a moment when Larry informed me that there was a window in the bathroom and Beats was most likely using it as we spoke. I ran outside to find Beats climbing out the window planning his escape. When his feet hit the ground, I surprised him by saying, "You could have used the door." He looked resigned at me and stated, "Larry ratted me out, didn't he?" I laughed at that, tried to cover for Larry as best I could. I knew Beats wasn't buying it.

I drove to the one place I knew Smokey would have gone when he left my place. I had offered him coffee and a chance to sit on the front porch and talk. When I got inside and saw the kitchen, I realized I had nothing I could serve him. The coffee was all emptied out and lying on the floor, along with the sugar and anything else that was stored in a container. The people that were searching for the formula left no stone unturned. I was hiding with Deke in a pantry that had a secret entrance while the children had a false wall inside the closet that they were hiding behind. It was a passage that led to a secret escape route. The wonders of old houses that were built in the time of slavery. Never knew when you would need to hide someone or provide them a way to escape.

Smokey seemed sad when I told him I had nothing to serve him. He bid me farewell and asked me to call him if I found out where the boy was. It broke my heart. We had one diner in this small town; it was close to the interstate and drew a lot of the locals as well as travelers. I stopped outside the diner, saw Smokey's car, and knew we had found him.

"I promise, this is going to be alright," I patted Beats' hand.

He pulled it away and said, "Let's just get this over and done with."

Smokey was sitting by himself in a booth, so there was plenty of room for us to scoot in on the other side of him. He offered to buy us something, so I said I would like a coffee. Beats wanted to eat. I think that boy has a hollow leg. He ordered up three eggs, hash browns, bacon, a bagel with cream cheese, and a short stack of pancakes with a large glass of milk. Smokey let the boy eat while we had some small talk. It was nice to catch up on some things. He looked at me and asked out of the blue.

"How did you remove all the tattoos?"

It caught me by surprise, I think that was what all the small talk was about, get me comfortable and then ask the real questions he was after. I saw Beats raise his head with that question, like he was paying attention the whole time but was pretending he was concentrating on his breakfast.

"I don't know what you're talking about. What tattoos?" I pretended to play dumb.

The truth was, I had no idea how that crazy junk that Maria had made up did any of the things it did. It did do several things. It removed tattoos and made you horny as hell if you took it in a large amount, which Deke and I had done. We thought it was moonshine. Taken in smaller doses it cured cancer. I didn't know that at the time, but found out later, after it had been discredited.

Smokey looked over his coffee at me. He could tell I was a lying bitch. He called over our waitress and had her fill our coffee cups back up. When he asked Beats if he had enough, the boy ordered another short stack of pancakes. Smokey just shook his head, the waitress looked confused, but he nodded, "Feed the boy. can't you see he's starving?" He said it with a smile on his face, so I knew he wasn't angry at Beats for running up a huge bill. It wasn't like he wasn't eating it. His plates were all clean.

"Another glass of milk, please," he said to the waitress as she was leaving. This time it was Beats with the big smile on his face. If Smokey wanted information, he damn well was going to pay for it.

Smokey began his story from the night before. I had gotten some sleep last night, apparently Smokey had yet to see any downtime. He told me how he thought Deke was the man they had been searching for. The killer with all the tattoos. He said from the video they had been shown that Deke used a concealer to cover up his tattoos. It was the video of him at the super bash singing with me. When they saw I was on stage with the man they thought was surely the killer, they had him arrested.

"You know what got your friend off last night, Jenna? He didn't have a single tattoo. Not one, no scars indicating he had them removed, nothing. Prison records show they were real and not henna tattoos. We had to let him go. He wouldn't tell us anything. Had identification saying his name was John Deacon. Explains why you called him Deke in front of a lot of people. He checked out. Funny thing, he didn't really check out. I can tell when documents have been forged and records have been compromised. Now can you tell me for the love of God what the hell is going on around here?!" he raised his voice in frustration. I had to get him calmed down.

"He is not the man you're looking for. That man died at the prison."

I thought I might have seen smoke coming from Smokey's ears. Must have been my imagination.

"John Deacon is a wonderful talent. He is kind and generous and wants nothing more than to sing out the praises of God to anyone who will listen. Get him off your radar and go back to your restaurant, Smokey. Leave this alone for everyone's sake."

I had just told him as much of the truth as I dared. He stood, called for the check.

"Young man, would you join me in my car? I have a few things I would like to discuss with you."

Beats looked very nervous, looked over at me for guidance.

"Thanks, Jenna. You piss him off and now he's ready for me."

He walked out in a hurry, me chasing him and Smokey trying to pay the bill and leave a tip. He finally threw a fifty on the table and chased us outside. He found me having a conversation with Beats. I heard him say that he wasn't going to do anything bad, and that Beats could trust him. They got inside the car and rolled the windows up so I couldn't hear their conversation. I stood nearby and watched. I knew everything was going to be alright when I saw Beats smile widely and start talking wildly with his hands. It seems his hands are always moving, like he's keeping a beat only he can see and feel. I watched them for nearly a half-hour talk. Finally, Beats got out of the car and came over to me.

"I like him, he's a nice man. I had to apologize for punching him in the ball sack. It was the only way I was going to be able to get around him so I could get to the phone and save Joey."

I had no idea what he was talking about. I didn't want to ask him to explain either. Beats does things you can't explain. The less you know, the better off you are.

I drove him back to the stables. He asked if we were going to take the record deal, the one we had won last night. I was all for it until Peter showed back up with the children. Now I didn't know what I was going to do. It felt natural to play with Savage Storm. I really liked those guys and they had been begging me to be their lead singer. Church Band and Peter needed me. Deke needed me. How was I ever going to make them all happy and take care of three small children?

Beats spoke like he was reading my mind, "You'll figure it out. I'll play for whoever you want me to play for."

I patted him on the head.

"You know, I think Peter knows Ben the best. I would like you to go with him up to New York and work out a deal together. I bet you he could get some hockey tickets for a game while you're in town."

Beats grew very excited with that.

"Mrs. Perkins has a clinic she has to put on in California next week. I was going to have to stay with Mr. Gould. I bet she wouldn't have a problem with me going with Peter."

He jumped out of the car and ran into the stables. He never gave me an answer, but I'm sure it was yes by the way he was acting.

CHAPTER 11

Now, it's Bob's turn.

Walter was getting tired of me, turned to Bob, and asked him to explain how he ended up in LA. Bob quickly took over with his explanation. This was something I was looking forward to hearing. Please tell us, Bob? How did you get to try the formula? I wondered if he would come close to telling the truth.

"Well, let me start with the phone call. I was back in Washington working as the assistant director. My boss was nowhere to be found. We searched for him, but he had gone missing. Rumors were being spread about his many misdeeds and that he might have flown the coop. I was being promoted to director. Effective immediately, I was to be the director full time. I was told to come to LA and meet up with some important people that would have instructions for me. I inquired about who I was supposed to meet. Was told to just get my ass to LA and I would find out. I purchased my ticket and was on my way in a matter of hours. I was met at the airport by a gay man with a sign. I don't mean to offend, but this guy was very flamboyant. He was not trying to hide anything about himself. With a limp wrist, he guided me to a waiting limousine and wished me luck. I got in the back seat and was greeted by a woman I knew as Miss Crenshaw. She told me I was going to be her new boss and she was going to be my personal secretary. I could see right off the bat where this was going. I may be the new director, but they were going to watch me very closely. I had a snitch and rat as my own personal secretary.

"I didn't want to let on that I knew the director had gone into hiding. I had my own problems with the Cartels looking for the man. He didn't just steal from the government and the taxpayers. The fool had stolen from some of the worse kinds of ruthless people. The Cartels. I was out in the DC area having a few cocktails with a friend of mine when I had my first encounter with them. I wasn't to be hurt because they needed me to do their dirty work. My friend was expendable. They grabbed us as we were staggering out of the bar and forced us into a waiting van. Once we had sobered up a bit, they began their interrogation. I was waterboarded while my friend was tortured. They did every unspeakable painful procedure they could think of to him. Once they were sure I could have no knowledge of where the director had gone to, they let me go, asked if I wanted to take my dead friend with me. They laughed as they drove away, leaving me to cover up the murder of my friend.

"I was driven to the house of a movie producer. His name is Adam Bennett. I think you all might have heard of him. He ran things for Helen Harrison who seemed to have her corrupt little hands in everything. I don't know what they had on the man, but he was a big part of their scam."

I hid the fact that I knew Bennett was doing everything in his power to make sure all of Helen's plans failed. He would counter things and make it look like it was just a stroke of bad luck that their plans would fail. I was next in line to carry the torch when the old man died. He had brought me into his fold. I couldn't reveal any of this.

"He told me of this grand plan that Helen had, and how I was going to be a big part of it now. I was to work closely with Urstin Trevosky and the man sitting next to you. I didn't know Ivan was undercover CIA at the time. I only knew he was Urstin's right-hand man. I was told I would go back to DC and wait for further instructions. I wasn't given any details of what the plan entailed, only that I would be a part of it.

"I was going to get back on the plane when I received a phone call. I didn't know who it was from, the caller ID was blocked. I heard a disguised voice tell me to lose the bitch and be at a certain hotel by 9:00 p.m. I was told not to be late."

I did all of this. I left out the details that I had drugged Miss Crenshaw's drink and had to undress her and put her to bed for the night. I wasn't sure how much detail I wanted to give. Seems Anna had held a few things back, maybe I should as well.

"I got to the hotel to find that Maria Gambella had rented out a few rooms for some homeless people and was about to partake in another experiment with these folks. Seems the first few times she had tried were a bust. Maria knew me from Richmond, knew I was ATF, at least I was back when she knew me. She played it off as if she was feeding the homeless and invited me to partake in the wealth of food she had prepared. Lots of vegetables and fruits. A very tasty smoothie, and some nachos that burnt the shit out of my tongue and lips and left me breathless. Then she brings in these steamed clams, shipped in from Iceland just that morning with some melted butter and encouraged us all to feast. She had found the empty box in her back seat when Joey had finally returned her car. Had been trying to figure out why the formula worked on him and nobody else. She took every possible difference that she could think of and added it to the formula. If it didn't work this time, she was just going to give up.

"I didn't know why I was there, tried to make excuses as to why I wasn't leaving. Maria seemed to be on edge and really didn't want me to be hanging around. I figured she had no idea how long this stuff took to work. The first thing that went wrong that night was that one of the homeless was a female, she had been the only one. The rest had been males whose ages ranged from thirty-five to the oldest of nearly seventy. I had just turned fifty a few short months before. The female began to have convulsions. We tried everything possible to save her. Before anyone could even dial for an ambulance, she was gone. Something had killed her, and I had a good idea it was something Maria had given her. I noticed that the whole time we were stuffing our faces with food, Maria ate very little. A few strawberries and some grapes.

"I jumped up and got into her face, yelled and screamed at her. 'What have you done? What did you give to us?!' I was in panic that I might be the next one that kicked the bucket. Maria just stared at me and told me I was a part of this, so just relax and wait. I was told that I was going to be quite surprised if what she gave us worked. 'I think she just had an allergic reaction to the clams or something like that.' That's what she said as calm as can be."

I was convinced it was no allergic reaction. I would find out exactly what this stuff did to you before the sun came up.

"Nothing was happening to the men in the group and we all figured it was another failure. I was getting good at concealing dead bodies. I was feeling bad about what happened to Maria when I was trying to get the information on her father after her husband had died. I figured I owed her a favor and hid the body in the desert. It was only a homeless person – who was going to miss her? I removed the body, stowed it in my trunk. With the help of another homeless man about my age, we headed for a midnight burial out in the desert.

"I stopped and picked up a shovel at an all-night shopping store. The first thing I noticed was that the man sitting next to me didn't look as old as when we had started out. The next thing I noticed was I had a tremendous amount of energy. It seemed to take no time at all to dig a nice deep grave. The homeless guy cheered me on the whole time I was digging. I could have used a little help. I stared at him staring at me. He said, 'Jesus Christ, you lost twenty years at least since we headed out.' I wasn't sure what he was talking about, but I could say the same for him. I rushed back to the car and stared at my reflection in the mirror. This wasn't good. I looked like I had just turned thirty. I was young. I was excited. I grabbed the homeless man and we jumped up and down for joy for what seemed like hours. It felt like we had just won the lottery. We got back in the car and were headed back when he notices a bar that hasn't reached last call yet.

"'Let's get a drink to celebrate. Can I borrow some cash? I'm a little short,' he said. I give the guy a twenty. He looks at me as if I'm a cheapskate. We get in the bar and he starts looking for any female that might still be alone. I sit down at the bar and order up a draft. I looked for him a few minutes later but he's gone, in the wind. This young lady sits beside me and we start to talk. Next thing you know we're in the hotel next door screwing like rabbits. I hadn't felt this good in years and she was quickly begging for mercy. I found it takes a lot of willpower to control yourself after you've been exposed to this stuff."

I didn't say what I did to Mrs. Crenshaw when I got back to the hotel. By the time we flew back to Richmond, I couldn't wipe that smile off her face.

* * *

Walter stood up and called for a break. I think he had heard enough to explain some of the bad behavior of the President since he had been exposed to the formula. He called over to me and asked me to join him in the same conference room I had fought off the advances of the President.

"Anna, please tell me you didn't hurt him or bruise his face in any way."

"What makes you think he did anything to me?" I had to play dumb. He just smiled.

"Go fix your hair. It's been a mess ever since you came back from your meeting with him."

I ran to the restroom and gasped when I saw my reflection. Not only was my hair a mess, my lipstick had been smudged and it appeared I might have been in a heavy make out session. I did my best to get myself back together. I wondered why both Ivan and Bob kept smiling down at me, like I had been a bad girl or something. Just because the President was young now didn't mean this was the first time that I had to fight off his advances. Even when he was still old, he thought he just had to have me. I guess I pushed all his buttons and he felt like he could have me just because of who he was. I had put a stop to it before, or he would do it again. The more I abused him, the stronger his desire. I couldn't figure out men. I thought about trying to use him to get my daughter back, decided that was probably a very bad idea. The fewer people that knew I had a daughter, the better. The last thing I needed was for someone to apply leverage to me to bend me to their will.

I walked back into the meeting room and held my head high. I was innocent and was going to act that way. We all sat down, and it was time to spin another tale. Let me tell them about the great Bethany Devlin. This might knock their precious President off his high horse.

CHAPTER 12

Bethany Devlin meets her maker.

I set up my playroom with everything I would need. It was time to show Franny a good time while we waited for Leon to arrive. I watched her through my one-way glass window, it looked like a mirror from her side. I could tell she had plans for me. I set up all the video equipment. I was going to make a video I would watch for years. I couldn't wait. I could tell her plan was to wrap that length of chain around my throat and slowly choke me to death. I had to counter that right off the bat. She had to believe that she wasn't getting out of here alive if anything ever happened to me.

"Hi dear, did you have a nice sleep?" I started out trying to be nice to her. I thought I might have heard her growl at me.

"I know I haven't given you a whole lot to eat in the last few days so I thought I would start by giving you some food and water."

I had a tray of crackers and a small bottle of water. I sat it down just out of her reach. I saw her strain to get to the offered food. I knew it would be useless.

"What's the matter, you not hungry?"

She screamed at me that she couldn't reach it and if I could push it another foot or so into the room, she would be able to consume it. I asked her to turn around and put her hands behind her back. When she did, I quickly cuffed her hands. I already felt a little safer. I let her eat like the dog she was. I watched her work a cracker into her mouth without the use of her hands. It made me giddy. I had to open the bottle of water and pour it into a bowl for her. I got to watch her lap it up like a pretty kitten.

I told her it wouldn't be much longer before her knight in shining armor returned to take her back to his castle in the desert. This wasn't something she wanted to hear and started begging me to not turn her over to a sheikh.

"It's already done, honey. He's on his way at this moment. You are going to make such a nice addition to his harem."

I watched her cry and almost felt sorry for her.

"I'll tell you what, you play a game of softball with me and if you can get a hit, just one hit, I'll let you go. Then you can run away and be free." I could see she felt like she might be able to do this. Then she caught on.

"What's the rules?"

"Well, let's see. I tie your hands to that hook in the ceiling over there. Then I throw this softball and you try to hit it with your bat."

She whined, "How can I swing a bat with my hands tied above my head?"

"Listen, honey. All men come equipped with a bat and balls. Just because you lost your balls doesn't mean you still can't swing that bat of yours."

She started to realize just what the game was all about. She would have to let me hit her penis with a softball that was traveling at a very high rate of speed. If she was to get a hit, it would hurt a lot, a whole lot. I got her to agree and she was attached to the hook and I was going to have my fun. I put a hockey goalie's helmet on her. I laughed.

"Sometimes I tend to over-throw and the ball goes a little astray. This is for your safety."

Leon said I couldn't do any damage to her face. I went to the other side of the room and got into position. My first pitch bounced right off the helmet. Good thing I strapped it on before I started this little game. My second pitch caught her right in one of her perk titties. I cringed, that was going to leave a mark. Franny started to heckle me and said I threw like a girl. I wound up and let it fly. I was going for a home run.

She moved her hips and got her bat out of the way. The ball just nipped her hip. I knew that it stung.

"I thought you wanted to get a hit and buy your freedom? I just threw the perfect ball."

I heard her say she was having second thoughts. I was getting mad and threw her a couple of more that she kept getting out of the way of.

"Enough of this. You're going back into your room."

I pulled her off the hook and wasn't prepared for her assault. She almost had me. I had gotten careless. If it wasn't for the fact that I was a blackbelt and was able to fight and defend myself, I might have been added to Franny's body count. I was able to flip her over my shoulder and drove her headfirst into the concrete basement floor. I heard her face crack when she hit. I knew I had done some severe damage, but it was her or me.

She was out of it and I dragged her back to the playroom and reattached the chain around her ankle. I had some explaining to do when Leon showed up. I locked her back in the room and went to get myself a drink when I saw the motorcycles pull up in front of my place. Leon and his right-hand man, Steven Lewis. At least Steve had succumbed to my advances. I was surprised he was still around after all these years. I ran to the door and greeted them warmly. I gave each of them a very strong and long hug. Leon seemed uncomfortable but Steve just hugged me back as tight as I held him.

"Where is she, Bethany? We have a tight schedule we must maintain."

"I was hoping we could catch up a bit and maybe you might invite me to LA to see some of my old friends."

"Fat chance, Bethany. You're lucky I came today. If it wasn't for the fact that I need Franny, I would have let you have her."

Leon wasn't being very cooperative. I was going to have to change that.

"Please come in and I'll show you where I have her. By the way, I didn't rough her up, she did that to herself. I told her she was being picked up by a sheikh, and she smashed her face into the concrete to make herself unappealing to him. Seems she wants to be a real girl now."

Leon said, "I highly doubt that."

"It's true, I have it all on film."

I led them down into the bowels of my home. I was on my turf now. I had just led my next prizes into my hell. I pulled up the tape of her begging to become a real girl and Leon sat and watched with his mouth open.

"I wouldn't have ever believed it if you hadn't caught it all on film. She has fought us every step of the way."

I looked at them puzzled. "She doesn't want to be a girl?"

Leon laughed, "Never has wanted it. She's been trying to kill everyone responsible for her being this way. It's her punishment for trying to kill a friend of mine. She started the process, I continued it."

"I still don't understand, when she came into my salon, I was convinced she was a girl. She even acted like one."

Steve had to get his two cents in, "She is an assassin, and a very good one. Part of her gift is she can fool anyone. I bet she might have even tried to kill you."

Boy did he get that one right.

* * *

Leon stared at Franny through the one-way glass and pondered what he was going to do. The mission would have to be postponed until he could get Franny's face back into perfect shape. He thought if she already had damage to her nose and chin that this would be the perfect time to complete the project. A little cosmetic surgery along with the final surgery would complete what Maria had started. He reached up to rub his chin and this might have been what saved him from capture. The scarf that was wound around his neck was caught by the fact he had rubbed his chin. Bethany was unable to choke him out quickly and he was able to put up a struggle. He whirled around looking for Steve and found him out like a light in the corner. She must have snuck up on him while he was deep in thought about what to do with Franny. He knew how dangerous this woman was, so he had been prepared. He reached into his pocket and withdrew a switchblade. A quick upward slice with the blade and he was free. Bethany countered his freedom with a sharp kick to his head, knocking the switchblade from his hands and over to the corner where Steve Lewis remained passed out. Leon wasn't a skilled fighter like Bethany was. This was going to be a fight to the death.

Leon fought as well as he could, but Bethany was playing with him and inflicting one painful kick after another. She also wouldn't shut up.

"Leon, we could have been happy together. We still can be happy together. Why won't you give me a chance and make love to me just once? I swear you'll never want another man again after you do it with me."

Leon was getting his butt kicked so badly he contemplated taking her up on her offer.

"Never! You're an evil witch that I could never love."

That only got him another kick to the head that really rung his bell. He almost went down for the count on that one and saw her coming in for the kill. Well, at least he had fought gallantly. He waited for her last strike. What he heard was her gasp for air. Then she gasped again. He felt her turn her attention away from him and spin and throw another roundhouse kick that put Mr. Lewis back in his corner.

Leon sat on the floor, blood running down his face, pondering what his next move was going to be. He had nothing left to fight with, all his energy was spent. He reached up to clear the blood from his eyes and realized it wasn't his blood.

Bethany was lying on the floor gasping for breath. She had been injured severely by the lost switchblade. Two stab wounds to her kidney area. Very good possibility a lung might have been pierced by the sound of things. Leon got up and looked down on her pleading face.

"I have never prayed to God, but I think I might have to start before I run out of time." Leon knelt beside her and took her hand in his. "I'm sorry for the way things turned out. I never wanted any of this to happen to you. We had fun as teens, but that's as far as it was ever going to go. I hope you understand and can forgive us."

Bethany glared at him with eyes full of hate.

"I don't give a damn about your useless apologies. What I need are my fucking Last Rites – I'm dying here."

Leon looked down on her and stated, "You need a lot more than Last Rites. I'm not a priest. I couldn't help you get into heaven even if Jesus was here himself to guide us."

With that final comment, he left her to bleed out on the floor. He started to gather the tapes that had Franny on them. He erased some others that he thought were very sick and abusive. If he had more time, he could have gone back to see who all her clients were. That was a mistake that cost many lives.

Mr. Lewis started to come around and Leon thought they both might have concussions. They gathered up Franny and her few things and left. Enough DNA evidence to hang all of them. If the cops hadn't been so greedy with what they discovered, Leon and Mr. Lewis would have gone to jail for sure. What the cops found on those tapes would have detrimental aftershocks to many people. Bethany had many influential clients that never wanted any of their sicknesses ever revealed. The two detectives that were assigned to the case were never very smart with what they had discovered. They saw a huge payday with a possible bestselling book to go along with it. When they turned over the evidence to their lead detective, they signed their fate. Being a police officer is dangerous work, sometimes cops get killed in the line of duty. Sometimes people set up cops to get killed in the line of duty. One will never know which it was with these two. All I know is the only money they ever collected was from the life insurance policies they both owned.

Now that the story had been told about Bethany, you can put two and two together and find out a presidential tape was out there with a confession to the murder of his wife. A tape that would find its way from one dead person to another. Seems whoever had the tape would turn up dead, and the next person would advance it up the ladder. The last person that held the tape that lived to tell about it was Helen Harrison. She used it to become Secretary of State. A very prestigious job if you couldn't hold the seat in the White House. You might as well say she held the seat, with as much dirt as she had on Stanley Adams. She was prepared to buy her time. First, she had to get America to love her again. Seems she had fallen out of favor with the public sector with all her tantrums and vile comments against the common folk. She had to reshape her image. The plan was put into place.

I looked up at Walter as I watched Ivan start to squirm in his seat. I knew he had a lot to do with the tracking down and deaths of all those people that had viewed those tapes. He would say he was protecting the President and the American image. I would say he was advancing Urstin's and Helen's agenda.

I threw it out to him, "Would you like to continue this story, Ivan?"

He shook his head and declined to put his two cents in. I knew it. He was as corrupt as the rest of them.

Let me walk you through what happened when Joey and I first returned from our trip to the other side. A few things had changed in that short amount of time. One of those things was Bob, which I already told you about. The other was very interesting.

CHAPTER 13

Our return.

Neither I nor Joey knew we had been gone for close to a week. To us, it had been but a few hours. I think Joey might have had an inclination that we were gone longer. Seems he had a problem with time slipping from one side to the other. It might have been why he was so cautious when we entered Scarlett's house. I thought it was Maria full of rage storming towards us. I didn't know Scarlett could act just like her. She was cussing up a storm at Joey telling him how insensitive he was to keep her worrying for almost a week.

"You couldn't pick up a gosh darn phone and tell me you were safe and when you would be returning. You just had to keep me worrying about you all damn week and with me with child."

I saw Joey throw his hands in the air and try to explain, and then he stopped.

"What was that last comment? Did you just say you were with child?"

"That's right, damn you. Even getting my tubes tied doesn't stop your soldiers from doing their job. You knocked me up again, and right before the biggest film of my life."

I watched her collapse in a mass of tears. Joey went over to comfort her. I wanted to tell her there was no possible way we could have called, but then I thought I better keep out of it.

"Are you going to keep it?" I heard Joey say. The look coming his way made me turn my head. Of all the stupid things he could have said. It was obvious she was going to keep it. If not, the baby would have been already terminated. She was getting her composure back and turned her fury towards me.

"Is this who you're shacking up with now?" I had to pipe up now.

"No ma'am, we were on a mission of great importance to the country. We were unable to access a phone or be able to make any calls in the situation we were in. I'm very sorry Joey was unable to contact you." Joey dropped the ball and confessed.

"I could have made a call before it all began. I got caught up in all the excitement and forgot."

"Finally, I get the truth. Well, take off all that makeup you have on. You look just like Peter with that getup."

Joey looked confused. I know I was. It dawned on me. She thought Joey was in disguise.

"Scarlett dear, I have something else to tell you."

I saw Scarlett brace herself for the big reveal. I truly believed she thought this is when Joey was going to tell her he was leaving her. I could see the look of dread on her face.

"I'm not in disguise or wearing any makeup."

Scarlett started to laugh. "Bullshit, you look twenty years younger than the last time I saw you. Hell, Peter looks older than you do."

"It's true Scarlett. Maria gave me something and I think it made me look younger. I don't know how long it will last." I elbowed Joey and asked to talk to him in private. "I'm in the middle of something here Anna, can't this wait?" I told him it couldn't. I had to tell him something right now.

He apologized to Scarlett and we stepped outside.

"Joey, when we were on the other side and Jesus asked to talk to me, he told me what happened to you. You're not going to age for the next fifteen years."

"WHAT! This can't be. Scarlett will look like she is a cougar with me in her arms ten years from now. We have got to find a cure. Something has to be done."

I watched him rant and rave for a few minutes. I told him the rest.

"I've been tasked with finding and destroying the formula so that it can never be made again."

"Does that mean you're going to kill Maria?"

I hadn't thought about that. I had only thought about securing the formula and ridding the world of it. I had to kill her if I was going to completely eradicate it from the earth. Joey said something that caught me completely off guard.

"She will know when you're coming, and she will kill you. I've seen what has happened to other assassins that tried to kill her. It doesn't end well for them, trust me on this one."

Could I trust her to give me the formula and never use it ever again? What happens when somebody else discovers what happened and tries to force her to give them the formula? I don't think she is the kind of person that could handle torture and not reveal the true formula. Yes, I was going to have to eliminate her. I couldn't let Joey know this. I would just have to do it, and let the pieces fall where they may. If it had been that easy, I could have lived with it. To say that I was about to walk into a hornet's nest would have been an understatement. Joey dragged me in with him. I got caught up in something that was way over my head. I began to do what Joey does and associate songs with situations. Bethel Music has a song called "Over my Head." It was the perfect song for me.

We went back inside with me deep in thought and Joey very upset.

"Where is Maria?" he asked angrily and forcefully. Scarlett told him that she had Katrina at the studio. Katrina was making the money in this family lately. TV series, commercials. Just wait until she gets older, like three or four years from now. I had seen her in a fabric softener commercial. People instantly fell in love with her. By the time she was five, she would have the hearts of all America.

Joey told Scarlett he had to go back to Richmond.

"I'm going to be fired from my job if I haven't already. I know I have voice work for an upcoming film, but Tom told me I could do that in a sound studio back in Richmond. Scarlett, I'm not like you. I'll never make a living in films. The Academy Award was a fluke – you know it,

I know it. Please come back and stay with me when you figure things out. I would love to raise our children together, but I can't do it here."

I don't think I had ever seen Joey so mad. Even when Urstin beat him up, he held his temper. Now it looked like he had smoke coming out of his ears. Scarlett asked him if it was something she had done.

"No, but something your mirror image did has gotten under my skin. If I don't leave, and I mean right now, I'm going to kill her myself."

Scarlett looked at me nervously.

"Is she going with you?"

"For now, but our mission is not over. She will be back, and when she does come back, make sure you're not playing any games and pretending to be Maria. I'd hate to see anything happen to you."

This just made Scarlett more nervous. It wasn't the threat of danger to Maria, it was the fact that Joey was going to be near me, close to me, enticing him to do things he wouldn't normally do.

"I hope it wears off soon. The older Joey was a lot kinder and gentler."

I watched him hug her and give her a big kiss. I heard him say he loved her very much and what Maria had done at the awards ceremony had him thinking. "It would be nice to have a family again."

I remember her showing her breast to the world. What else had she done to make Joey say that? I just remember the disrobing part.

We left shortly on foot after that and Joey began to make phone calls. I was glad I was wearing a pair of sneakers because I think we might have walked about four or five miles before a ride showed up for us. We were headed for the airport and a flight to Richmond. Now let me tell you this had made me just a little bit nervous. I watch the news. I knew who was on all those planes. I knew Joey's history and his bad luck with flying. I tried to talk him into taking a train or a bus. He wouldn't have any of it. I couldn't just walk away from him. I had nowhere to go and Urstin was going to kill me the minute he found me. I thought my chances might be a little better with Joey, so I went with him. I should have known better. Let me tell you about the plane crash. We had gotten off the flight when the plane was still in the air, just barely. Need a bathroom break, because this is a whopper of a story and no one in their right mind is ever going to believe it – not even me and I was there.

* * *

The story, it's all true. Trust me.

Bob knew where I was going with this next part. I could see him beg me not to go there. The big hero was going to be taken down a notch, but no one outside this room was ever going to find out, right.

Mr. B had a car come and get us. We would be transported back to his place because Joey was going to have to wait until morning to get his flight with the only man willing to fly him around. That man had survived two flights with Joey. You would think he would have learned his lesson by now. We would find out that the third time was the charm.

Bob stood up and asked if he could tell his part of the story. He then looked at Ivan and said, "I would like Ivan to tell his part as well. Do we have a deal?"

He looked right at a very nervous Ivan. He never said a thing, just nodded his head.

"Okay, then. I woke up at that hotel with a woman I didn't even know, or even what her name was. I dressed and slipped out of the room. I searched for the other guy, but I must admit I didn't really look very hard. I found a young kid filling his gas tank at the gas station just down the street and made him a deal he couldn't refuse. I wouldn't hurt him if he gave me a ride back into the city. In fear for his life, he gave me a ride back to LA and the hotel. Everyone was gone and the rooms were being cleaned. I asked the owner where everyone had gone. She told me they had checked out.

"'An elderly man paid me. Thanked me. Gave me a very large tip for the inconvenience and the mess. He said someone might stop in and he gave me an envelope for a gentleman by the name of Bob, is that you?' she asked. I told her that was me, showed her my ID, because she didn't quite believe me. I ripped open the envelope and read the instructions. I was to be at a certain address that evening. I was to bring Joey and

Anna with me. Failure to show up would get a lot of people hurt. I didn't know at the time who the elderly gentleman was, the owner couldn't tell me. There was a phone number on the note. I dialed it and got Joey. Told him what was going on and that I thought Maria and the homeless people were being kept as hostages. He told me he would get back to me, said he would call me right back. A minute or two later he called back, said he would meet me.

"He had called Scarlett to verify that Maria had dropped Katrina off before she left the house. She had. Joey was now motivated. Mr. B had lent him a car and told him to have fun. We had fun alright. By the time Joey showed up to pick me up, it was going to take a miracle to make the assigned time. Anna took over the driving and even with all the traffic, we were still five minutes early. My knuckles were solid white. I hate the way she drives. I was scared shitless. Joey on the other hand was having trouble breathing and I had to help him calm down. Anna just looked at us and called us lightweights.

"I checked the glove box and found a couple of loaded weapons. A Glock for Anna, a .45 automatic for me. Joey said he didn't need a weapon. I left them to enter this side of the building. I circled around and was going to enter from the other side. I had no idea what we were going to find. All I knew was we were entering a warehouse in an industrial section of town.

"I entered to find that I had been set up. Mr. B was waiting with a bunch of MS-13 gang members. They were all armed to the teeth and ready to kill me on the spot. They had orders not to at this time, but that my time may run out if I didn't do as I was asked. He looked at me and said, 'Bob, I see she has worked her magic on you as well as these folks. I can't have that.' Behind him was a full-sized cage with the other homeless people and Maria. They all looked petrified. Maria was filing her nails like she didn't have a care in the world. I thought I would sacrifice myself and create a distraction so that Anna and Joey could get a jump on them. I raised the gun and fired at Mr. B. He didn't even flinch, he just laughed at me. 'You think I would give you a gun with real bullets in it? I'm a movie producer, we don't use the real stuff.' The gang bangers grabbed me and threw me in with the homeless. I had been defeated rather quickly. Anna, would you like to tell him what you did?"

* * *

Anna took over.

Joey and I entered from the near side. We encountered a dead man within a few feet of entering the building. The man was armed with an AR-15 that hadn't even been used. Somebody had gotten the drop on him. Bullet hole in the back of his head. I had no intentions of turning him over to see what his face looked like. I handed the Glock to Joey, grabbed the rifle for myself. We silently made our way through the warehouse to see Bob was arguing with Mr. Bennett. I saw him raise his gun and shoot. The damn guns had blanks in them. Good thing I didn't need Joey to use his weapon.

I was about to make my move when I felt cold steel on the back of my head. A hoarse voice told me to drop my weapon and stand up. I put the weapon down and slowly turned my head to see Joey with his hands in the air covered by one man and another with a weapon trained on me.

"Mr. B. has been expecting you," he said.

He ordered me to join the party. Joey was mumbling something to himself, it was like he recognized something. I looked at him and he had a big smile on his face.

"What's up?"

He laughed. "Of everything she has ever written, I read one story. They scare the shit out of me, so I try not to read her stuff. We are now in the one story I ever read."

I thought, well at least he knows how we're going to die.

"Gentleman, welcome to the party. I hope Mr. B has let you sample the product we just stole from the Cartels."

The MS-13 members had an uneasy look on their faces. Mr. B just stood and listened.

"He didn't tell you guys what this is all about did he?" he said. I heard more mumbling amongst the gang. Joey looked at one gang member and asked him if he had a knife. It was just seconds before Joey had one pressed against his neck.

"Not me fool, that package right there, slice it open."

The gangbanger removed the knife from Joey's neck and sliced the package open. Pure cocaine. Uncut and most definitely not ready for distribution. This stuff was an overdose ready to happen, but the gangbangers didn't realize that. All they knew was this junk belonged to the Cartels and they were all dead men if it ever got out who had hit this warehouse. I thought they were going to kill Mr. B.

"Try some gentlemen. It is some of the best you will ever have."

I watched in horror as one after another of those idiots started snorting large amounts of death. Joey sat with his back against the cage and watched as every one of those gang members put themselves on the list of unfortunate people that overdose from drugs every year. Street stuff is cut so much that its strength is severely lessened. The stuff these guys were devouring was the pure shit. Within a few minutes, it was just Mr. B, Joey, and I outside the cage still breathing. The gangbangers were all dead or on their way to death.

Then Mr. B said, "Nice work Anna, Joey. You as well Bob."

He opened the cage and let Bob out. He whispered something in Bob's ear and then turned to me.

"Anna, you and Bob are going to take credit for this seizure of almost forty-five tons of pure cocaine. The biggest bust in US history. I'm sorry how I had to go about getting you here, but I couldn't use these gang members and you guys at the same time. We lost a lot of men taking this place."

I was in disbelief at what he was saying. It was all a double setup. I looked at Joey and asked him if he knew all along. He said, "I told you it was the only story I ever read."

I still don't know what the hell he was talking about, but it sure appeared he knew everything that was going to happen.

Mr. B left Bob and I to get the authorities in to secure the place. Bob dropped me off several hours later after we briefed the agents that showed up. They were told I was undercover and would be in mortal danger if it was known I was involved in the seizure. He left me at Mr. Bennett's house and Joey was somewhere inside. I wanted to crawl up beside him and hold him. In his funny sort of way, I was very attracted to him. I wasn't going to search every room in the house, so took the downstairs bedroom and waited until morning to fly to my impending doom.

A knock on my door woke me from a restless sleep of pleasure and nightmares. I had dreamed that I was floating through the air and found some high-tension lines on my way back to earth. The pain was awful, and I woke drenched in sweat. I had a hard time falling back to sleep until I felt Joey's wonderful equipment sliding in and out of me. That orgasm woke me drenched in sweat once again. I couldn't go back to sleep now. Good thing I could see the sun coming up. I lay back and closed my eyes. Played back the things I was going to need to do and found myself in Joey's arms once again. I forced myself awake. I stood and paced the room. I lay back down again and drifted off until the knock on the door. It was Joey. I called him to come sit beside me. When he did, I grabbed him and forced myself on top of him. He fought me and threw me to the floor.

"What is the matter with you Anna?" he asked.

"Bad dreams Joey. I needed to feel your touch to calm me. I'm sorry about that," I replied.

He got up and walked out of the room saying as he went, "Breakfast will be ready in about ten minutes. Grab a cold shower. You need it.'"

He was right, I so did need that shower. I stunk from sour sweat and body odor. My clothes weren't exactly clean but in the closet was the sexiest blue dress I had ever seen. It fit perfect along with the matching panty and bra set. Pushed my assets right up. I wasn't used to a thong, it kept slipping into my ass crack. I found a vanity with all the makeup I would need. It felt like I was going to the prom. I couldn't explain why I was fixing myself up. All I knew was I would be spending the day with Joey and I wanted to look my best. I walked out and Joey smiled and shook his head.

He let out a whistle and mumbled, "I'm in so much trouble."

I hadn't known what the formula does to men when they first take it and how it makes them act. I was about to find out.

Joey hadn't had any downtime with me since he became young. It was one thing after another, and he hadn't had time for his hormones to take over his brain. He would have plenty of time today.

I sat holding his hand all the way to the airport. I saw Joey doing everything he could think of to distract his mind and take his attention from me. Nothing he did seemed to be working. I wasn't discouraging him at all, instead, I moved my body closer to him and remembered my awesome dream from last night and felt my panties becoming moist. It was now time for me to distract myself from thoughts of Joey before I ripped his clothes off right there in the limo.

We arrived with our clothes still on, just barely. Joey ran for the terminal and I tried to keep up. The last thing I borrowed were high heels that I barely wear, never mind run in. I almost landed on my face several times. I decided it wasn't lady-like to run in heels and walked the rest of the way. I had to save my dignity. I caught up to him leaving the bathroom. I noticed he still was having trouble getting everything put back inside his pants. I sure hope his zipper doesn't break.

Billy was waiting for us and apologized that he was unable to get the private jet. The insurance company was taking its sweet time paying for the last jet. We would be flying in a cargo plane. I heard Joey groan. Billy told him he brought extra blankets and even brought enough parachutes for all of us. I didn't care for the joke. The bad dream still very vivid in my memory banks.

The cargo plane was loaded with stuff that was destined for Colorado. Billy said we would transfer that cargo off and pick up another shipment meant for Baltimore. He said we could finish the trip from there with a couple-hour drive. The plane was going to be tied up for a few days and he would drive us the rest of the way in his car.

"Shouldn't be but a couple of hours layover in Denver," he told us.

The flight to Denver was uneventful and very boring. I couldn't get Joey to take his clothes off and have some fun with me. He claimed he was already a member of the Mile-High Club. I wanted to be a member as well. He fended me off and I had to devise a plan. A two-hour layover would be plenty of time for me to loosen my prey up. When we landed, I dragged Joey straight to the bar. I was going to order up some red wine when I noticed the bottle of Patron. Ever heard of the song by Joe Nichols? "Tequila Makes Her Clothes Fall Off." It does you know. I can attest to it. Joey ordered Rum and Coke. I ordered him a few more and before long Billy had to come and drag our staggering butts back on the plane. He warned us that if either of us puked he would make us clean up the mess.

As soon as the plane was in the air, Joey had lost all his clothes. Mine were gone long before that. We were screwing in drunken bliss when something weird happened. It got very quiet. You could no longer hear the jet engines purring away. Just the wind over the wings. Billy came back and found us naked as jailbirds and started cussing.

"We've been hit by an EMP. My pilot said he would stay with the plane and make sure it doesn't land in any residential areas. Quickly, get these on."

He threw us the parachutes. I was barely conscious and giggled myself sick as Joey tried to get some clothes on me. He gave up trying to find my stuff and pulled his shirt over my waiting breasts. I made him fondle them some more before I would let him put the chute on me. Time was running short and Billy came back out and said we had to go now, time's up. All Joey had gotten back on was his boxers but that was enough. Billy slipped the chute over Joey's shoulders and threw us both out the loading door. I can't tell you if he went with us that time. I died on the way down. My dream came true and I fried on those power lines. I woke up drenched in sweat. That was such a vivid dream, or was it? According to the story Joey gave me, it was all very real. Let me explain.

What I'm about to tell you all came from Joey. Did he lie to me, tell me some wild made-up fantasy of a story? Once you hear it, you might say yes. Others will say they believe every word. Gentlemen, I'm one of those people who believe every word he told me. Why, you say? I was involved in so much of this wild fantasy, how could I not believe every word he told me? Please remember, this came from Joey, not me.

CHAPTER 14

Joey has a tale.

I couldn't believe it was happening again. I can't fly anymore. I turned to see if Billy had followed us out the loading door, but it was so dark I couldn't tell. Anna's chute had opened as soon as we left the plane. I had my hand on her ripcord and when the wind caught her and yanked her out of my grasp, the cord was pulled, and she was safely floating to earth. I had to get my own chute open. I had no idea how high we were when we exited the plane. I pulled, it opened, and about a few seconds later, I hit the ground. It wasn't a soft landing. Another second and I would have been roadkill, flattened like a bug on a speeding windshield. My ankle was sore, I was alone. I looked around for Anna, but I couldn't find her. What I could find was the smell of burnt flesh. I looked up and saw her hanging from some power lines. It wasn't a pretty sight. I hung my head in sorrow. I liked her. This was no way for anyone to die. Such a tragedy. I got up to make my way to civilization. I followed the powerlines until I found a street. I sat and waited for a car to come by. The first one was a county sheriff. I was dressed only in my boxers, so to say I caught the police officer's attention would have been an understatement.

He got out of the car and we had a little talk. I got my ride and spent some time in a cell. The nice officer even gave me a bright orange jumpsuit to wear. The cell had a couple of other men inside with me. Rednecks, some people call them. I called them assholes. These two guys started on me almost as soon as I arrived. It was like throwing a new stuffed toy into a kennel of puppies. They just had to play with it. I wasn't in the mood. It was two against one. I was roughed up and bleeding from a cut above my eye. The two guys were lying in a corner crying like babies. Jacob has a way with people. What he did was even the score. He can't interfere, but he can give me things I might need to help, like a baseball bat. The one he gave me was a nice aluminum bat. It made this weird sound when it struck bone. I had become very good at swinging a bat.

When the guard came back in after hearing all the blood-curdling screaming, he thought he would find me lying in my own blood. What he found was two tough guys crying and whining about being beaten by an imaginary bat. I asked him if I could get an ice pack. He just shook his head. I told the officer he put me in a pen with a bunch of pussies. I didn't have no bat, where would I hide it? Nervously, the officer left me. I had my ice pack. The officer never gave it to me. When he came back in with one, he nearly pissed himself when he saw I had one already.

"I don't know what kind of shit you got going on here. I sure will be glad when you're gone."

I could tell the man was ready for a good stiff strong drink of bourbon, maybe more than one. In another minute, I would be ready for one myself.

Urstin and his right-hand man Ivan came walking in dressed as police officers. They had come up with this story about a missing mental patient and gave my description. I fit the profile, but I was younger than who they were looking for. They asked to see me. Urstin smiled broadly when he saw me, Ivan never gave away what he was feeling, remained straight-faced without emotion. Urstin told the guard this was without a doubt the man they were searching for. He asked if they had found a woman, said she had the most amazing green eyes. No one has seen anyone that fit that description.

"Keep a close eye out for her. She is extremely dangerous."

The two guys in the cell with me shouted to Urstin as he left, "Don't bring him back, please!" It sounded like they were pleading with him.

I was taken to an interrogation room. They sat opposite me and stared.

"Nice work, Joey. You have a very good surgeon in LA. I can't believe how young you look. Maybe you could give me the number so that I can have the same work done, what do you say?"

Urstin was asking for the number of my plastic surgeon. Was he being serious?

"I don't think you could afford him. He's very expensive."

Urstin let out a very long and loud belly laugh.

"You crack me up Joey, you know that? You also might have put me on the Cartels' most wanted list tonight. I was trying to kill my bitch wife. You were just collateral damage, a bonus. Why would you choose to fly with a man that transports product for the Cartels?"

I didn't know what he was talking about.

"Joey, stop looking so confused. You can't possibly tell me you didn't know Billy was a mule for the Cartels?"

I was dumbfounded. I really didn't know.

"You're lying."

"You think I'm lying? Here, let's watch the news together."

He flicked on the television and we watched the report of the plane crash. Two confirmed dead, an estimated twenty tons of unprocessed cocaine spread all over the mountainside.

"He was taking it to Baltimore to be processed and distributed to those poor citizens. How does that make you feel Joey?"

I knew I had nothing to do with it, except I didn't ride for free. I paid fuel cost. So, in all reality, I was involved somehow.

"Be a shame if the world found out the great Joey Hopkins was in cahoots with the Cartels."

"You know damn well I'm not."

"I do, but the world Joey, they might not believe all your stories." Urstin was really hitting a nerve. "Joey, tell me how you got to be the way you are right now. Maybe we can make a deal. I want to be young again."

Could I really make a deal with the devil? This man has been my nemesis since my days in the Navy. This guy was pure evil. I couldn't do it.

"I have this plastic surgeon in LA."

"Enough of the lies!" Urstin screamed at me. He got right into my face. He was so close I could smell the vodka on his breath. "Listen to me, you piece of shit, you're going to tell me everything I want, or so help me, I will destroy you. Do you understand?"

I nodded and took a deep breath.

"I have this surgeon –"

I got a backhand to the face.

"I don't think you took me seriously, did you Joey?" Another punch to the face. "I want to know the truth, and you damn well are going to give it to me!"

I was saved by a knock on the door. The officer at the door motioned for Ivan and Urstin to follow him. When they came back in, I was gone. I had disappeared into the wind.

The officer that had been dealing with me all night said, "I knew something wasn't right about that man, downright weird I tell you."

Urstin and Ivan searched the whole room, where there was no place to hide and no exits except for the one they were at. How did I get by them and escape? Urstin was so mad he punched the officer in the face and accused him of helping me escape. I was still in the room. I just was on the other side of the curtain standing with Jacob. He had reached through and pulled me to the other side.

"Jesus wants to speak to you."

I looked at him, "Now? He wants to speak right now?" I was badly beaten, still slightly drunk, dressed in orange prison garb and in no shape whatsoever to be meeting with my Lord. "Can I get something better to wear and maybe cleaned up a bit before we go?"

Jacob laughed. "Trust me on this. He's seen you in a lot worse shape than this."

I shook my head. I didn't like this one bit. What had I done now that warranted this meeting?

When I arrived at the yellow house, I was told he was at the cathedral down the road. I walked with Jacob and he was telling me that I had really messed things up this time. I couldn't figure what I had done wrong. I was about to find out. Jesus waited for us at the doorway.

He told Jacob that he could wait for us. This was something only he could do with me alone. I thought this was just great. All my life I dreamt of having one on one time with my Lord and here I was now dreading every moment.

"I want you to meet someone. He is the only one who can fix what has happened," Jesus calmly said to me.

I wanted to know what we had to fix. What had I done?

"We need to do a reset. The only one that can do it is my Father. We are going now to meet with him together."

I was being brought in to meet the Holy Father, the one and only God, the I AM, my Creator. I was a mess. I wasn't dressed for this occasion! I needed to shave, a shower. At least a decent set of clothes and a comb through my hair. I started to resist, pull back. Jesus took my hand and started to pull me along. I fought him. He kept telling me it was going to be alright. I kept resisting. Finally, he left me in the cathedral, said he would be right back. I sat and listened to thousands of angels sing. It was the most beautiful sound I have ever heard. As I looked around, I noticed just how big and glorious this one church was. I felt truly at peace.

I looked up and saw Jesus pushing a cart with a burning tree on top of it. I instantly recalled the Desperation band song called, "Burning Tree." I fell to my knees and begged God for his forgiveness. I begged and pleaded that he give me another chance. I would do better, try harder. Whatever it takes God, I'll do it. Has anybody ever told you that God has a sense of humor? I heard the voice of James Earl Jones asking me to stand. I hadn't looked up yet, but slowly rose to a standing position. The burning tree was in front of me, but the voice was behind me. I turned and saw him, he laughed and said he sure did love that prop. I didn't know what to say. I wish I could describe him to you, would like to very much. I was so overwhelmed I don't remember exactly what he looked like. He looked like us. I was sure I had met him several times in my life. He assured me that I had.

"I am always with you, Joey. Always remember that first and foremost. I will never abandon you, no matter what."

THE TRUTH

We talked about some things that needed to be addressed. Other things were just small talk. He finally got to the root of the matter.

"I'm going to do a restart for you, Joey. It is very complicated, and I rarely do it. I'm going to take you back to just before you got on the plane in LA."

"I thought we couldn't go back in time," I remember saying this to God.

"I am timeless, Joey. If I say it, it is done. I gave free will to my children, they in turn now have the choice to turn to me or to turn to Lucifer. In the end, which is close at hand, I will determine who gets to stay with me and who gets to live in Hell with him. Joey, we must save as many as possible. I wish I could save them all, but if I did that, I would be bringing hell to heaven. Remember all that we talked about. Good luck. I'll always be with you."

I closed my eyes and I was sitting in the car with Anna holding my hand. I looked at her pretty face and those piercing green eyes and smiled. All was right in the universe again. It was to be a day of déjà vu. Only something had to change today, or all would not be right in the universe once again.

Now if I only knew what it was that caused the need for a restart. The other thing was, why was a restart rarely done? Would it cause more problems than it solved? Did it disrupt the flow of the universe? Maybe a ripple effect where things that might have happened are now changed forever. Some for the good and some for the bad. How come I remembered, but no one else did? They were all living this day for the first time while it was my second pass through this day. It felt strange. I didn't want to get on that airplane because I knew what was going to happen. Once again, a plane that I was on would crash.

I ran for the bathroom. Anna tried to keep up but kept turning her ankle, so she had to slow her pace. I stared at my reflection and tried to figure out a way to make things right. I was coming up with nothing. I guess I'll make it up as I go. I walked out to find Billy was waiting with Anna for me to come out and join them.

Anna said, "You alright, Joey? You look a little frazzled."

"Fear of flying lately," I responded. This got a bunch of nervous laughter.

Billy said, "Don't worry. I brought parachutes for all of us this time."

I thought to myself, make sure you pull the ripcord a lot sooner than you did last time. I almost splattered myself into the ground I had waited so long. The power lines were also a concern. Must make sure I steer Anna clear of them this time. We shouldn't drink or have sex. Yes, must make sure we behave ourselves this time around.

That was my plan when we landed in Denver. I even ordered a coke before heading to the restroom. Anna was doing a number on me. I was sure she was going to break the zipper on my pants. When I returned, she was on her second tequila, and that made me nervous. I grabbed my coke and drank it in one gulp. I think she had gotten the bartender to make it a double, so I could catch up to her. This wasn't good. I had to keep fighting off her advances. It wasn't easy. The little head started to do the thinking even though I fought hard with it. I knew I hadn't had as much to drink as the last time, but I still had more than I needed. When Billy came to get us, he seemed a little perturbed that we had gotten drunk.

While he was assisting us back to the plane, I asked him, "What are we transporting?"

"I have a customer that ships this cargo once every two weeks. It's something from a pharmaceutical company that they use in a drug they manufacture in Baltimore. I'm not exactly sure what it is, but they pay on time and it's steady work."

I wanted to scream at him that he was being used to transport cocaine to the East Coast and was supplying the whole northern corridor from DC to Boston. I really hoped that he was being honest and wasn't trying to pull the wool over my eyes to hide the fact that he was a drug mule.

He left us to be alone, but only after leaving us a bucket and telling me if I make a mess, I'm going to clean it up. Anna couldn't wait and my clothes were flying around the cargo hold. I knew I was going to need them, so I tried to keep track of where she was tossing my stuff. I carefully removed her clothes and made sure I would be able to find them quickly when the shit hit the fan. She picked her stuff up after I had neatly put it to the side and flung it to parts unknown. I tried to go and get her things, I really did, but was pulled back down and consumed by Anna. I lost track of time until the silence hit the plane. This time I knew what was going on and jumped up to find our clothes. Nothing had changed, we were going out the door barely clothed, but this time Billy went with us. My ripcord was pulled as soon as I cleared the plane. Billy followed Anna down and pulled hers. He made sure she cleared the power lines, but he ended up hanging about twenty feet above the ground in a spruce tree. I found Anna, then Billy. He wanted to cut himself down. I knew that was a bad idea. I told Anna to stay with Billy. I was going to find a ladder and help him down.

I found the ladder, was taking it when the cops showed up. A man in boxer shorts stealing a ladder from a garage was arrested today. I could already read the headlines. Another trip to my familiar jail cell. I was ready for my two redneck friends. For some reason, they didn't want to tangle with me this time. Something about a bad dream and a crazy man. I of course fit the description of crazy man quite well. I waited for Urstin and Ivan in my orange prison garb. They were right on time. The story changed this time.

Urstin was mad that he was set up. Seems he had gotten bad intel from Mr. B about what and who was on the plane. He knew Anna and I were on the plane; the drugs and who owned it was what had him aggravated. He thought Anna was going to confiscate the drugs when it got to Baltimore. The drugs were supposed to belong to a different group of bad people. These folks were supposed to be American businessmen. He would be doing the Cartel a favor by taking out the plane and the bitch that was responsible for them losing so much product in LA. When he found out it all belonged to the same Cartel, he almost had a stroke. This was revealed in a phone call shortly after the plane crash. Somebody was going to pay, and if they didn't, somebody was going to die.

Urstin didn't want to die, so he needed a fall guy. He also needed Anna. Her body hadn't been found on the plane. One person was recovered from the wreckage. It was the pilot. He thought I was the man with all the answers. He tried to beat those answers out of me. I told him Anna knew nothing about the plane or the cargo and I had no idea about her whereabouts at this moment.

My story about the parachutes and Billy being hung up in a tree were all just that, stories. Nothing had been found in their search of the area. I thought this was strange, at least they should have found my chute. It was like it never happened. Urstin decided he was going to play unfairly. He showed me a live feed of Madison Square Garden. It was of a hockey game between the Rangers and Bruins. A large fight had broken out before the game and several people in the stands were clearly visible in the footage. Ben Bennett, Peter, and Beats were all clearly seen in a shot of players duking it out.

"I'll give you to the end of the game to give me the information I require. Once they come out of that stadium, if I don't have what I want, they will die. Do you understand, Joey?"

I understood all too well. I couldn't save them. I had nothing to give to Urstin. I pleaded my case only to get put harshly back into my cell. The rednecks were gone, but a very feminine-looking biker was lying on the floor severely beaten. His jacket had the Queen Bee insignia. I checked on him to see if he was still alive. He was. I put my ear close to his head, he wanted very badly to tell me something.

"They are both safe now. We got them out." It was all he managed to say before he passed out. Okay, little I could do with that information. I called out to Jacob, maybe he could help me.

It took him a few minutes to show up, but he did.

"I need your help. Peter and Beats are in grave danger. We must save them."

Jacob laughed at me.

"My friend, they are in danger because of you. The universe is out of whack and it might take a few days to settle it back into place. We can do nothing." That wasn't the answer I was looking for. Urstin came down shortly after that, asked again for anything I might want to add. I sat dejected in the corner of the cell. My cellmate had passed away just a few minutes ago and now more would die because of me.

"So be it then. I'll let you watch the aftermath on the news."

He wheeled a television over so that I could see it, placed it on a channel that would have the news coverage he wanted.

"I hope you enjoy. Maybe next time you won't lie to me."

He walked out, leaving me to view something I didn't want to see. I prayed for them to find a way out of their predicament. What I saw that night was a night of miracles.

CHAPTER 15

Ivan tells a white lie.

"I could barely get Urstin to listen to me. I knew we were in very hot water. In Urstin's rush to kill his wife, he had discovered they would be on this cargo plane that was loaded with cocaine bound for Baltimore. If Urstin had dug a little deeper, he would have known it belonged to the Cartel we were having problems with. They supplied us with large sums of money to fund Helen Harrison's campaigns and in return, we provided them with some protection. The warehouse in LA had them on edge. Now losing the cargo plane had them incensed. This was unacceptable. I was in fear not only for my life, but Urstin's and Helen's as well. We had a very big problem.

"Urstin decided to call in a few favors and put a hit out on some folks close to Joey. I knew he couldn't give us the information we needed. I begged Urstin to go in another direction, but he insisted on teaching Joey a lesson. I made notes of the people he called so that I could turn all that evidence in when I came in. I watched in disbelief how the night had unfolded. I checked in on Joey several times to make sure he hadn't somehow disappeared. He sat in his jail cell all alone, head between his knees praying to God.

"Urstin was done with him. He was doing damage control and trying to line up a big score so that he could come up with some cash to give to the Cartels. I didn't think he was going to be able to come up with a hundred million to save our worthless lives. He did, he devised a plan with Helen to do just that. We would get to live another day. The things that I was seeing were making me want to fold my tent and call it a day. It also was making me think that the country was in terrible danger and I must do everything in my power to save her. I stayed on for a few more months. Barely made it out alive. I'll turn it back over to Anna and let her explain the details."

* * *

Anna must avoid the truth.

I knew if I said the wrong thing here, I would be putting a fine man in danger. He had already pleaded with me to keep him out of it. I knew Ivan had his suspicions. The Queen Bees being in place to facilitate our escape was way too much of a coincidence. If anyone knew the full extent of his involvement it might lead to his death.

Walter asked the question I so dreaded.

"How did the Queen Bees know just where to find you and that you were in trouble?"

I threw the old man under the bus. "It was Mr. B. He knew what Urstin was up to, knew that Billy would be prepared whenever he flew with Joey now.

This was the third time Billy was on a doomed flight with Joey. The Queen Bees just had to wait and watch to see where we landed. We could have gotten Joey out as well if he hadn't been caught taking the ladder."

Now that was a whopper of a lie that was as close to the truth as I dared to get.

"Where did they take you, Anna?"

Here we go with the part of the story that no one was ever going to believe, including me.

I began once more.

"I was taken to California to a horse ranch owned by Mr. B. It was out in the desert and very remote. Before I get to that part of the story, you must understand how all the players ended up at the ranch, including our President."

I paused. I cast a gaze toward Ivan, watched him squirm in his seat. Bob didn't appear to be all that comfortable as well. I thought this might be a good thing. Now how was I ever going to get them to believe what Beats had done? When a boy as young as eight does what he did, there is no way to get a single person to ever believe. I thank God for him everyday, because if he hadn't been there, I would have been dead a long time ago. The boy saved my life several times, put his life in jeopardy more times than I can count, and still came out of it with a big smile on his face.

I continued to tell them the story.

Well, let's go back to where Beats and Peter go to New York to meet up with Ben. Jenna had talked to Mrs. Perkins. She was taking care of Beats now. She had a conference in California and Mr. Gould was going to watch the boy while she was gone. Jenna told her of the trip and Mrs. Perkins thought that was a great idea since Beats always seemed to get caught up in some scam that Mr. Gould came up with to make all kinds of money off the poor child. That was a whole other story that was told a long time ago but was the beginning of when we discovered just how special of a child he was.

Peter was excited. Beats was even more excited because Peter had promised they could see a Rangers game and Beats' favorite player played for the Bruins. The two teams would be meeting each other while they were in New York. When he talked to Ben before they left, he had said he would get them the best seats in the house. Ben had one favor – he wanted Beats to play this new drum set he had. The one catch was, he was to do it in front of a group of friends Ben had visiting the studio. Peter asked Beats if that was alright with him.

"If it gets me the tickets to the game, I'm fine with it," he said.

Peter relayed the information to Ben and he got them the tickets. He also got a Led Zeppelin tribute band to agree to be at the studio the same time as Beats. Everyone that had heard Beats play the drums had compared him to the late great John Bonham.

On the plane to New York, Beats had a very bad dream. He woke up crying and as much as Peter had tried to console him, nothing seemed to be working. Peter had his own bad dream and he could still taste the blood in his mouth. When he wiped his mouth, he realized he had bitten his tongue and that was where the blood was coming from.

"Beats, listen to me. It was just a bad dream, nothing more than that," he had said it more for himself than Beats.

The boy started to calm down, but also, he was formulating a plan. The dream had foretold him of what was to come. He knew he couldn't change much that was to come, but he could make it so that they would live instead of die. The key to it all was that everyone in the car had to survive the original attack. He knew the driver would be Turkish. All he had to do was learn one word. *Gelen*, it meant "incoming" in Turkish. If he shouted it loud enough, he knew the man would duck and take cover. It would save his life for now. The rest would be in his hands.

They arrived at the studio right on time. Ben took Beats right back to the sound room where he had set up the new drum set. Beats couldn't wait to jump in the seat. They were a little early. It was okay. Peter and Ben got to work out the details of Jenna and Church Band performing once again. This time Peter had to break some bad news to Ben.

"I think she wants to play with Savage Storm and Deke's band Truly Blessed," he said.

This caught Ben by surprise.

"I thought you two were an item. Weren't you going to marry that girl?"

Peter tried to explain, but that seemed to be a difficult thing to do.

"It's complicated. She is more comfortable performing with Deke and singing lead for Savage Storm."

Ben scratched his head.

"What about the boy? Who is he going to play with?"

Peter just shrugged.

"I have no idea. Nobody has asked him. Besides, he's just a kid. How will he be able to handle a tour?"

"I'll tell you how, Peter. He will do it like he was born to do it," Ben replied.

The guests had arrived. It was now time to see if his theory was even close to being correct. Ben introduced Peter to the tribute band for the classic rock group Led Zeppelin.

The guys were distracted. They had their eyes set on the sound room and the noise that was emanating from it. Peter noticed one of the guys had a tear rolling down the side of his cheek. The guys all had their instruments with them. They wanted badly to go into the sound room.

Ben said with a huge smile on his face, "Be my guest gentlemen."

Peter watched them interact with Beats. He had no clue who they were, but he greeted them like they were long lost friends. The memories of Beats first playing the drums for him was rolling around in his head. It was a Led Zeppelin song that he had first heard Beats play. Ben and Peter watched them agree on a song to play. Ben was ready and hit record, no way was he going to pass up this opportunity. They played the song "Rock and Roll." Peter and Ben watched with their mouths hanging open. Ben kept doing fist pumps and Peter kept saying over and over, "I can't believe what I'm seeing."

After one song, the guys had played enough. Beats wanted to do more, but when you're in your seventies, it's hard to keep up with such a young man.

The guys thanked Ben and walked away shaking their heads and talking to each other in rapid and excited speech. Peter watched them walk away. Ben called him over.

"Listen to this," he said to Peter. Ben had isolated the drum track and played it for Peter, then he played it again. It sounded the same to Peter.

"I just played the original track and followed it with Beats' track."

Peter looked puzzled.

Ben said, "They sound exactly alike! John Bonham was one of the greatest drummers of his time. I think we have the next greatest drummer of our time sitting in that sound room Peter. You've got to get that kid to play with you guys, do whatever it takes."

Peter pondered his advice. Ben told them he was going to the game with them. I guess to further try to talk Peter into making sure the kid played with one of the bands under his control. Ben talked Beats' ear off on the way over, but once inside, Beats was in game mode. His favorite player was winding down his career. A few goals short of seven hundred. A milestone that Jason Craymore greatly wanted to achieve. This game had playoff implications. The winner would most likely get to play at home to start the playoffs. It was already determined they would play each other in the first round of the playoffs. The players were doing their pre-skate when the first of the bad blood began. Beats was cheering loudly for Jason and they weren't exactly in Boston. One of the rookie players for the Rangers made the first mistake. The kid was going to be a superstar someday and had been called up for the playoff push. After just five games, he already had eight goals and ten assists. To say he was a major part of the team would have been an understatement. He also was very cocky and had a big mouth. One that someone was going to put a fist into very shortly.

The phenom skated up to the glass in front of Beats and yelled at him to keep his mouth shut and show some respect to the Rangers. Jason Craymore's best friend, Sergie, heard what was said and him being of Russian descent didn't exactly like the kid using ethnic slurs against one of Jason's fans. The first punch thrown was by the Bruins and the game hadn't even started. The Rangers couldn't have anyone going after their rookie all-star and jumped in. The Bruins weren't shy and joined into the fracas. Bodies were flying everywhere and it was game on. The referees looked at each other and just started to jot down on a notepad who was going to get tossed and who was going to get to play. The crowd roared loudly and the mob mentality started to take control. They wanted blood and they were going to get it. If it wasn't going to be out on the ice, then it was going to be in the stands. Many people had traveled to New York for the game and many fights ensued between New Yorkers and Bostonians.

Beats noticed that Jason Craymore had been injured in the pregame fracas. Just by the way he was holding his arm, it looked like it was a season-ending injury. Beats had to do something.

"Peter, I need you to get me down to the locker room," Beats said.

Ben looked at Peter and shrugged his shoulders.

"It means the world to him if he could get to meet Jason," Peter said to Ben. He knew the man had some influence in this town.

"I'll see what I can do. Wait here for me."

Ben left to work his magic. Ben hoped if he did this favor for the boy that the kid would stay under his control and play with one of the bands he had signed.

Moments later, Ben came back and led Beats back to the locker rooms. The first period was close to being finished so they had precious little time. Once all the players headed for the locker room, the meeting would be over. Jason Craymore sat dejected at his locker with his wrist wrapped in ice. Fresh from x-rays, and confirmation of a broken bone in his wrist. His nose hadn't faired too well and his right eye was swollen shut. Jason was a mess. Sergie wasn't doing much better. He laid on the trainer's table with a bag of ice on his face.

Jason smiled when he saw Beats. Ever since he first met the boy in DC, he knew the kid was special. Beats sat down next to him and said, "I can take all the pain away if you would like. I feel responsible for everything that happened tonight."

Jason patted him on the back with his good hand.

"It wasn't your fault. I gave it everything I had. It was a great career," he said.

Beats replied, "What I'm telling you is that I can make it all go away."

Jason looked at him puzzled and said he didn't understand.

Beats said, "Let me show you."

Jason thought that the kid seemed determined. What did he have to lose? Make the kid feel better is what he thought.

"Okay kid, show me what you can do."

Beats moved over to him and placed his hands just above his broken wrist. Beats was only going to fix the wrist but got a little carried away. He pulled everything from Jason. The years of injuries had caused severe arthritis. The knees were surgically repaired so many times he wondered how they stayed together. His broken collar bone caused stiffness quite a bit. When Beats was done, it was all gone. He felt terrific like he hadn't since he was playing Peewee hockey. Jason opened his eyes to tell Beats all this when the door to the locker room flew open and his coach came plowing in shouting obscenities. The first person he saw was Beats and he blew a gasket. He grabbed Beats by the collar and ushered him from the locker room. Outside the locker room, the coach kneeled in front of Beats.

"I'm very sorry, but you can't stay inside. I have some things I need to tell this team that young ears were never meant to hear," holding onto Beats' hands as he said this.

Beats said he was sorry as well and said, "I hope you don't feel too bad after today."

The coach stood up feeling a little woozy. He stormed inside the locker room screaming once again. Five minutes later, an ambulance showed up to take the coach to the hospital.

Beats was escorted back to his seat to watch the rest of the game.

"Did you have a nice talk with Jason Craymore?" Peter asked him.

Beats smiled and said, " A very good pep talk. I think you'll love what you see from here on out."

Ben and Peter looked at each other and shrugged. They knew what Beats was talking about when incredibly Jason came skating out for the second period. The Rangers weren't very happy to see him, especially when he was playing like he did in his rookie year. Jason lit the scoreboard up three times in the period and now the game was tied. His coach got to watch from the hospital. One eye swollen shut, a broken wrist, and a nose that needed to be set.

The third period started like the previous and the rookie phenom felt he had to do something. Jason was in the corner and the kid took a run at him. The elbow was high and connected with Jason's head and drove it into the boards for a double impact. Jason Craymore was once again out for the season, this time with a severe concussion. The kid was suspended, but the damage was done. Jason had finished two goals shy of seven hundred. The playoffs were also now in question for him.

After they carted Jason off the ice, Beats didn't want to stay for the rest of the game. Reluctantly, Peter and Ben were talked into leaving the stadium. Beats was prepared for the rest of this exciting evening.

The taxi pulled up just as he had dreamed with the Turkish driver. Ben climbed into the front and Peter slid into the back.

Beats stood at the door and screamed, "Gelen!"

He ducked down and so did the driver. The barrage of bullets lit up the side of the taxi. Everyone inside the vehicle was hit. Glass was flying everywhere and the sound of metal giving way to powerful rounds was deafening. Beats was outside the taxi and wasn't hit by any of the lead. Some glass scratched his brow and he had blood flowing down his face. The gang members had to be quick. It was a quick strike and then take off, so you didn't get caught.

Beats was able to quickly get into the taxi and evaluate the damage. The first was to check on the driver to see if he was still alive. He was, but barely. He didn't have much time. First, he would save Peter, then if he still had enough time, he would save Ben. It all depended on how long the Turk lived. He held his hands above Peter and pulled his injuries from his body. Peter stared at him and watched what he did. He had seen this once before. Poor little Jacob had taken a bullet and was dying. The dog Jake ended up with the bullet and death. Jacob walked away like nothing ever happened to him. It was his turn now.

"No, Beats. Who are you going to transfer it to?" Peter asked.

"I got this Peter," he replied.

He moved to the front still holding on to Peter's injuries, checked the Turk was still breathing, and pulled Ben's injuries from his body. He quickly gave it all to the Turk before he died, for if he didn't, it was all coming to him. It had to be transferred or held.

"We have to go now," he said to Ben. "You know where to get us to a safe place, we must go now."

Ben seemed to understand. If they didn't get to safety, another attack was imminent.

The three of them walked away from the taxi and headed for the subway. The whole event had been caught on camera. Joey got to watch it all on the news from his jail cell. The police had questions for our three heroes. They caught up to them in the subway. Sometimes you think the police are the good guys, but sometimes they can be the bad guys. They all wear the same uniform, so it's hard to tell which is which.

When they fire their guns at you, Beats figured they were the bad guys. He dragged Peter and Ben down onto the tracks and into the tunnel.

"Follow me! We have got to get to safety. The subway has many passageways and places to hide."

He led them into the bowels of the city and away from the pursuing officers.

"It's your turn, Ben. Make a call. We need a place to hide for the night."

Ben pulled out his phone and made the calls. They had a place to hide. It turned out it wasn't all that safe of a hideout.

CHAPTER 16

Deke's side of the story.

After winning the contest that Jenna had set up with Ben, things in my life started to take a downward spiral. Firstly, Jenna liked to play with Savage Storm and pushed me out of the way and played with them when Peter decided to show back up with my wife Ellen. If that wasn't bad enough, Ellen found me, and I still had to answer to her for why they left us in the first place. The reason of course was, Jenna and I were under the influence of that evil concoction that Maria had made up. It was a super Viagra kind of substance that drove both men and women into a sexual frenzy. We were making enough noise behind that wall that the whole town knew what was happening, including Peter and Ellen.

I tried to smooth things over with her once the police finally released me from custody. They thought I was the Deke with the million tattoos – I was, but don't tell them that. The only good thing that evil formula did was remove all my ink, like I never had a tattoo in my life. It was the weirdest thing ever to happen to me. I was a freak with all those tattoos. Now without all the ink, I look like a wimpy white guy. The fake ID I acquired said my name was John Deacon, that's why people called me Deke. If the cops had done a thorough investigation, they would have easily found I was indeed the man they were after. I got lucky. My band members thought we would never win, and when we did, they got cold feet on me. Now it's just Zach and maybe Beats. I can't find him to ask him if he's in or not. That boy is about the best there ever was, he would not be easy to replace. Jenna, she could sing like an angel. I felt so comfortable when I was on stage with her. I can't explain it. Seems like we were meant for each other. I used to fantasize about her. Then we drank that damn stuff and she nearly killed me. The sex was great in moderation, but she couldn't be satisfied. It was more, more, more. I thought my rod was going to fall off from overuse. She wouldn't let me sleep and I felt like I was going to die. That behavior lasted nearly the full two weeks they were gone. She claims she got some medical help and now doesn't have any desire at all. It was feast or famine with her. Now I'm afraid to be alone with her in case the medicine doesn't work.

I dread going to see her. I need to ask her what her plans are. Ellen's plans apparently don't include me. She got on a bus this morning and is on her way to see her mother. She claims she needs time to heal, and I need time to get Jenna out of my head. Until I no longer desired Jenna, there wouldn't be enough room in my tiny brain for them both. I guess that means she's leaving me. She left by telling me she still loves me, but things needed to change. I kissed her goodbye and told her I would work on it.

I needed to play in a band, it kept me focused. In order to do this, I had to visit Jenna. I stopped at Niko's house first. I didn't want to take the chance that Peter might not be there, and if he was, I didn't want to get shot. That is why I asked Niko to join me. I thanked God he was home.

I explained to him why I was there and asked him if he would help me.

He said, "I'll tell you what son, you got to go and see R.J. Ted after we're done. He needs some help in the worse way. I think you can help him on one of those projects he's working on. Do we have a deal?"

I thought that it would be a simple and easy task that he was asking me to do. If I knew exactly what I was getting myself into, I might have passed and went to see Jenna myself. Pastor Ted is more than a handful. His mission is to help people, but some of those people are beyond help, or so I thought. I would find out soon enough.

We headed over to see Jenna. That was when the fun began. When we knocked on the door, we could hear complete chaos coming from inside. Niko didn't wait for anyone to answer the door, we just walked in. Jenna was chasing one of the twins around the house. The other two children were running in opposite directions. Seems that Joey, or maybe it was Jacob, had found a gun in the house and was running around pretending it was a toy. Niko grabbed me by the shirt and pulled me down to take cover just in time. The gun went off and a bullet whizzed just above our heads. Jenna was screaming at the child and he began to cry and dropped the gun. It went off again when it hit the floor and the bullet ended up in the wall between the two of us. Niko wiped his brow and let out a sigh.

"Never a dull moment with those children."

We stood up and Jenna let out another scream. She was now holding the gun and Niko dove for cover once again. It wasn't necessary. She put the gun up out of the reach of the kids and invited me in. Niko, where are you? I need you now, I thought to myself nervously. Niko stood and let it be known that he was there as well.

Jenna apologized for the commotion. She had been cleaning the mess the bad guys had made. Apparently, they left behind one of their weapons and the kids found it before she did. We sat and she made us coffee. Small talk ruled for the first few minutes before I got down to business.

"Jenna, I have no band that I can use to fill the contract with Ben. My guys from the bar never bargained we would win. They've had their fill of touring with the metal band they played for. Now they just want to relax and enjoy life and get drunk as much as possible."

Jenna gave me a warm smile and said, "Deke, I might have a solution for you. Savage Storm wants me to be their lead singer. I don't want to leave Peter out in the cold. I would like to play and sing for Church Band."

I started to protest, but she held her hand up to let her finish.

"I can't sing for both bands, my voice would never hold up. What I would like to do is this, play for both bands with you. You can sing and perform better than anything Savage Storm has to offer. I'll tell them we are a package deal. You'll sing the lead on most of the songs while I play the keyboard. I'll jump in and sing lead on a couple of songs in between. When Church Band plays, now we'll also have Peter. We'll spread the workload amongst the three of us. What do you say to that?"

"Do you think Peter is going to go for that after everything that has happened between us?"

Jenna smiled, "I have a wild card, his name is Beats. He said he'll play for whoever I ask him to play for. Peter would be a fool to pass on him. He doesn't play for him without me giving my blessing."

I shook my head. This was a lot to grasp. I would be living my dream life with my dream girl by my side and never again be able to hold her in my arms. This would mean I would never be able to talk Ellen into ever coming back to me. I was in a conundrum. I'm sure Jenna thought I was going to jump at the chance. I didn't.

"I'm going to have to get back to you on that one Jenna. I have to seriously think about it."

She played my bluff and said, "Take your time. Let me know what you decide."

I thanked her and left her to ponder what I was going to do. Niko was on my tail and gave me the answer.

"Pastor Ted awaits your arrival. I told him you would be there in about an hour."

I was going to protest, but I bit my tongue. I had agreed to do something, maybe this would help me decide what I was going to do.

"You're right, would you like to join me, Niko?"

"Hell no, have you seen the kinds of people that man is trying to help?"

I watched him walk away from me shaking his head and mumbling about some damn fool, probably get his head shot off. This was not the confidence builder I was looking for from him. He told me he was going to walk home.

"Have fun," he said as he waved goodbye to me. My day wasn't getting much better, so how could Pastor Ted make it any worse? I'm so stupid.

CHAPTER 17

Beats sees it all.

Ben got us to his safe house about an hour later. I was tired and exhausted from everything that had happened today. All I wanted to do was grab a little shut-eye. I found a pillow and crawled between the sofa and the wall. It was my own little safe place. Out of sight, out of mind. I don't think I was asleep more than a few minutes when the Cartels found us. Ben doesn't have very good friends. They cave under the least bit of torture. I hid where I was at while they rounded up Peter and Ben. The plan was to take them to this alley where they like to kill people. It had become almost a nightly ritual to drag someone down to this little spot and put a bullet into them. The neighbors never even called the cops anymore for fear they would be the next ones standing against the wall waiting for their final breath.

I couldn't let them go without me, so I made myself known. Hindsight would have been a very good thing to have right then and there. I could have got away scot-free, they never knew I was there. I just had to be the hero and expose myself. Now I was being dragged to my final resting place along with my two adult companions who were shamelessly begging for their lives. I wasn't going to waste my time and energy on that nonsense. I had to come up with a plan. So far, I was coming up with nothing. If only I had stayed behind the couch, I might have lived to become an adult and have a family and a wonderful life. They call it a crossroad, the place where you get to make life-changing decisions. I made my decision to die with my friends tonight. What was I thinking?

My time was quickly nearing its end when I decided it was time to dial up my namesake. He told me I could call him anytime. I didn't need those stupid phones all the guardian angels were carrying now. I could use telepathy. He answered on the first ring. I told him I could really use his help now. You know what he says to me? "I'm on it." Three simple words. I had no idea what he was about to do, but I was confident that he was with me and everything was going to be alright. Even if I took a bullet in the head, I knew he was with me. This gave me the confidence to run my big mouth.

"You guys have no idea who you're dealing with. If you let us go, I promise you no harm will befall you."

This made those gangbangers laugh so hard they could barely stand. I was fuming. How could they not take me seriously? I stomped my foot, and the walls all around us began to shake. I looked around bewildered and wondered what the hell was that. I stomped again and this really got some attention. Things started to fall off the buildings and down upon us. It was like I was playing the biggest bass drum ever. I stomped again and again, and I could feel the beat reverberate off the walls. I watched several of our executioners run for their lives. Not all of them ran, one man, which is all it takes, was determined to finish the job. He lined us up against the killing wall. How do I know it was the killing wall? It was covered in dry blood, and who knew what else. Pockmarks, where bullets had hit the wall, were all over it. This wall got a lot of use.

I told Peter I was sorry.

"I tried my best."

He patted me on the head and told me he loved me. Ben just stood there and cried. He was making me sick to my stomach. The one brave soul that stayed behind asked us if we had any last requests. He laughed when he said that.

"How about a song? They say that music people are so into their music, so how about singing me a song before you die?"

I thought about it for a minute. I looked around and saw an empty five-gallon bucket. I had my sticks in my pocket. I asked the man if I could use the bucket. He kicked it over to me. I looked up at Peter and asked him to sing, "Battle Cry" by Imagine Dragons.

Peter looked at me strangely and asked, "Are you sure?"

I nodded my head. I know many songs, but this one has an intense drum line. I needed intense if this was going to work. I started up my beat, Peter sang the words, and before it was over, we were in California. All I remember before being knocked to the ground was the flash of light. We all lay on the ground slightly confused. What had just happened?

Peter said he saw a flash of lightning come down from the sky and fry our executioner. It was such an intense strike it knocked us all back. Our backs were against the wall, but we still flew backward away from the lightning strike. It blew us from New York all the way to the California desert. Ben was rubbing his eyes and saying he couldn't believe it. He was looking down at his father's ranch. A place he spent many days at after the death of his mother. He hadn't been back here in many years. We all stood up and shook the dust off. I looked up and said a thank you. I knew what happened even if these idiots didn't. Jesus had saved us. He had pulled us all through the curtain and to this place. I knew this would be a place of significance. One that was full of purpose and danger. I would nearly die several times while spending time here. I loved every minute of it.

CHAPTER 18

Back to Anna.

Walter stared down at me. I could see on his face he didn't believe a word of what I had just told him. I think any normal person wouldn't believe anything I said. I could see Bob was taking it all in. He had no choice but to believe. Now he was beginning to understand the things that happened to him. Ivan was a contrast in emotions. First, he wanted to know how Joey had gotten away so many times. The man had luck like he had never seen. Always, there would be something to foil his plans. It drove Urstin crazy. Ivan had to put up with Urstin's violent mood swings. I'm surprised the man survived his time with him. I was in the middle of a lot of those times when I was the bride of the psycho. I had given enough information to the former director to have Urstin put in jail for life. He would always thank me and ask for more. Still not quite enough for a conviction he would say, get me more. When I had stuff on Helen Harrison, he got excited.

"You must stay and gather more Anna. This is national security we're talking about."

I didn't know he was gathering stuff for his blackmail portfolio. He wanted to go out a very rich man. I think he did, disappeared into the wind never to be seen again. His ex-wife disappeared along with him. I heard rumors of his demise, but I couldn't confirm anything. I was sure Ivan knew what happened to the man. Bob had a pretty good idea as well. If he screwed over the Cartels like Bob said he did, I had no doubt he was dead.

"Anna, it's getting late. Are we anywhere close to wrapping this up?"

Bob laughed. Ivan put his hand to his forehead to try and cover his smirk.

"No sir, I'm just getting warmed up."

Walter blew out a sigh. He called to one of his staff members and had him order some food.

"Looks like we're going to be at this all night."

He sat back down and pulled out a bottle of aspirin. I think he took twice the recommended dose.

"Go ahead, let's get this done with." He waved his hand at me, like I was an annoying fly. "Continue."

When the three of them had arrived in California, it wasn't the time they thought it was. The ripple in time and space was still unstable and they were five weeks into the past. This was about the time I arrived at the ranch. Franny had arrived several weeks before me. They couldn't go home because they would meet up with themselves and that couldn't happen. So, until time caught up with them, they would have to stay hidden at the ranch. Mr. B somehow knew all of this before it happened and had everything in place for us. When questioned on this, he would say it was something that he read. Now that was two people that said they had read something that was going to happen. At the time, I didn't know they were reading Maria's manuscripts. Each one foretelling in detail everything that was about to happen. The one thing they didn't count on was the ripple in time. It had changed a whole lot of things. Now Maria's manuscripts weren't as accurate as they had been. We were all going to find that out the hard way. Maria included. Nothing was as it was before, except it was. Confused yet?

Things continued along the line that Maria wrote, but slightly different, until finally they went in a completely different direction. She had written that I died. As you can see, I'm alive and well. Other people died in her story, but they're still breathing today. Some of them that were to walk away, are buried out in the desert. The ripple had changed everything. I won't get into details of what was supposed to happen in her stories, because of course, it didn't happen. What I will get into was what did happen.

Leon had arrived with Franny. Mr. B had set it up for her to be able to recover from her surgery. He said that once she was on her feet, that she would get a personal trainer to get her into shape for her mission. He never said what her mission was going to be. I arrived shortly after that. I needed a place to hide, as Urstin and his people were searching for me. The Queen Bees had delivered Billy and I to hide out until everything quieted down in the outside world. This is about the time Billy discovered he had been a mule for the Cartels. He never knew he was being used. The Cartels now wanted the both of us found and killed with extreme prejudice. Some idiot on the news had leaked that I was the agent responsible for the biggest seizure of drugs in the nation's history. I looked up at Bob when I said this. I knew at that moment he was the idiot.

Bob stood up to protest.

"If I hadn't, the Cartels would have killed me before I reached Richmond!"

Walter started to bang his gavel, "Order, order!"

"You see Mr. B had set me up. He knew I was dirty, and he wanted me taken out. That's why he hid you and left me to dangle in the wind."

I listened to the gavel bang as chaos ensured. I stood and cussed him out. Ivan began to put his two cents in, and that is when things had gone completely out of control. Walter started to hit Bob on the head with his gavel. Ivan was trying to constrain Walter. The staff was beside themselves not knowing who to restrain and who to let blow off some steam. They just sat there in complete confusion. I thought about getting into the fracas, but I was enjoying the show much too much. I sat and giggled.

As time usually does, cooler heads prevailed, and we took a recess. Bob needed an ice pack and Walter needed to go get his blood pressure medicine. I thought I would use this time to take a bathroom break. He was waiting in the stall beside me.

"Anna, as you can see, this isn't going to be easy. You may mention my name, but please keep from them all of what I did. I won't last the week if they find out what I did."

"I told you, I'll keep you out of it as best I can. I owe you that much."

I heard him mumble a thank you and heard the toilet flush from his stall. What the hell was he doing in the ladies' room? Wasn't he concerned that he would be seen leaving here? Then I thought about all the extremes he had gone through in the first place. He must be in disguise. I laughed out loud at the thought of it. I jumped up and raced for the door to try to get a glimpse of him. The hallway was empty. He was gone. I turned to wash my hands and freshen up when the door opened, and he walked in. I thought I was in the ladies' room.

"Anna, I must have you. Can't we get in a quickie before you return to the hearing room?"

"Mr. President, I already told you no. Now please don't make me tell you again."

He begged me from his hands and knees. He looked so pathetic. This had been going on nonstop since we met up at the ranch. I knew his weakness for dominant women. I also knew he wasn't going to stop until I gave in and gave him a little something. I pulled up my skirt and dropped my panties and ordered him to put his big mouth to work. I felt so powerful in those few minutes. How many people can say they had the President of the United States on his hands and knees servicing them? I let him have his pleasure for a few minutes. I would need a couple of minutes myself after he finished to recover. I swatted his head away before he could drive me over the edge. I looked in the mirror and saw my face was flush. I tried cooling off with cold water, but the damn President had gotten me quite worked up. I stormed out of the bathroom and worked on my composure as I walked back into the hearing room. It felt like everyone was staring at me and knew exactly what I had been up to. I was so embarrassed.

Walter was back in his seat. He looked at me and just shook his head. Ivan didn't look like he had a care in the world and Bob had an ice pack on his head but was ready to continue. I wish I was. I had to get my focus back and I had to do it now. I decided that to tell about the ranch now wasn't going to be the best place to continue, so I went back to what happened in Richmond with Deke and Pastor Ted.

Deke had arrived at the foundation office where Pastor Ted now worked. After what happened at the church, R.J. had been told never to set foot in that church ever again. Thankfully, he had set up the foundation and it had money coming in that he could use to survive with and do good in the community. He had been on the phone with a priest from South Richmond. They had three people that were in dire need of the Make a Way foundation. R.J. Ted was just the person to help them find their way back and become worthwhile citizens once again. Now he had Deke who could help him make that happen.

CHAPTER 19

Deke's new mission.

"Deke, we have a lady who has lost her children and the love from her family because of drug addiction. I know you were a heavy user. I think you can help with that one. I also have a former soldier with extreme PTSD. I think you can relate to that guy as well. The last one is a hoarder that has shut himself off from the world. We are going to try and dig him out from all the stuff he has accumulated over the years and see if we can get him back into the mainstream. Do you see anything here that you feel you can't handle?"

I listened to everything R.J. presented to me. This didn't seem like it was going to be so bad. I was all in. The memory of what Niko had said and done was still fresh in my mind.

"Has Niko ever helped you with any of your projects?"

R.J. laughed. He started to say something, but was having trouble getting the words out.

With a big smile on his face, he said, "He tried to help me a few months ago. Things didn't go quite as planned and they might have gotten a little rough. Did he say anything to you about it?"

I answered him with, "Well, he mumbled something I didn't quite catch, but it didn't sound good."

I looked to see what R.J.'s response was going to be. It looked like he breathed a sigh of relief.

THE TRUTH

"Good. At least he didn't tell you any wild stories that might have scared you off."

I had never gone out with R.J. on any of his missions. After today, I wish I had never gone on any with him. I was feeling uneasy with the responses that I was getting from him. I thought he might be hiding some very important details I might need to know. I would soon find out. We started with what we thought was going to be the easy one. The Hoarder.

When we arrived at the house, I had a hard time finding it. There was stuff piled high in front of the house, along the side, and packing the backyard to overflowing. I thought, if this was how the outside looked, what might the inside look like? We were about to find out. There was a narrow path that led to the front door. I looked at what was piled high and could only determine it was a bunch of junk. I thought we could get a truck in here and make a small fortune just in recycled metal.

R.J. knocked on the door. He knocked again and called the man's name. Nobody was coming to the door. He was about to knock again when I grabbed his hand.

"Listen, do you hear that?"

R.J. put his ear to the door and said it sounded like someone was crying for help. The door was locked, but I have a heavy foot and opened it up with a good hard kick. It moved only a few feet and was caught up in debris. I reached inside and was able to clear a few things out of the way so that we could enter the house. Small paths led around the room of junk. Barely any light was coming through the windows where stuff was piled so high. I thought this would take nearly a month just to clean up the inside, never mind even attempting the outside.

We listened for the feeble voice calling for help and found the man under an avalanche of junk. R.J. and I started quickly removing the items that had fallen on the man. I couldn't help but notice that one box contained comic books from the fifties and sixties. This box alone was probably worth more than this house. The next box had baseball cards from the same era. This guy was sitting on a gold mine. We dug him out and got the poor guy some water. He told us he had been trapped for several days. From the smell of him, I couldn't disagree.

We got him cleaned up and R.J. spoke with him while I looked around. I saw antiques and stuff I hadn't seen in years that would make a collector salivate. All this stuff was probably worth millions and it was all piled high collecting dust. We had to tell this guy what he had. I was getting excited.

R.J. grabbed me and pulled me outside.

"This guy will never part with his stuff. It's an illness. We need to work on the illness before we can get him to clean up and rejoin the world. I've seen all the things you have. I know he has stuff that would make several men very rich. We are not going to be two of them. Do you understand?"

I did. This was like finding a million dollars in lost money that no one was ever going to claim and turning it in to the authorities. It was stupid, but it was also the right thing to do. This gold mine belonged to this very sick man. We were sent here to help him, and damn it, that's what we were going to do. Already I was thinking about how this man was going to have an accident and how I would volunteer to clean up the place.

I had to walk outside and get myself back under control. The thoughts in my head were very unhealthy. I gathered myself and returned to find R.J. kneeling over the man doing CPR. Oh my God. R.J. had killed the guy to get the money for himself! I went to assist him and try to save the guy's life. R.J. had already called for an ambulance before I had gotten in there.

"Did you do this, R.J.?"

He looked at me like I was kidding.

"No, he started to have convulsions. Last thing he said to me before he passed out was that he was a diabetic. I can't find anything in this mess. I think he needs insulin or maybe sugar! I don't know which!" he screamed at me as we frantically tried to keep him alive.

"The paramedics will never be able to get a stretcher in here. Grab his legs and let's carry him out to the street."

We grabbed the man's legs and slowly made our way outside. As soon as we were clear of the debris field, we began our life-saving treatment. When the ambulance took him away, he was still alive. His sugar had dropped into the low twenties. The paramedics were good at their job and stabilized him for transport to the hospital.

"I'm sorry I thought you had tried to kill the man for his money. I was having evil thoughts and I was thinking about knocking the man off and stealing his stuff. Can you forgive me?"

R.J. looked me up and down. He looked up to the sky and asked the Lord.

"What do you think, Lord? Can we trust him?"

As soon as he said that, we heard the squeal of tires and the unmistakable sound of two vehicles coming together. We looked up simultaneously to see the ambulance get T-boned by a drunk driver. It hit so hard the ambulance rolled over on its side. We ran with R.J. once again dialing 911 and telling them what happened. I could only think that if the man died, were we destined to receive this money? R.J. said the man had no family. So, who would be getting the riches that were inside that dump if he died?

I couldn't think about it. I had people that were in desperate need of my help. The driver in the car was mangled beyond repair. He didn't need any help anymore. The smell of liquor was heavy in the air. R.J. had gotten the driver out of the ambulance. He wasn't hurt that bad and was able to assist us with the other two. He had more medical training than I did, so I let him take charge. I held a compress on his forehead to keep the blood out of his eyes while he worked on the other two. R.J. assisted with his other needs. They all lived to see another day, much to my disappointment. I thought it might have been a sign from God. It was a test. I passed with flying colors. I could be trusted.

I thought after the first stop that R.J. would be done for the day. Not going to get off that easy. We were off to the drug addict's place of residence. Not a very good part of town I might add. I hadn't thought about that. I sure hope no snakes are hiding about this neighborhood. Even my own people wouldn't recognize me now that I didn't have a single tattoo. This made me twice as nervous as I already was. I didn't have any weapons with me. How was I going to defend myself? We were in the van that R.J. used to get around in. It belonged to the foundation. It was armed to the teeth.

We pulled up to the apartment and R.J. reached into the glove box and handed me a fully loaded Glock 19. He then removed a semi-automatic Ruger SR9c.

He smiled, "This is one of my favorites." He dug around a little more and pulled out two flashbang grenades. "In case we need to get out in a hurry."

I was ready to get out in a hurry and we hadn't even gotten out of the car.

"Her name is Crystal. Her nickname is Crystal-meth. She lost her two children to CPS. Her parents have given up on her. Seems the only thing she cares about anymore is getting high. I thought that you might take the lead on this one since you were such a heavy heroin user."

I thought back to my life in those days. It wasn't going to be easy getting through to her. I knew I couldn't be told a thing. Even if someone said something, I wouldn't have listened. Most times you either die, or you hit rock bottom before you'll start to listen. Then after you have beaten it, it still stays with you to fight day after day for the rest of your life. After recovering, most people find themselves right back in the thick of addiction. It's not their fault. The disease is so strong you must have the willpower to fight it. You must also have a support team to go to when you feel like you're slipping. These are the cracks that addicts fall through every day. I relied on God to save me from myself. His personal visit to me in my jail cell got me on the right path and I've never looked back. Many folks don't have the faith that I was given. Without God, they flounder lost in a sea by themselves. What I thought we had to do with Crystal was to get her to believe in God and the power He holds to win all battles.

It was a good idea until she opened the door. A cross hung from her neck. Nice start, now all we had to do was turn it right side up. The cross hung upside down from her skinny neck. I could tell from her face that she had been a user for several years. Addicts get the look after a while. It's unmistakable and never goes away, even after you stop using.

"What do you two clowns want?"

R.J. began to say something, but I put my hand on his shoulder to stop him. I said, "We would like to come in and have a chat about your children. Would you like to get them back?"

If she said she did, then we had hope. If she said she was better off without them, then I was going to have R.J. call it a day with this one.

She invited us in, two stoned addicts sat in her living room. I noticed they could barely move. I also recognized them as Snakes. Once you battle Snakes, you always battle them. I grabbed them by the collar and threw the two of them out of her house to the angry protests from behind me. She was screaming at me for throwing her friends out of her house.

"Listen to me very closely. I'm only going to say this once." I glared at her and moved my face so that it was just inches from hers. "You keep trash like that in your place, you're never going to see your children again. Do you understand me?" I said it in a way that meant business. If you try to be nice to them, they just blow you off.

I reached up and grabbed the necklace from around her neck and pulled it off.

"This has got to go as well. He will never be your savior."

I pulled the gold cross from around my neck and place it around hers.

"This is who you're going to pull your power from. I was once very much like you. He was the only one that could save me."

I had spent a lot of money on that cross, I thought if I gave it to her it would be well worth the money to replace it if she recovered. She held it in her hand and gazed at it. She lifted it back up over her head and gave it back to me.

"He turned his back on me many years ago. I have no need for him now."

I stood there with the necklace in my hands.

"I think it was you that turned your back on him. Did you have some difficult problem and you couldn't figure out what to do?"

She turned back to me and said, "Yeah, my husband was murdered, the killer was never found. I had to raise two children without a father.

What God would do that to someone he loved?!" she screamed at me. She made a good point.

"A loving God." It was R.J. now putting in his two cents.

She whirled on him and I don't have any idea where the knife came from but there it was, shining in all its glory pressed to R.J.'s neck. He had been seated on the sofa when she attacked him. Now she had advantage and leverage. R.J. never blinked or showed worry.

"My God is always testing us, making us stronger. Like he is today. You could take that knife and end my life in two seconds. It wouldn't change a thing for me. I will always love my God to my dying day. Now I would like you to ask him back into your heart and pray with me for his forgiveness and his help to get you cleaned up."

"You think that your bravery is going to save you, that you can come in here and try to fill my head with all your bullshit. It isn't working. Now take your buddy over there and get the hell out of my house before I run this blade across your throat."

I was very relieved that we both made it out of that house alive. We got into the van and R.J. said to me. "She likes you. You should make another visit without me next time. Give her a few days. I think we can get this one back."

"Are you kidding me? You nearly got your throat slit! Now you want me to go back there by myself and try to clean her up."

"That's right, you're the right man for the job."

I looked at him in disbelief. He just smiled at me. I could see just a small bit of blood on his neck. He didn't seem to notice.

"Okay, one last stop. I just love PTSD cases."

I thought the man had lost his freaking mind. This was going to be a disaster. I still battled with nightmares from the war. He had said this was an extreme case. I thought we were in more danger than ever. I swallowed hard and readied myself for the next stop. This turned out to be the kicker. We never had a chance with this guy, but he changed my life forever.

We were in the nicer part of Richmond. All single-family homes. A lot of old brick ranches. The house we were looking for was another brick ranch among the many. This place was set alone at the end of

THE TRUTH

the street. His backyard ended at the tracks. A heavily traveled set of double tracks just north of the James River. It looked like no one was home. No car in the driveway, but it had a garage, so a car could have been parked inside. We didn't see any activity, no lights, but it was just early afternoon.

"You ready?" he asked me.

I told him the truth. "Nope, never ready for something like this. Maybe you can help me with my PTSD?"

He patted me on the shoulder and said, "I already did. Your eye healed up nicely."

I remembered he had beat the crap out of me twice in one night when he was trying to help me. My eye was swollen for a week.

We knocked on the door. Well, at least he didn't have a dog that could rip us to shreds. We heard nothing. He knocked again. Still nothing. I turned and saw a heavily bearded man hold a shotgun pointed right at us.

"Um, R.J., I think we found him."

The man called out to us.

"You two Jehovah's Witnesses?"

I was ready to say something, but R.J. stopped me.

"No, sir. We are with the Make a Way Foundation. We were asked to come and see you. We are here to offer up our services."

The man looked at us suspiciously.

"You sure you're not with them? I warned you I would fill you full of lead if you ever wandered onto my property ever again."

I was sure he was serious.

"Sir, I'm a fellow veteran. I was with the First AD in Iraq."

The man smiled, "I was First Cavalry. I got to go to both Iraq and Afghanistan."

Okay, the man had seen more than most. Just a little was enough.

He put the gun down and invited me inside. He looked at Pastor Ted, "Who did you serve with?"

"I'm sorry sir, I never served. I have served God my whole life."

"Coward, you stay out here. I don't need your kind in my house."

I could see the hurt on his face, but he took it like a man and made himself comfortable on the porch steps while I went inside and tried to find where the guy had left his sanity. We entered his kitchen to find two life-sized blow-up dolls sitting at the table. These are the kind that you find in adult magazines that sell sex toys. The expensive kind that are so life-like they appear to be real.

"I would like you to meet my ladies. This here is Annabelle, and her twin sister Jezebel. Now she is a handful let me tell you. Be careful around her."

He talked to them like they were real people and expected me to do the same.

"I'm cooking up some lunch, you hungry?" he asked me. I told him I was. "I'd cook something up for them, but they hardly eat. You know women, always watching their figure."

I was feeling sorry for the guy. He was very delusional. He was also very dangerous. He was cutting up some cucumbers when the knife slipped and cut his finger. Just the sight of blood caused him to go into a full-blown rage. I ducked as the knife flew over my head and stuck into the wall. I had to jump up and tackle him to get him to calm down. As fast as he went berserk, he calmed down.

"Let me up young fella, I've seemed to have dropped my knife." I went and pulled it out of the wall and reluctantly gave it back to him.

He says to me, "The girls are looking for a good time tonight. I sure could use your help. It's hard enough keeping up with one, but they both need loving. All they do is whine and complain about sex. They're killing me I tell you. I need all the help I can get with them."

I could sympathize with him, but I wasn't going to have sex with no blow-up doll.

"I wish I could, but it's getting late and I have some more people I need to visit before the day is through."

"Okay, maybe a raincheck. When do you think you can come by again? I sure could use someone to talk with. You know, someone that was in the shit and can relate. Not like them fake doctors that have never seen the bodies and all the blood. You've seen the blood, haven't you?"

"Yes, I've seen it. I made it flow many times."

The question had caught me by surprise, and I found myself sinking back into those very bad times. I understood where he was coming from and wanted to help him.

"Thanks for coming by. I hope to see you again."

I wanted to say I could stay longer, but I had already made the excuse to escape his presence.

I walked out and R.J. had all kinds of questions for me.

"I need a beer, how about you?" I asked him.

R.J. had been on the wagon for some time now. He was an alcoholic.

"I'm sorry, forget about it, let's grab a sandwich and a soda."

"You know, I would have been alright if we went to a bar," he said.

"Why tempt fate, better this way."

I didn't want to be the one that knocked him off the wagon. It would be very painful for me. The guy is as big as a house. He threw me around like I was a rag doll. No sir, I have got to keep this one sober.

CHAPTER 20

Gainesville, Florida. Several weeks after Anna gave birth.

The doorbell rang and Kimberly Jacques was awakened from a sound sleep. The doorbell rang again. She pulled herself out of bed and grabbed her robe. A quick look through the peephole showed a delivery man standing there with a clipboard. She had been working all night at the crew management desk and had just gotten to sleep a few hours ago. The man asked if she was indeed Kimberly Jacques. She said that she was.

"Here, sign here for a very important delivery."

She hadn't been expecting anything, but in her state of mind, she grabbed the clipboard and signed without reading. The man turned and said he would be right back. A van was waiting out on the street in front of her home which was in a very rural part of the state just outside of Gainesville. It belonged to her deceased husband – a police officer gunned down while he was having lunch.

The man got into the vehicle while a woman carried a heavy package to the house. Kim thought she could hear a baby crying. The woman spoke no English but pointed to the box and spoke in Spanish, "Aqui esta el bebe." She put the box down in front of Kim and walked away.

The man drove off very fast as soon as the woman was back in the car. Curious, Kim opened the box, which wasn't sealed to find a very young baby girl. The poor thing couldn't have been more than a month old. There was clothing and formula in the box along with a note.

THE TRUTH

It read:

> *Please take care of this baby and let people believe it is your own. Her name is Isabella. She is in grave danger. Joey will be in contact as soon as he can safely do so. Until then her safety is in your hands.*

It wasn't signed and there wasn't anything else to go along with it.

Joey hadn't worked in weeks. She didn't even know if he still had a job with the railroad. Things seemed strange whenever it involved Joey. That Rocco character showing up in the field tied to a stake with fire ants crawling all over him still gave her the willies. Now this. She brought the baby inside and checked her out. The little girl seemed to be in perfect health. Kim noticed she had the most beautiful green eyes she had ever seen.

"What am I going to do with you little one?"

The baby squealed and let out a tiny laugh.

"So, you're in danger and I need to protect you, but why are you in danger?"

She didn't get an answer. I guess we have got to wait for Joey to show up and give us some answers. The answers she was waiting for didn't come quickly. When they did, it was duck and cover, then ask questions.

* * *

More stories for Walter.

"I'm getting very tired of this Anna. What do all these Deke and Pastor Ted stories have to do with the President?"

"That's what I'm trying to tell you. How it all went down and what everyone was doing when it happened. In case you didn't realize, I'm in love with Pastor Ted. He is truly incredible."

"Yeah, yeah, tell me more," Walter said dismissively.

"When I'm done, you'll be wanting to give him a medal."

Bob was drinking coffee when I said that, and it went everywhere. He just blew it out all over the place. He started choking like it had gone down the wrong hole or something. One of the staff quickly went to his assistance and they got it cleaned up. So, you think this is funny Bob, do you?

"I think I'll tell you how Joey got back to Richmond now. Mr. B had sent his son to Denver by airplane. He was instructed to get Joey out of jail and back to California. That didn't happen as planned. Tom didn't like being ordered around by his father. He liked to be his own man. So, begrudgingly he went to get Joey. He rented a car and started searching all the police stations until he found the right one. A young officer agreed to help him, and they went and found Joey staring at a television set that had been set up outside his cell.

"This is highly unusual," the officer said. "Why is he in orange overalls?"

Tom was irritated and blurted out, "How should I know? The man does the most stupid things sometimes. One time he ran down the streets of Richmond in his birthday suit. Maybe he did it again."

Joey just stared at him and said, "Your brother was almost killed tonight. Did you know that?"

Tom didn't and suddenly grew quiet. He had been threatened as well as Ben. Their father was being manipulated by some very powerful people and the two boys were being used as leverage.

"We have got to get him out of here. Some people are looking to take our lives and we are in danger," Tom said excitedly.

"Well, good thing you're in a police station. Not much danger here." He smiled like he knew what he was talking about. So young and so stupid.

"I don't think you get what I'm saying. If we stay here, we are all in danger. You ever hear of the Cartels being afraid of a little old police station?"

This got the young officer moving. His life was in jeopardy as well as ours, and now he didn't want to stay at the station any longer. He unlocked the cell and escorted us out to his police car.

"I have a rental, where are we going?"

"I'll take him over to the local superstore. He needs clothes and he can't be seen outside the station wearing the orange overalls. Get in the back sir."

Joey climbed in the back while Tom went and got the rental car. He followed the officer for a few miles. Once at the store, Tom raced in and found Joey a few items to wear. As fast as he could, he had Joey in some clothes that almost fit him. They would have to do some more shopping later on. The shirt fit like a glove O.J. Simpson might try to get on.

Joey stared at him and said, "Do I look like a medium to you?"

Tom didn't have an answer and he didn't have time to argue. The officer removed his shirt and gave it to Joey.

"It's a large, but it's better than that shirt." They traded. It was very snug on the officer, but at least he could get it on. Joey thanked the officer and bid him farewell.

The officer called to him and said. "I just want you to know how much you inspired me with that movie you did with the baseball team. The speech you gave made me want to become the best person I could be and so I joined the police force."

He saluted Joey and drove off. Joey sat with a huge smile on his face. Tom knew why. Joey can't read a script to save his life and just said whatever came to his head. The director loved it so much he scrapped the original script and left Joey's lines in. If Joey didn't ad-lib all his lines, he was sure he never would have won an Academy Award.

"Joey, I need to get you back to LA. I have a safe place for you to stay until this cartel business is resolved."

"Tom, you know as well as I do that the Cartel is not after me. You blew so much smoke up that cop's ass I thought he was going to catch on fire. I need to get back to Richmond. Are you going to take me, or do I have to find another way to get there?"

Tom thought about it for a minute. He stopped the car. He got out and walked around to the side and opened the door.

"Go, do it your way. Don't ever tell me I tried to tell you so." He seemed a little perturbed.

Joey walked away with no money, no ID, and no way to get to Richmond. Good thing he was a railroad man. He wondered how far it was to the nearest tracks. He had kicked his fair share of free riders off his trains. Now he was going to be one of them. Should be a piece of cake. He just needed to find the right car. He had seen many a dead body that hadn't found the right car to ride on. Sometimes it can get a little rough back from the locomotive engine and a little slack action up front is a whole lot of slack towards the back. If you're not careful, you get knocked off the train and roll around under the wheels coming apart in a thousand pieces. He had seen what some of these folks looked like after falling off. It's not pretty.

As for how good those engineers were, he had to laugh to himself. He personally knew more than a handful of guys that should never be in control of a locomotive. It's not that they were bad guys, it's that they weren't cut out to handle the weight and size of these monsters. The computers do most of the work for them now, but those systems don't always work. Sometimes they go out en-route and they have got to take over. Even the most experienced operators get complacent, having not run an engine in weeks. It's all a recipe for disaster that the government in all their wisdom figure that it is safer this way. Joey says it's all bullshit. They are trained for six months to run these things. Once they know how, then the computer runs the train and they slowly lose their skills. Finally, when something goes wrong, it all goes to hell and they have rail cars all over some suburban neighborhood. With the stuff they carry, how can anyone feel safe living near railroad tracks?

* * *

Joey's journey.

Now that I said all this had run through my head, it was time to do one of the most dangerous things I could think of – hop on a moving freight train. I had walked maybe ten miles before I came across some tracks. My feet were sore, and my stomach was growling. These tracks had promise. Now, which way was east? I had better not get on a westbound train. If I did that, I would be back in LA the hard way. I looked to the sky to see where the sun was at. Getting my bearings, I started to walk down the tracks. I needed to find a signal where a train might stop. One thing I learned as an engineer is that only stupid people walk down the gauge of the track. It's the quickest way to get run over. Walk to the side and you'll never get hit. Walking on the side of the track is grueling and you quickly get sore feet. It's so much easier to walk in the gauge. Now I was one of those stupid people.

An hour later, I almost was one of those dead people. I never heard the train coming and I think Jacob might have pushed me off the tracks because it wasn't me that threw myself into the ditch filled with stagnant water. My luck being what it was. The train was coming to a stop and would have stopped before it got to me. The crew got out on the platform and were yelling all kinds of things at me. I heard stupid idiot more than a few times. I stood up and waved to them.

I yelled back, "I need a ride. Mind if I sit on the second engine?"

The conductor got down and walked over to me. I don't know if he recognized me or if there was another reason. He looked me square in the eyes.

"You look a whole lot younger than I remember."

I laughed.

"Hollywood, they use a lot of makeup. Tried to make me look older than I was."

"Hot damn!" he exclaimed. He yelled up to his engineer and said to him. "Ray, we got us a Hollywood movie star asking us for a ride, what do you think? Should we give him one?"

The man whose name was Ray looked down at me and wanted me to do a few lines to prove who I was. I couldn't remember what I said in that damn film. I never read the script. I improvised.

"Well, I'm not sure what part of the movie you liked. Some people are always asking me about the speech I gave right before the big game. Others want to know what I really said to the relief pitcher and the catcher to start the big fight."

"We want to hear what you said to your love interest after your heart attack in the hospital."

This was a part of the movie no one had ever asked about. It was fill in space, had nothing to do with the story, or did it. My girlfriend, played in the movie by this young and up-and-coming sweetheart of a girl, her name was Abbey Shore, wanted to know what I was going to do now that the season was over for me. I remember it well, because it was the last thing I wanted to do.

"I guess I'll retire and take you to that beach in the Caribbean you keep bugging me about."

That was the line I said. The script read that I was to say.

"I love you so much and I want you to be happy. Let's go to the Caribbean to that beach you keep talking about. It's about time I retire and start enjoying life."

Funny, the director kept my lines in and didn't make me redo them.

Ray laughed at what I said.

"That, my friend is Joey Hopkins, get his ass up here. We got things to talk about."

The conductor held his nose and asked Ray if he was sure he wanted me up there with them. He threw down a couple bottles of water and a bar of soap.

"Get him cleaned up before you bring him up."

I sat with my two new friends for the next two hundred miles talking railroad stories all the way. The guys wanted to know all about Scarlett Davis and what she was like. They kept saying she had a nice rack. I guess the whole world had seen them after her Academy Award performance. I couldn't tell them it was Maria that they had seen. Scarlett never would have done that.

Ray made me run the train the last twenty miles. He was tired and wanted to take a nap. His conductor wasn't qualified to run a train, but I was. I had no idea what their territory looked like or any of the speed restrictions, but like I said, the computer runs everything now, so all I had to do was monitor the system, which I could do. I looked over and his conductor was fast asleep as well. I guess these guys trust me with their job in my hands. I shook my head. If they had heard some of the true stories from Richmond, I don't think they would have let me on their train.

We arrived at their off-duty point and I had to get off. Ray gave me some cash and a leftover sandwich he hadn't eaten. I thanked him and asked where we were at.

"You are in Brewster, Kansas. Get the next train into Kansas City and the rest will be a piece of cake. Make your way to Saint Louis and from there you'll be able to get to Richmond."

"Thanks, Ray. You are a real-life saver."

"My pleasure, my friend. Stay safe."

He walked away and I never saw him again. It's funny how you meet people that help you out along the way in life. If only for a moment or a day. People that if they weren't there for you, your life might have gotten turned in a completely different direction. I often wondered if it might not be divine intervention? Sometimes, I truly believe it is divine intervention. He told me he would always be with me, didn't he? How do we know when the Lord is wielding his mighty hand in our favor? I think it happens every day in our lives and we never realize it.

It took me a week, but I arrived back at my place in Richmond. I had a spare key hidden in a fake rock by the back door. Nobody was home at my place. As far as I knew, Samantha was still staying there. The house was cleaner than I had ever seen it. I could tell right off the bat that the twins hadn't been here in weeks. Neither had Maria, if so, I would be stepping on her clothes thrown all over the place as soon as I walked through the door. I needed a shower and my bed. The bathroom was immaculate, and my bed was made. I finally felt like I was at home.

As soon as my head hit the pillow, the fun began. All I wanted to do was get some sleep. I heard my front door open and someone walk in. I thought it might be Samantha, so I called out to let her know I was back. She opened the door with a warm smile and screamed.

"I thought you were Joey! What are you doing here, Peter? Last time I saw you on television, I thought you were dead."

"Calm down, Sam. It's me."

She looked very closely at me.

"No way. Joey is much older than you. Peter, what did you do to make those people want to kill you?"

In frustration, I stood up and tried to talk to her. That wasn't the best idea I had that day because I sleep in the nude. Samantha looked me up and down.

"You have the same scars as Joey."

How did she know what scars I had? Did she ever see me in the nude before? I covered up and went to her.

"Listen to me. Strange things have happened to me to make me look younger. I'm going to be this way for a very long time. Nothing I can do about it."

She says, "It was something Maria did, wasn't it?"

Smart girl. She learns fast.

"Yes, it was. I'll tell you about it in the morning, now can I please get some sleep? I'm exhausted."

I settled into a nice deep sleep. I wish the next event had been a dream, but it wasn't. My neighbor Derek and Samantha were engaged to be married. At his bachelor party, he had a sort of coming out with the Queen Bees. Now Samantha lives with me. The two of them are still friends, so when she left me, she went over to his place. He called Jenna and told her I was back. Jenna was in a fret over what had happened in New York and not hearing a thing from Peter in over a week, came rushing to my house to talk to me. This wouldn't have been so bad in itself. They failed to tell her what I looked like now. Samantha has a crush on me and will climb into my bed. I didn't know this at the time, I found out when Jenna came storming into my room. I was as surprised as she was to find a naked Samantha in bed with me. Thing was, I looked like Peter now, and she thought I was him. Until I was able to convince her I wasn't Peter, I was. Now I know what Scarlett goes through with Maria looking so much like her. The one difference, nobody can tell them apart. Peter and I have many differences. One is all my battle scars. The one scar that Helen Harrison gave me when we were young teenagers in love is the most predominant scar I have. I had decided I had enough of all her lies and broke up with her. I now sport a six-inch scar where the two by four with the nail sticking out of it hit me in the chest. It was headed for my head. I knew she was trying to kill me. I didn't know why. I thought it was because I had broken up with her. I didn't know there was another reason.

Anyway, that scar is what most likely saved my life that night. Let me set the stage for you. Samantha had come back to the house and slipped into my room and stripped naked, climbed into bed with me and cuddled. I didn't even know she was there. Jenna had gotten Niko over to the house to watch the kids and rushed to Richmond to talk to me. I had no house phone and no cell phone, so she came in person. She still has her key. I'm not sure if she moved out yet or not.

She comes storming into my room all in a huff and needing to talk about Peter. She finds Peter butt-ass naked in bed with Samantha. I'm trying to wake from my deep sleep, and I couldn't have been more confused. Who is Peter and who is this son of a bitch she is screaming at? The door slams. Samantha is trying desperately to wake me up. Startled that somebody else is in the room with me, I stand up and the covers fall away from me. Jenna returns with a butcher knife from the kitchen. Peter is in so much trouble I think to myself.

"She thinks you're Peter! Joey, do something," I hear Samantha scream at me as she tries to hide under the bed.

My senses are starting to come back when I realize she thinks I'm Peter. The butcher knife is on its way to end my life when Jacob slaps me beside the head to wake me up. I grab the pillow, my favorite down pillow, and swing it like you would in a pillow fight. It catches the knife and pulls it from her grasp, leaving feathers flying everywhere. The pillow hits the wall with the knife inside. I fall to my hands and knees and Jenna jumps on top of me and starts pounding me with her fist. One shot after another is hitting me in the back of the head and shoulders. My only thought is – thank God this isn't Maria, I'd be dead already.

I have got to get this enraged person off me and under control. I stand up and rush backwards into the wall. I heard the wind knocked from her sails. Thankfully, she weighs about 120 pounds soaking wet, so that wasn't much of an effort.

I spin and mount her, looking into her sexy eyes. Somehow, I found this stimulating and began to rise to attention. This was not the time for this. She had almost killed me.

"Jenna, listen to me."

She squirmed beneath me and I knew if I didn't grab her hands and secure them, she would be grabbing something of mine, and it wouldn't feel good.

"I'm Joey. I know I don't look like it, but I am. Maria put something in my drink, and it made me look younger. You have got to believe me. Look at my chest, does Peter have these scars?"

I let up a bit so that she could look closer. This took a lot of the fight out of her and I felt safe to release her from my grip. I should have held a little tighter. When I started to get up, my excitement had started to show. This was quickly resolved with a knee and a tongue lashing.

"How can you get excited like that when I'm trying to kill you?"

As I lay on the floor in pain, all I could do was blame Maria.

CHAPTER 21

Anna at the hearing.

"So, you told us this story so that we can all fall asleep," Walter whined.

"No sir, you wanted to know about the strange behavior. Joey had been the first to take the formula. I was telling you this so that you could see some of the behavior traits that he was taking on, the danger he put himself in, and the sexual way he felt when he was in the fight for his life."

Walter steepled his fingers and thought about it.

"We can't do this all night. I'm tired and I can see the staff is exhausted as well. I wasn't planning on this going all night and into the next day. Nobody is to leave this building, not even the staff. I don't want leaks getting out to the media. I'll arrange for a place for everyone to sleep." He stood up and left the room.

Great, another day of this was a given. I wasn't going to rush the story for no one. If they didn't completely understand, they would when I was done. I asked one of the staffers if it was possible to have a fresh set of clothes brought to wherever I would be sleeping. The staffer sympathized but had to inquire just how much outside contact was going to be allowed. I sighed to myself. I would be sleeping in the same building as the President. How was I going to keep him out of my room? I called out to the female staffer.

"You think they'll bunk us up together?"

It was an innocent question. She looked at me like I was a lesbian. I didn't even want to argue with her about her misunderstanding. I let it go.

Walter came back a few minutes later and gave us our assigned lodging. He called over to me and said that he had a private room for me, while everyone else was going to have to bunk up together. He said that the President insisted.

"Mind your P's and Q's tonight, young lady. We have enough problems with him as it is. Don't make it worse. Do you understand?"

I nodded that I did, now if he would only keep his end of the deal. I had fought him off twice today. Once letting him have a little taste, my mistake for sure.

"I hope the door has locks."

Walter just glared at me, turned, and walked away. The room was nice, and I noticed the door did have a lock on it. Thank God. It also had a bathroom, so I didn't have to leave the room to get freshened up. I walked into the bathroom to find it had everything I needed. All the products I used at home, like this room had been set up just for me. A nightgown hung from a hook on the door that was very sexy and sheer. I knew who had left it here. Damn him.

I would have to sleep with one eye open tonight. Must be a secret entrance or some way of getting in here unnoticed. I walked around the room to see if it held any clues. I couldn't find any. Satisfied I might be safe after all, I lie down and fell into a light sleep. I awoke to someone sliding in behind me and was ready to cuss him out when another more familiar voice spoke into my ear. It was Ivan.

"I wanted to let you know that Urstin knows you had a baby. Don't ask me how he knows, just know that he does. When he finds this baby, if it's not his, he'll kill it. I hope you have this baby well hidden." He laughed. "I'm sure it's not his."

He slid out and was gone. I jumped up in panic and looked around. How did he get in here? How did he get out? I couldn't see any possible way. I checked the door and it was still locked. I paced the floor, my heart beating a mile a minute. They knew about my daughter, but they knew very little. Somebody with a big mouth must have told him. The

Queen Bees must have known they had a mole and that was why they came in the middle of the night and whisked her away to safety. I prayed that she would be okay. I wanted so much to hold her. I started to cry, and I laid back down. I cried myself back to sleep.

In the morning, he was standing over me looking down at my body that was covered only by the sheer nighty. He was holding a package that contained a fresh set of clothes that were all tailored to my exact size.

"Thank you for keeping me out of this," he said to me.

Startled, I sat up and covered myself with a blanket. I didn't even ask him how he got in here. Why bother?

"I was visited last night by Urstin's right-hand man. They know about my daughter. You told me she was going to be safe."

He stood there without emotion on his face and simply stated, "If he finds her, it will be because somebody made a mistake and didn't listen to directions. I told you, as long as you follow the plan, she will stay safe."

He paced the room once or twice then said, "I will have Urstin taken out of the picture before the year is out. Until that time, follow the gosh darn plan!"

He threw the package at me and walked out the door. The door that had been locked all night, and it was still locked when he left.

I dressed and walked back into the hearing room. Walter had brought in a caterer to serve us breakfast. I grabbed a huge cup of coffee. I needed it after that restless night. What would today bring? I was about to find out. The President beat me to the punch. He had just gone into Baltimore with the National Guard. An audit of all the books was the task of the day. He knew where the crooks were at. Now he had to expose them. The books held it all. They say follow the money. As much as they try to cover their trail, there is always a trail. That is why the President had used the National Guard. They were able to keep the secret of the audit. Before the day was through, many would be in handcuffs, and many would be involved in the riots. If you didn't believe they wouldn't fight back, you would be sadly mistaken. No, it was game on, and this President had just signed his death warrant.

The media started to spread the lies. See, the President was a little over-ambitious. He had also wanted to help as many people as he could along the way. The schools were a mess and many people were living with disease and hunger. He brought two doctors with him to help with the medical problems the city was facing. He also brought in tons of food and water to feed the hungry, many of them children. Illegal immigrants were rounded up and put on buses to be deported. These weren't your average run-of-the-mill immigrants. No, they were the worst of the worst. Killers, criminals, sex offenders, rapists. The media said they were just poor folk trying to make a living in a rundown city, innocent of anything they had been accused of. These were family people. Their poor children would be separated from them and locked into cages until someone found them decent housing. The lies led to the riots that led to the discourse that led to the many deaths and looting that sprung up, spreading like a disease along the East Coast.

It was hard to concentrate that day because of all the chaos at the White House. Walter said to me, "I told you this was national security, look what he has done now!"

I wasn't going to take the blame. I didn't give him the damn formula to drink. I tried to get them not to use it, warned them not to do it. Nobody listened to a damn thing I said.

"Walter, I'll try to wrap this up before they burn this place to the ground. Maybe Bob would like to tell you about his behavior and how this damn stuff affected his state of mind and all the things he did that he wished he hadn't done."

Bob looked at me like I was throwing him under the bus. Maybe I was. I knew there had to be a reason the President hadn't visited me last night. He was busy setting this up. I sure hope he knows what he's doing. Joey told him way too much. Things I'll never be able to reveal to this panel. I was there the day he brought us all in for a little chat. Joey had told him about the doctors and how Helen had destroyed their lives. These were good doctors, he said. Their nicknames were Mutt and Jeff. Their real names were Scott Mutter and Jeff Stein. The President had said he would have a job for them, we didn't know what he had planned.

THE TRUTH

Now I think I was beginning to understand. To get rid of cancer, sometimes the cure is worse than the disease. Chemo can make you feel like you want to die. Sometimes it doesn't work, or it does, but the cancer still comes back. This country was suffering from a cancer, and the President was out to cure it. I thought of the human body as the country. It was going to fight the cure. The doctor knew this wasn't going to be easy. Given a chance, the treatments would work. Now if only the patient would let us treat her, we could rid the body of the cancer.

"Bob, tell them how we all got to the ranch, even the President you coward!" I screamed at him. He stood and protested that he couldn't do it. Walter banged his gavel over and over. Finally, after he had enough, he had security take Bob away. I looked and watched Ivan smirk at me. He mouthed so only I could see, "Well played Anna." I shot him a dirty look. The next one to be taken out of here in cuffs was going to be him.

"I don't know what that was all about Anna, but I wish you wouldn't do that. I need as many people in here that knew what happened as possible. I need desperately to get to the truth."

I stood to speak.

"Bob had many answers to your questions. I know the story, but it is hearsay. Do you wish for me to continue with the story?"

He let out a sigh. "Please continue with the story."

I watched him pull out a bottle of Tums and pop about half a dozen pills into his mouth. Good, we felt the same way, maybe he would share.

"I told you about R.J. and the foundation, Deke and how he came to volunteer to help. Now you know that Joey is back in Richmond and about ready to go back to work. What happened in these few days is how we all came to meet up at the ranch. Please bear with me as I explain."

"Do I have a choice?" Walter said as he threw his hands in the air in frustration.

Deke had felt the need to continue to help Pastor Ted. They went out a few more times and these were much simpler and easier people to deal with than that first day. Deke had asked about the hoarder and if the man lived.

"Yes, he is back at home living with all that mess. Would you like to repay him a visit?"

Deke had pondered this and finally said that he would like to do just that.

The two of them headed back to the house of junk. If it was possible, Deke would swear there was more stuff piled high in the backyard. Chances are he was right. They knocked and the man answered the door this time. His name was Charlie and he lived off a disability check.

"You know Charlie," Deke began, "I think I can help you clear out some of this old stuff so that you can gather more new stuff. I noticed the pile is a little higher in the backyard."

Charlie laughed and said he was indeed running out of space.

"I have a truck I could swing by with and maybe we could recycle some of those old stoves you have out front. You can keep the money. I'm doing this to help you out."

Charlie said he would think about it. "I could use a little extra cash. Do you think they pay much?"

"You'll be surprised how much money you have in junk around here, Charlie," Deke said as R.J. elbowed him in the gut.

"Okay, come by tomorrow and I'll dig out some of the stuff I want to recycle."

"I can help you if you would like?"

"No, I got this. Some of that stuff has sentimental value."

R.J. thought to himself that there wouldn't be a damn thing in the recycle pile when Deke got here tomorrow. They left Charlie to start searching through his piles of junk and went to a restaurant.

"Have you visited Crystal or the soldier yet?"

Deke didn't want to admit that he hadn't. They made him very nervous. Finally, R.J. got him to confess that he had stayed away from the two of them.

"It's important that we follow through on our people. I'm counting on you Deke to do the right thing. I'm sure we can save at least one of them."

Deke thought they were both a lost cause, but he promised he would try.

R. J. dropped him back off with his truck and said to him, "Do the right thing Deke. The more you give to people, the more you get back."

Deke thought about it for a minute. It all made sense to him. When he gave of himself to other people, his life was good; when it was all about himself, life was a bit on the rough side. He decided then and there, he would go and visit Crystal and the soldier, and he was going to do it today.

First stop, Crystal Meth. He was greeted outside by two Snakes. They must have known he would return and were lying in wait. This was their prize. Deke wasn't allowed to mess with what was theirs. Deke had other ideas. As soon as Deke walked down the walkway to the door, they greeted him. A punch to the stomach and then a kick when he was down.

"Stay away from her Church boy, or we'll kill you."

It was said more like a snarl, trying to be tough guys. Deke looked up at them and whispered.

"Do you know who I am?"

"Yeah, you're a pussy on a mission. Now get up and get the hell out of here."

Deke stood and stared right into the eyes of one of the men.

"Take a good look. You thought you killed me before, but here I am, alive and well. Picture me with a lot of tattoos."

The man he was staring down pissed his pants. His counterpart couldn't figure out what was going on.

"Diablo, he is the devil."

Tough guy pushed his buddy out of the way to make eye contact with Deke.

"Better believe your friend."

The other snake felt the hair on his neck stand up. Deke gave him the willies.

Deke went up to the house and knocked.

"I can't let you do that."

Deke turned to see tough guy was pointing a Saturday night special at him. Deke smiled and wondered if the guy had ever shot it before. These guys were very dangerous, but sometimes they were lazy and stupid. If he never tried it before, did he know if it would work? Had it been cleaned in ages? Deke turned to face the man.

"I'll tell you what. Let's have us a little gunfight. I'm not armed so if you shoot me that makes you a coward. If I was to also have a gun and you killed me, then that would make you a big name here in the streets. I have a gun in my truck, let me get it out and let's have us a duel. That is, unless you're scared or something like that."

He had called him out, now the punk had no choice. If he backed down, his friends would call him a coward. If he dueled with Deke, he most certainly was going to die. He just didn't know this. He thought Deke was a Christian choir boy, nobody to fear. His friend felt different, but he knew his friend was a crackhead coward. Time to make a name for himself.

Deke walked back to his truck and pulled out the gun that R.J. had given him. He had fired a Glock 19 before so was familiar with the gun and how it felt in his hands. Like his punk friend, he didn't know if R.J. had ever fired it before or how long since it was cleaned. He was going on faith now.

They lined up facing each other about thirty feet apart, each of them holding the gun in his right hand. Deke gave him an out.

"You can walk away now and live. Do the right thing and walk away."

"You're just saying that because you're scared," the punk said as he swayed back and forth nervously.

Deke stood straight as an arrow. "Should have listened to your friend."

They both raised their weapons at the same time. Only one gun fired. Now there was only one snake left, and he was running as fast as he could away from Deke. Deke walked over to the punk and checked to see if he was still alive. A hole in his forehead just above his nose told the story. Deke never missed. Now he couldn't visit Crystal because the cops and more Snakes would surely be all over this place within a few minutes. He calmly got into his truck and went to visit a fellow soldier. Once again, Deke had blood on his hands. He needed the soldier to talk to as much as the soldier needed him.

When he arrived, the soldier was waiting for him in a panic.

"Thank God you're here. Jezebel has gone crazy. I can't control her no more."

Deke thought this was going to be a long day. Let's try and talk the man down.

"We got off on the wrong foot last time. I don't even know your name."

"Sorry for my manners, son. I'm Roscoe, Jerome Roscoe. My friends just call me Ross."

"Okay Ross, now my name is John Deacon, but people just call me Deke."

"Well Deke, like I was saying. I woke this morning and she was in a foul mood. I think she might be having that time of the month thing. I swear I saw her head turn a three hundred and sixty. Annabelle was crying and I was trying to get her settled down when Jezebel comes storming into the house complaining about some fool named Joey. Says he's planning on killing her. Nothing I say can calm her down. It was so bad I had to get out of the house. Can you go inside and check on Annabelle? I sure hope she isn't hurt."

Now Deke wasn't no fool. He knew that the two girls were just blow-up dolls. What could be so evil and sinister about a couple of dolls? When he walked in, he found Annabelle. Her head was stuffed inside the refrigerator. He opened the door and pulled her out. He could have sworn he heard her let out a sigh of relief. He sat her at the table where he had first met the girls and searched around the house for the other doll. Where did this crazy Ross hide this thing? He searched the whole house and couldn't find her anywhere. Just when he had given up, she dropped down from the ceiling and landed on top of him. Scared him so bad he practically soiled himself. He picked her up and yelled at her to behave. Now he was acting as crazy as Ross, pretending she was real, and treating her that way. He sat her down in her seat and went out to get Ross.

"Hey, buddy. I got her. She said that she will behave and wants us to come inside and have some lunch."

Ross let out a nervous laugh but came inside with Deke. When they got to the kitchen, Annabelle was in her seat, but Jezebel was gone. Somebody was playing with this guy's mind. No way that doll got up and walked away. He turned to ask Ross, but he was long gone, ran back outside where it was safe, or so he thought. He heard him scream and found Jezebel outside with her arms around his neck. How did he get her outside? Maybe this guy was playing with his mind. Deke hated mind games.

"What are you doing outside with her? Bring her back inside," Deke called out to him.

It was useless. Ross was down on the ground crying he couldn't breathe. Deke ran outside and pulled the doll off a very frightened Ross.

"I thought you told me you were going to behave."

Deke could have sworn he heard the doll let out a tiny laugh.

"You have to take her away before she kills me. I can't handle her anymore. Please Deke, take her away!" Ross pleaded.

Deke loaded her into his truck and said to Ross that he would find her a good home. It was time for some more target practice. He figured he was going to need it if he went back to see Crystal.

He drove away with the doll sitting beside him. It was quiet for the first mile or so. He was going to go over to the rock yard where there was a deep quarry and shoot her a few times and toss her into the quarry. That was the plan. He nearly crashed when she attacked him on the highway. It must have been the wind that blew her on top of him, yeah, that was what happened. When he got to the rock yard, he set her up in a standing position in front of a rock formation. He left the truck running as he felt this was going to be a quick job. Fire a couple of quick shots. Toss the remains over the side.

He turned to walk about fifty feet away and when he turned around, she was gone.

"What the hell is going on here? I must be losing whatever is left of my mind. Did she blow over?"

He walked back to search for her when he heard the truck rev up and start moving toward him. He looked up in amazement as he found

Jezebel behind the wheel driving right at him. He dove out of the way and the truck hit the embankment and slowly rolled over on its side.

"I've lost my fucking mind!"

Deke paced all over for a few minutes. He got his phone out and called for a tow truck.

The driver showed up and was ribbing him about having way too much of a good time with his girlfriend. Deke didn't find it very funny.

"Just roll it back on its wheels, please."

The driver did as Deke asked and he checked out the damage.

"Looks like a ding here and there. Should be fine to drive."

"Thanks. You want a blow-up doll?"

The driver laughed at him like he was the biggest wuss there ever was.

"Buddy, I got the real thing at home. No thanks."

He walked away laughing at a very embarrassed Deke.

She was sitting on the front seat like nothing had ever happened. Just a doll out for a ride. Deke was rattled. If he tried to kill it, would it kill him first? He decided to take her back to Ross. He needed more answers about this doll. When he pulled back into Ross's driveway with Jezebel, he thought the man was going to cry.

"You promised me you would get rid of her, you promised."

Deke hung his head.

"I tried, but she tried to kill me several times along the way. If I didn't bring her back, I think she would have."

"Damn right she would have, the evil bitch."

Now Deke had sunk into the depths of mental illness with Ross. He was sure this had something to do with that incident with the snakes earlier in the day.

"Maybe we can do something else with her."

"I'll take care of her, no thanks to you son. Now, leave me. I've got to prepare."

Deke was none too happy to leave Ross by himself with that doll. His brain had been rattled beyond anything he had ever experienced. It was time for a drink, maybe two or three. He lost count after a dozen. The only thing that sobered him up was the news. Jezebel had struck for the last time. She was right, Joey was going to kill her. He used the train, his first day back on the job, just several miles into his trip. Ross was with her to the very end.

Ross had a plan. He got a length of rope and tied her up. He carried her to the tracks behind his house. The plan was to leave her laying on the tracks and let the next train run her over. When he laid her down, she broke loose and grabbed him and wouldn't let him go. He struggled with her as the train came closer. The feeling of the train getting closer and closer was vibrating through his bones. The feeling of doom lingered in his soul. He broke free of her grasp just in time to look up and see the engine right in front of his face. His time had come to an end. Jezebel was going to lead him straight to hell hand and hand. The time had come to pay for all the sins he had committed while in the service of his country. He knew there were many. The Grim Reaper had appeared and now he was going to get his comeuppance.

Deke watched in horror as the news told the story of a former soldier with severe PTSD committing suicide on the tracks behind his house. They told of the man's many service medals and accomplishments. He was a hero. It was too bad nobody bothered to help this hero after he had served his country with pride and honor. Deke knew he had tried, or did he? He ordered up another drink and drank it in shame.

"Crystal, you are my last hope. I must save you to save myself."

This wasn't going to be easy, but nothing worth doing in life is easy. Like getting up and walking out of the bar. The last thing Deke remembered was falling flat on his face after he stood up to leave.

CHAPTER 22

R.J. Ted gets a call.

I was working out a plan to make what was left of the money I had on hand stretch for the rest of the month. I would have to tighten the belt to make it. My phone rang and it was my office manager, Desiree Freeman. She was upset about a call she just received from the police chief. Seems Chief Mondale wanted to speak with me, and the sooner I got down to the station, the better it was going to be for me. I sighed, wrapped up what I was doing, and asked Desiree if she wanted some unpaid time off.

"We spent too much money this month. I can't make it stretch all the way to the end of the month."

She looked at me and blew me away.

"You do so much for so many people, it's my turn to sacrifice. I'll be by your side whether you pay me or not."

I was speechless.

"I can't let you do that. You have too many mouths to feed. I'll pray to God to make a way and we should be fine."

She laughed at me.

"I like how you used that play on words, seeing we're the Make A Way Foundation."

I blushed. I didn't even realize I had done that. I bid her farewell and headed with dread downtown.

Things seemed very quiet when I got there. Crime in the city had gone down so much since Deke took to the rooftops and started to pick off one bad guy after another. It seemed all the bad guys had left town to find some place safer. I walked to the desk to find a very bored police sergeant.

"I need to see Police Chief Mondale."

I introduced myself and the man stared at me and drank some coffee.

"I know who you are. First time I've met you in person. You sure are a big son of a bitch."

I didn't know how to respond to that, so I kept my big mouth shut.

"Follow me, we've been expecting you."

I followed the sergeant into the lower section of the station where they keep people for the night when they misbehave. I had stayed here a few times myself. I knew it well.

"First off, you know this guy?" He pointed at Deke who was passed out in a cell. I noticed he had wet himself and he stunk to high heaven.

"Unfortunately, I do. Has he done something wrong other than to get shit-faced?"

The sergeant looked at his paperwork and laughed.

"Not last night, but you might say he has some very interesting history with us. When we are done here today, I need you to remove him from my jail cell and make sure he never returns. If he does, next time he's never going to get out. Do you understand what I'm saying?"

I did. If they knew Deke's real identity, I was surprised he was getting out at all. The chief cleared it all up for me.

I sat at his desk while he lectured me on everything he knew about Deke and what he thought he had done. This also included me, and how I aided him in doing the things he allegedly was being accused of. I protested of course, but I was scolded and told to sit my fat ass down. The Chief was upset.

"Pastor Ted, I could lock the two of you up and throw away the key, but what would that accomplish? Crime in this city is at an all-time low and you know who is getting all the credit for that?"

He stood up and pointed to himself.

"If I announce that I've apprehended the vigilante sniper and his cohorts, this will bring the criminals out of hiding and back wrecking my streets. I kind of like the way things are now. If only I could keep Hopkins out of this town, I might be able to get a solid night's sleep. Do you know Joey has been back at work for one day now and already he's killed someone with that train he operates? The man is a one-man wrecking ball. Can't you convince him to move to LA permanently, please for me?"

I was embarrassed by the way the chief was begging me to do something I had no control over. I know all about Joey Hopkins and his bad karma, experienced it more than a few times. I thought the further I stayed away from the man the better off I was. I lied to the chief.

"I'll talk to him, see if I can get him to believe he would be better off in LA."

It was just a little white lie. Funny thing about lies, they tend to get bigger as you go, until they swallow you up and spit you out in disgrace. I should have been truthful with the chief and told him I had no control or influence over the man. What I did was talk to Joey and I got caught up in a tidal wave that dragged me straight across the country and almost killed me once or twice. I needed money. Joey knew a way I could make some and continue with my foundation I so wanted to keep up and running. God had made a way for me. I should have ducked and run for cover.

The sound of a key in the cell door woke Deke. He struggled to his feet and moved to the entrance. I helped him walk out of the station and found his truck waiting just outside the entrance with the police sergeant at the wheel.

"I thought you might prefer to take him in his truck rather than your vehicle. Get the man cleaned up." He held his nose as he walked by us. "Jesus, does he stink." He laughed as he walked by us. "Check out the toy he has in the back. She's a beauty."

I looked in his truck bed and saw the blow-up doll. It belonged to Roscoe who so tragically lost his life last night. I wondered what Deke was doing with it. I tried to ask him, but he was still not quite functioning properly. I drove him back to the foundation office and got him sobered up. The rest of the day turned out to be quite interesting, especially when I told him about the doll in the back of his truck. I thought the man was having a heart attack. I couldn't get him to calm down. The last time I saw him that day is when he sped off for parts unknown. This was bad. I hadn't had a chance to explain to him how close he had come to going back to prison for the rest of his life.

CHAPTER 23

Anna back at the hearing.

I stood up to stretch and asked for some more water. Walter stood as well. He asked if I needed a break because he sure as hell needed one. He had run out of aspirin. While I had been telling this part of the story, the President had expanded to two other cities. The auditors had now invaded Detroit and Chicago. The soldiers were only there to protect their own people, which when they showed up were fired upon. The government officials knew they had to do something to protect themselves so had called in favors to some of the most ruthless individuals they could find. The President had been prepared for this. The auditors were vital to the operation. It wasn't going to be hard to take down many corrupt people in power today. The evidence was all in the books that were now in the auditor's hands. Stuff that never was meant to see the light of day. It was all-out war. The President had more firepower, but if they had been given time and been forewarned, this would have been a bloody revolution. The speed in which they were hitting these cities was giving the corrupt individuals no time to cover their tracks. So, they contacted the media to do their dirty work and spread lies that made the people come out in force. The bad guys figured if they could tell enough outrageous lies, it would slow the President's forces down enough that they could burn all their books and cover up as much of their bad deeds as possible. They hadn't figured on the

President being one step ahead of them. He had the plan in place, and nobody but his people had a clue as to what the plan really was.

The President knew what he was facing. He knew this because he had already read it. The small ripple in his plan was the ripple in time that Joey had caused from the reset. Maria's manuscripts had saved the President before, and from this last story he read, would save him again from the ruthless Urstin Trevosky. This little war on corruption was going to propel him into a second term and stave off Urstin and his cronies. If it failed, he was going to be forced out of office in disgrace.

How was I going to tell this committee what was going on?

"Well you see, Maria writes these stories that seem to come true and that is why the President has acted the way he has."

Come on, that would be the most unbelievable thing I've told them today, or would it? I would have to work it into the story somehow.

I went to the bathroom and this time I was intercepted by Ivan.

"Your guy is screwing up, you know it, I know it. This is all going to end in disaster. Many lives are going to be lost today. How come you couldn't have just told them last night and saved us from all this mayhem? I know why you did it. The blood shed today is all on your hands."

He walked away from me shaking his head in disgust. I was also shaking. It was from fear. I didn't read any of her stuff. Joey had always said it was better if he didn't know what was coming. I felt the same way. Mr. B felt differently, and he orchestrated us into position to foil the plans of the other side. He had to have her stuff as soon as she wrote it. Maria would write her stories, bring it into Tom Bennett. He would then take it to his dad to see if he wanted to make a movie out of it or shelve it for a later time. Some of the stuff she wrote was so good they filmed it right away before the events could take place. Some of it they used to slow down Helen Harrison, who had been putting the squeeze on Mr. B with Urstin and his communist friends. Tom had told me they had killed his mother when he was younger to get his dad to do their bidding. He told me that he and Ben had been used as leverage. Don't do as they ask, one of them would die a horrible death. Mr. B did their bidding and a little more.

I came out of the bathroom to find the floor in chaos. The people had made it to the White House and were rioting outside. I saw Walter come running down the hall and pull me into the hearing room.

"We are almost out of time. I need you to tell me about what happened at the ranch and how the President was given the formula."

"I can't rush this story. It must be given in small doses or you will jump to conclusions and people will get hurt. I can't make it any clearer than that."

He pulled me back inside and threw me in my seat.

"Start talking, sweetie. We don't know how much time we have left."

I began as the sound of automatic weapons being fired above my head from the second floor rang out. Well, isn't this going to be an interesting last part of the story? I stood and requested that Bob be brought back out for this part. Walter was in no position to argue, so screamed at one of his staff to go get the man.

"Please Anna, he is on the way. Begin before we are all killed by those lunatics outside.

CHAPTER 24

Anna at the ranch.

I was given a room at the ranch and instructed on what my duties were going to be. I had to train this woman who had been in an accident and get her back into shape for some mission that they had planned for her. When I had first seen her, she looked rough. Her face was swollen and bandaged. It looked like she might have had some internal injuries as well as she walked with a stoop for a few days.

The first few days, all I was able to do with her was some minor strength training and muscle stretches. I wasn't feeling all that well and found myself bent over the toilet a few times with nausea. My breast seemed sore and I was in a foul mood. I explained it all to myself as being in the situation I was in was the cause of all these symptoms.

We were finally able to go outside and do some running. Franny was a little smaller than me. She tried to keep up but struggled to get her breath. I figured she was out of shape and if I kept working with her, she would come around. Within weeks I was chasing her, and I was trying to figure out why I couldn't keep up with her. She had so much energy and pep. I felt like I was drowning in mud. My breast hurt so bad and felt so heavy, I would have to take breaks in the middle of my run. I grabbed a handful and it appeared I had gone up a cup size. I had a suspicion about what was happening to me, but I didn't want to tell anybody what I was thinking.

THE TRUTH

When I was younger, I had very bad menstrual problems. I was diagnosed with endometrial disease. The endometriosis was severe, and I needed surgery. After the procedure, the doctor took me aside and broke the news to me that the chances of me being able to have a child were slim to none. I was in fear that the disease had once again risen its ugly head.

I didn't want to explain to the panel what was really on my mind. I thought somehow, someway that I was pregnant. The only two I had been with were Joey and Pastor Ted. If I was indeed pregnant, one of the two was the daddy. I told Leon to bring me a test kit so I could confirm my suspicions. He took his sweet time getting it for me.

When I was running, I would see Beats out riding one of the horses. They still had a week or so before time would catch up with them and they could go home. Ben was getting extremely anxious and wanted to get back to New York in the worst way. Peter just relaxed and treated it like a vacation. I asked him several times if he would like to run with us, but he would say he would never be able to keep up. The way Franny was running lately, I was having trouble keeping up.

It was what might have saved me in the end. That day Franny was way ahead of me and I was struggling to crest this last hill before we got back to the ranch. The ranch had an underground river that ran under it and came back out about a mile south of us. I was about to see the underground side of it. I waved to Beats and he raised the Stetson he was wearing to let me know he saw me. The ground below my feet shifted and I lost my balance and fell. Then the ground shifted even more, and that's when I realized we were in the middle of a very large earthquake. I watched Franny tumble down the hill to the dirt driveway. I held on to a rock for dear life. The ground below me started to split and I frantically tried to crawl away from the hole that was opening below me. I almost made it until I was rocked back and down into the crevice. I felt like I was falling forever until I hit the ice-cold water. It took my breath away. When my head emerged from the depths, I took in big gulps of air. It was very dark, and the only light was coming from above. I struggled to keep my head above water and try to stay below the hole. The pull of the current had other ideas for me and was pulling me towards darkness and a very uncertain future. It might get me out to safety a mile downstream, or it might drown me before we got there. I couldn't take that chance. I had to stay below the hole anyway I could do so. My feet were able to find something to slow my progress into the dark and I was able to grab a handhold along the wall to hold me in place. My only hope was that Beats had seen me fall through the earth and go and get me help.

I felt a rope hit the water beside me and I desperately reached for it and grabbed it. I tied it around my waist and ran it in front of me so I could use it to guide me up and out. I pulled on the rope twice to let whoever was on the other end know I was ready to exit this watery hell I was in. The rope slowly grew taut and lifted me from my potential watery grave. Either he was very strong, or more than one person was pulling on the rope. I reached the top and was able to use my hands to get me up and over the edge.

I saw just who my hero was. It was Beats and the horse he rode in on. He had used the rope and tied it to the horse. The horse had slowly pulled me out of the hole. Beats had just directed it. The fact that a little boy could think on his feet that fast in a life or death situation with little to no guidance was incredible. I lay there for a few moments gathering my faculties. When I was once again able to talk, he told me not to.

"We have company. Bad people are here. We must hide."

He grabbed the blanket he had used under the saddle and wrapped my cold body in it.

"I will get you to safety, then I will go back and get food and water. These are people you don't want to be around. Very dangerous folks."

I watched him struggle to get the saddle back on the horse. I was amazed he was able to do it by himself. I was useless at that moment, otherwise, I would have helped him. He assisted me up and onto the horse and then he walked us down the hill and south to where the river came back above ground. He knew of an old storage shed down by the water that once was someplace they stored supplies for the boats they would launch into the river from here. It was run down and hadn't been used in years. The door was unlocked, and we entered. It would provide shelter, not much else. A window on the backside was broken, but otherwise, it was a good place to hide.

Beats said, "You remember that bad Russian man? He is here with a bunch of people. Somebody had to call him and tell him we were here. Peter is in danger along with everybody else at the ranch. Nobody will suspect me as being a threat to them so I should be able to move about freely. At least I hope that is how they will perceive me."

I held his hand and thanked him for all his help. I told him to be very careful.

"I know Urstin very well, be very leery of him."

"I'll be very careful. Don't you worry about me."

He left me to hide out and I must have fallen asleep. When I woke, the fun had just begun.

I heard something bang against the front door. I opened my eyes to see it had grown dark outside. In the dim light, I could hear something, very odd and almost silent. Like the wings of a bee. I looked up in time to see a drone above me and it was carrying something. It released it and started to move very quickly back towards the opening in the broken window. I had no doubt what it had just released. I had just under five seconds to get out or die. It had released a grenade. A broom handle with very little broom left to it was beside me and I picked it up and swung it at the drone like it was a piñata. I hit it as it was about to escape, and it crashed inside. I dove for the window and what was left of it gave way quite easily. As I was hitting the ground outside, the whole shed blew into a million pieces. I wasn't quite out of the woods yet. The whole side of the shed that wasn't torn apart landed on top of me. I was stuck below some very heavy debris. Once again Beats was there, just in time.

He apologized. He didn't know that he was followed by the drone. When he saw it, he could only think to throw the food against the door and keep riding. He hoped the sound would warn me of the impending danger. The boy was in tears. He said he felt so stupid that they had tricked him.

"It will never happen again, I promise."

He said those words like he had a plan or something. I knew very little about the boy. I would learn what a formidable opponent he could be.

I was very hungry, so he dug through the rubble and found the food he had brought. I offered him some, but he said he already ate. While I ate, he told me what was going on back at the ranch. I lost my appetite.

CHAPTER 25

Beats tells the story.

I rode into the stables to see Peter and several other people waiting for me. Peter was worried sick I might have been hurt and they had searched in vain to find me. There was a man there. His name was Ivan, along with a couple of his men that were either bodyguards or henchmen. I could see everyone was well-armed. Peter berated me for not coming right back to the stables after the earthquake. He wanted to know if I had seen Anna. They claimed how worried they were for her safety. I told them I hadn't seen her, but I could tell them where she wasn't.

"I rode along the river all the way back here. I'm sorry I was so far out when the quake hit. If I had known it was going to hit, I would have been closer to the ranch house."

Peter cuffed me in the head for being a smart ass.

We all headed inside to find the big Russian dude on the phone. He was talking to Helen Harrison. I could hear her shrill voice from the other side of the room and Urstin didn't have it on speaker. I tried to block her voice. It gave me the willies. I heard her say that she would get the President and be at the ranch before the sun sets tomorrow. That didn't leave me much time.

The many other thugs that had shown up with Urstin and his men had fortified the windows and set up positions to defend the ranch. Were they expecting an attack? Were they afraid of little old Anna?

I had to gather some information so I could figure out just what was going on here. Ben Bennett was trying to act like he was in charge, this was his family's house. He was beaten and tied up and I could hear him whine that he wished he had never called them. I now knew who the biggest idiot in the house was. I walked over and gave him a kick.

I stared at him and said, "I want to thank you for letting me play with those old guys. It was fun and I really liked them. It felt like I was with old friends. I also want to thank you for calling these thugs to come visit us. You must be the stupidest person in this house. What the hell were you thinking?"

He whined, "The cartel was after us. As soon as we go back to New York, they will try to kill me again. I knew this Russian man has influence on them. I was looking to have him call the dogs off. I didn't realize he hadn't set the dogs on me yet. He asked where I was staying, and I accidentally told him. I think we're still a week ahead of time."

He started to cry. Urstin couldn't get here fast enough when Ben said the things that he said to him.

I pondered this in my head. I had to think. If we were still a week ahead of the incident in New York. That meant we couldn't go back until at least a week from now. That gave Urstin and his men that much time to get as much knowledge of the things to come in the next week from us as he could. I started to think and that's when it came to me. The earthquake, it happened the day before we left for New York. Urstin had lied to Ben. We just had to survive one more day, then we could go back. I could make that happen. I also knew I had to disrupt things so that nothing changed from here on out. I liked my life. I wanted to go back to it. I wasn't going to let some Russian bully ruin it for me.

I walked out to find Billy was the first they wanted to interrogate. He was tied naked to a sheet of plywood. They had drilled holes in it and tied him spread-eagle to the board. The holes were aligned in a way that it held his hands above his head and his feet spread so that he could stand but not move his legs. It looked very uncomfortable. They would ask him a question, and when he gave them an answer they liked, nothing would happen. When he lied, they threw a dart at the board. Sometimes it hit wood, sometimes it hit flesh. I could see they had played this game before. They were very good at it.

All Billy would tell them was the date he flew Joey and Anna along with a shipment to Denver. He refused to tell them about the crash and the aftermath of it. That doomed flight was going off tomorrow morning. Urstin made some notes. When it was apparent Billy was not going to reveal any more information, they untied him and walked him outside. When I heard them shout to run, I looked out the window to see that they had given Billy a ten-second head start. They counted very fast and shot Billy several times in the back. If Billy wasn't supposed to die until tomorrow, but now he was dead, was that going to cause another ripple? I felt the ground shake once again. Aftershocks they said. I thought ripple in the universe. Who would be next for their board of torture? I didn't want to stick around to find out if it was going to be me. I ran into the kitchen and started to prepare some food. A quick sandwich, some fruit, and a bag of nuts.

I saw them dragging Peter into the house. He was going to be the next victim. I had been here long enough to know where the guns were hidden. I had long since found the ammo. A Remington 783 .30-06 would do the trick nicely. I grabbed it and headed for the stables. I had a backpack full of ammo, a gun, and very little food. The stables were being watched by two of Urstin's men. What was I going to do?

I ran inside the stables in a panic and told the fools that Urstin was in trouble. Peter had somehow broken away and was preceding to kill them one by one.

"Please help! There is blood everywhere inside! Be careful. He's an animal."

I fell to my knees like I was a frightened child in need of comfort. They ran to the house and I ran to grab my stuff. No time to saddle up, we would be riding bareback tonight. The horse was so tall I had to climb up on the side of the stall to mount the animal. I had already unlatched the gate and we were off and running into the darkness of the night.

What I didn't know was that Urstin had planned this all along. His real prize was Anna, and he wanted her dead or alive, mostly dead. Ivan had brought the drone and had it set and ready for flight as soon as I made my break for it.

"The kid will lead us right to her and I plan on giving her a big surprise."

Urstin rubbed his hands together and laughed a maniacal laugh. The drone was loaded with a grenade with the ability to drop it and pull the pin at the same time. All they needed to do was find their quarry.

CHAPTER 26

Anna waits. Beats plays Urstin like a drum.

After Beats had told me what was going on back at the house, I wondered what Franny was doing. His whole story never included her. I asked him, but he said he never saw her when he was there. I asked him if he had a number on how many people Urstin had with him. He said he counted five men, Ivan and Urstin. I could work this out, but he said they were prepared for an attack. I knew they wouldn't stop until they found me. My only hope was that drone was the only one they had.

Beats said he was going to reduce their numbers so that we could rescue Peter and Franny. He said they could have Ben. He was the traitor that had set them all up. I tried to tell him not to pass judgment on the man, but he waived me off saying, "The man did things to get us killed, he has to pay."

"From what you've told me, he has paid. He knows he screwed up," I tried to explain to him.

"You stay here. I'm going to work."

He acted like a grown-up man, being brave and stupid all at the same time. I called out to him, but he was off into the wind and the dark swallowed him up. My leg was cut badly. I tried to salvage some stuff from the debris of the storage shed. I found some clean rags that I used to treat my leg. I had the bleeding stopped, but I was going to need stitches sometime in the very near future. The blood-soaked rag that I first used was discarded for a new one and I had the cut covered well this time. It was about that time that I heard them out in the woods. The first yip, and howl. Coyotes – and hungry ones at that. I needed shelter and I needed it now. I looked around but I could find very little to use in the dark. I squirmed back into the debris of the shed and tried to use what was left of it to protect myself until the sun came up. I would be able to better defend myself in the light of day, or so I thought.

The sounds of the coyotes grew louder as they crept up on where the smell of blood was coming from. I was on the menu now. You could say I was their prey, which I was doing a lot of now. Praying that is. I could hear them just yards away searching for me. It was so dark I couldn't see them. I pushed myself in under the debris as far as I could get and used a board to close the opening. I could feel them walk over the pile of debris and start digging to find me and get me out of my hiding spot. It was going to be a very long night. My only hope was that I could make it until Beats returned.

The coyotes were fighting among themselves, frustrated that they were unable to dig me out of my hiding spot. I could feel one digging at my feet and then I felt the first bite. I pulled my leg in close to me. Another chunk of flesh bleeding and exciting the animals. They dug more feverishly. I was panicking and knew my time was near. The moon had risen late that night, or maybe it was the cloud cover that let the light shine down on me. I wasn't sure. The light was dim, but I wasn't in complete darkness anymore. I felt the board that I used to conceal me being torn from its spot exposing me to the hungry animals. I was done for. The coyote was practically in my face, I could feel his teeth just inches from me. His breath came in rapid puffs as he dug deeper to pull me out and start to feed on me.

I closed my eyes and screamed as loud as I could. It was the only thing I could think of. The coyotes were excited and started to yip and howl a victory tune. It would soon be time to eat. I felt his teeth bite and scrape the top of my head and pull my hair. I screamed again and again. I was screaming so loud I guess I never heard the shot. The next thing I heard was Beats telling me it was okay now, come out, they're gone. He moved the dead coyote from the front of my hidey-hole and offered a hand to help me out.

"I told myself I never wanted to kill again. Yet here I am killing people and animals once again."

I wasn't sure what he was getting at.

"Urstin is down two men. We need to move. They will be coming here first light. We need to find another hiding place," he said in such a way, I wasn't sure if I believed him. Yet here was a dead coyote that was trying to eat me, and I was sure two of Urstin's men were dead somewhere out in the desert.

"You lead the way, I'll follow. You seem to know this area a lot better than I do."

An hour later, we were hidden in a cave along the riverbank. When the river was high, this cave would be under water, but at this time, it was accessible. The last thing we needed was a flash flood. The whole cave could be underwater in a matter of minutes. Beats said he needed to hide the horse. It would give away our location if Urstin's men were to see it. He left me for an hour, then returned with more food and water. I drank greedily finishing almost every drop. I was so thirsty.

"I have another bottle, but don't drink it. We're going to need it for later."

It was so tempting to drink that down as well, but I resisted.

"We have more problems now. A helicopter landed with about ten more men and I think the President and Helen Harrison, they have Maria and Mr. Bennett. I could tell they didn't come willingly from my vantage point."

I thought about this. If they had Bennett and Maria, that could only mean one thing.

"Beats, we have got to stop them. I'm sure they are going to torture her for the formula. If they get it, God is going to destroy the world. Jesus told me this himself. It's my job to stop it from happening."

"If you say we are on a mission for God, then I'm with you. I must warn you though. I'm in it to win it. Once I start, I will not stop. Many will die, many have died in the name of religion. I have talked with Jesus personally myself. He gave me a gift. It was a gift to heal, not kill."

I held his hand in mine.

"I know this is hard on you. You are just a little boy. One that should be playing and having fun with other children. I'm so sorry I dragged you into this."

He looked at me confused.

"You didn't drag me into anything. I have free will and I plan on using it."

I hugged him and cried just a little bit. I was so proud of this little guy. He scared the shit out of me later that day. The kid was a natural-born killer. He was right, many would die.

CHAPTER 27

Beats.

Anna was trying to put on a brave face, but her injuries were severe. I had checked out her legs. The coyote had taken a chunk of flesh from one leg. The other leg was even worse. It had a nasty jagged cut, most likely when she jumped through the window to get away from the grenade. If she didn't get medical help soon, infection was a sure thing with no way to properly clean her up. I had to do something. I told her I was going to try and find us something to eat. What I planned on doing was praying. I got out of her view from the cave and got on my hands and knees. I begged for a way to help her.

I opened my eyes to see he was on the other side of the river calling out to me. He had a very happy disposition and a huge smile on his face.

"You're incredible my boy," he called out to me.

I waved to him. I could barely hear what he was saying.

"Watch this," he pointed to the sky and I saw an eagle approach from above. The eagle swooped down and plucked an enormous fish from the river. It was so heavy the eagle was having a hard time getting it back up in the air and when it flew just feet above my head, dropped its prize right in front of me. Discouraged that it lost its dinner to me, it flew away making high-pitched whistling noises.

I heard Jesus shout to me, "For this cause, use it wisely."

I shouted out my thanks and ran with the fish back to the cave. The longer I kept the fish alive, the better my chances to save Anna.

I thought about what Jesus had said. It was a name of a song I once heard. "For This Cause/Eagles Wings/Carry Me." It was a song I heard Hillsong London perform when I was younger. Jesus had laid down his life for me many years ago. Now he had given me a gift to heal and a mission. I couldn't let him down.

The fish was heavy and very much alive. It squirmed and twisted in my hands and I dropped it several times. I had to hurry. The fish wouldn't live much longer. I climbed the few feet back into the cave and found Anna was sleeping.

"Wake up Anna," I shouted to her. "Hold this for me. When I tell you, give it back to me."

I was excited and very demanding. She grabbed the fish from me, and I got to work. First, I unwrapped the bandages on one leg, the cut immediately started to bleed. The other leg was wrapped, but it was where the chunk was taken out. The rag was soaked in blood. This wasn't going to be pretty. Once the wounds were exposed, I held my hands above them while Anna protested my removing of her bandages.

"Quiet Anna," I shouted. "Let me do what I do best."

She squeezed her eyes shut. I could tell she was in extreme pain. It doesn't take long, a minute or two is all that is required, but I had to concentrate, and Anna's cries were making it very difficult.

I hoped the fish was still alive, because if he wasn't, I was next in line to feel the pain Anna had just endured. It was, I was then able to transfer all her injuries to the fish. It was too much for the fish and it died almost immediately. We now had something to eat. No way to cook it without being discovered.

"Do you like sashimi?" I asked her.

"I don't even know what that is," she answered me while rubbing her leg, not even finding a hint of even a scratch.

"How did you do this?"

She was pointing to her healed legs. I avoided the question and told her sashimi was raw fish. I was cutting it up into slices to serve to her.

She wasn't buying my avoidance. She asked again.

"I was given a gift from Jesus a while back. I can heal if I have something to transfer it to. The fish was the perfect thing to pass your injuries to. Now you're healed and we have something to eat."

I watched her just shake her head in disbelief. I knew what she was thinking. Every time I went to heal someone, I thought for sure this would be the time it didn't transfer. I remember just how bad that could be at the Kentucky Derby. I screwed up and didn't transfer the horse's injuries and kept them as my own. I could heal from a broken leg. The horse was about to be put down. I had to do something, so I did. It was very painful.

"Now that you're healed and can fight, we must go on the offensive. I don't want to be hunted down. I want to be the hunter."

She looked at me in disbelief. The words that came from this child were something that she probably never heard before. I was not an ordinary child. As soon as she realizes this, the better it will be for her.

We packed up what little we had and struck out. They were very close and it's a good thing we moved when we did. A party of four guys had found the horse and were searching the area we now occupied. The recently vacated cave was the first place they found. The blood-soaked rags made them overconfident. It was to our advantage. I set Anna up in a sniper's favorite spot. A high place overlooking the kill zone. I took cover in a hollow tree. My backpack now contained some treasures I had acquired from my first two kills. A 9mm FNS-9 Luger semi-auto pistol fully loaded with seventeen rounds. I was about to put it to good use.

Anna took the first shot, I cleaned up the rest. She may be a girl, but she fights like a man. The first shot nearly took a bad guy's head off. The other three scrambled for cover right into my waiting arms. I had to think fast, my cover had been blown. I started to cry.

"She's crazy! I've been hiding from her for hours. What took you guys so long to come and rescue me?"

I balled my eyes out while keeping my backpack close. They tried to comfort me, but I cried louder.

"Quiet kid! She'll be able to locate us if you keep making so much noise."

I had two guys right beside me. The third guy was on the other side of this small clearing where we were positioned. Anna took her second shot and nicked the guy in the arm. He screamed out in pain and called to the others that he had been hit. When Anna had taken her shot, I was ready and placed two quick headshots on two unsuspecting villains. The only man still alive took a quick look my way and raised his weapon to finish me off. He knew it was me, I was holding a freshly fired weapon. I didn't have time to take another shot and dove for cover. Anna had plenty of time. It was game over for these four henchmen.

Anna came down from her high perch and we gathered a couple more weapons we might be able to use later.

"Nice work, Anna. Two of these guys are the President's men, two are Urstin's. He has Ivan and one other. If the President's men are out here hunting us, that doesn't bold well for us." Anna agreed.

"Let's cross that bridge when we get to it. I have a feeling that the President is not the bad guy here. You say you saw Helen Harrison get off the helicopter with him?"

I shook my head, "That's right."

"We know for sure what team she plays for. I think she is controlling the game right now. She must have some very damaging dirt on the President."

I found my horse along with four other ones. At least we had saddles to ride in now. Anna and I gathered the horses and made our way back to the ranch house. It was only a couple of miles, but it felt like an eternity. When we discovered they had sent out more than one search party, I was caught with my pants down, literally for me. I had to go and was in the woods taking a crap. Anna never had a chance. It was only by luck that I was still wearing my backpack. She was captured and I was saying and doing the same thing.

I was now all alone out here. God only knows what they were going to do to her. I could see her naked body on the dartboard now. Asking her one question after another. I wonder what part of the body they were going to make a bullseye out of. I had a pretty good guess as to two spots. One on each side of her chest. I shuddered at the thought.

THE TRUTH

I could do this, I had to do this. It was up to me now to save them all. I got into position to scope out the area when I saw some motorcycles coming down the road. The Queen Bees. I never knew which side they played for. I sure hope they play for our side. It was only a few moments before I was going to find out. It was then I realized why they were fortifying the house. They were waiting for this attack from the Queen Bees. This was going to be a slaughter. I had to stop them, but how? I took the shot.

CHAPTER 28

Franny does what she does best.

When the earthquake hit, I was sprinting down the hill toward the ranch house. I saw the vehicle at the bottom of the hill. I lost my footing and tumbled the remaining distance head over heels. I lay just in front of the car, trying to gather my composure. I had to will the pain from the fall away. Once the ground stopped shaking, someone got out of the car and came to my assistance. It was Ivan. He helped me to my feet and brushed the dust from my body. I felt like I was being pawed. The dust from my breast was long gone but still he had to make sure to get every single speck. I knocked his hands away. I had to retain my dignity. That was when he decided it was time to knock the dust off my ass. I dropped him with an elbow to the jaw and walked in the house in a huff. I didn't even turn around to see if he was alright.

I knew something was up when they showed up. I played the part of eye candy that was staying at the ranch. It's easy to play like you're stupid when you're dressed and look as girly as I was. When Maria had first done this to me, I hated it with a passion. I had well over six months to get used to it. With this last operation they did to me, I now didn't have a bit of maleness left. I never would again, so I embraced what she did and made the most of it. When I was male, I was just invisible. Now that I looked like I did now, I had men and women coming on to me all the time. I liked the women, endured the males.

Ivan was very persistent. He followed me into the shower. He wanted some and I was going to give it to him. I cupped his chin in my hands and checked out his split lip. His hands were all over my naked body. I wonder if he had seen me two months ago if he would have stayed in the shower with me. I played him up, got him all excited, and when I had my chance, head-butted him into the twilight zone. He lay on the shower floor with the water hitting him in the face. He had no idea what had just hit him. My forehead was a little sore, but it was well worth it.

He found me less than an hour later and I was raped as a woman for the first time. I was hoping to save myself for Leon. I wanted him to have the first taste before I ended his life. I still planned on giving him everything he asked for, but he just wasn't going to be the first now. I played out his death as Ivan violated me. I had to disconnect, or I would've killed Ivan that night. I wouldn't have gotten away with it. The price to kill Ivan would have been my own life. I still had too many people I needed to exact my revenge on before I was ready to die.

When he finished, he spat on me and called me white trash.

"I hope you had a good time big boy. Maybe next time you can take some Viagra and we can have more than a minute of fun." I was such a bitch. This comment got me a backhand across the face, but I wasn't done. "Tough guy, I don't think so. When Anna gets back here, she'll castrate you and fill your mouth with your own ball sack. I'll make sure she knows what you did here tonight."

I thought this was going to bring a rash of more violence my way. It didn't. I think my man was afraid of her for some reason. I would find out he had good reason to be afraid of her before our time here was through.

I stayed in my room for a couple of hours. I was trying to formulate a plan. When I heard the helicopter land, I peeked out my window and to my surprise found the President's own personal helicopter parked on our front steps. It was time for me to make my appearance.

The first person I saw was Helen Harrison, thank God she didn't recognize me. She did take a long hard look at me. Maybe she did see some of Francis Boucher under all my makeup. I sure hope not. Urstin was another story. Leon said I was being trained to take him out. The guy wouldn't give me the time of day. I tried hard to make him like me. He pushed me away like I was a leper or something. I knew that I would have to find another way to take this man out.

I was strolling around the house greeting all my new guests when I saw her. Sweat instantly broke out on my jaw and my legs got weak and I nearly fell. One of the President's men grabbed me to keep me from falling.

"My, I got lightheaded there for a moment. I sure hope I'm not pregnant," I said as I stared at Ivan.

My nemesis was sitting in the parlor, talking up a storm with the President. I wanted to kill her then and there. I sat down and someone brought me a glass of water.

"You alright, miss? You look awfully flush."

I told her I was okay and stared at Maria. She must have felt my eyes upon her as she slowly turned and looked at me. I could see her recognize me and let out a squeal of delight. She stood up and dragged the President over to me.

"You must meet my best friend Franny. She is just such a sweetheart."

I got to meet the President while clenching my fist and doing my best not to jump up and strangle her right there. I smiled my best fake smile and endured some more. I would have my revenge. I just had to wait for the perfect time.

The President was very talkative. I listened as I watched Maria. They had brought all the ingredients to reproduce the fountain of youth formula. Urstin and Ivan had an important meeting they had to attend to in Denver, said they would be back tomorrow. They wanted to be here when Maria made the formula. That meant I had time to disrupt their plans. I had no idea what it was, but if Urstin and Helen wanted it, I had to make sure Maria was unable to reproduce it.

I also found out that Bob was on his way. Urstin had called him and insisted he come right away. This wasn't good. He knew who I really was. Would he rat me out, or would he remain silent and see what I was up to? All this was going through my mind as the President was asking me to join him in the bedroom. I wasn't really listening to what he was saying, just answering yes to his questions without really hearing what he said. When he grabbed my hand and led me to one of the backrooms, it dawned on me exactly what was going to happen. I screwed up. I had no idea how I was going to get out of this predicament.

I was trying to figure out if I could use him as an ally or if he was the enemy and quite possibly need to be taken out. As our clothes were hitting the floor and his tongue was invading my mouth, I started to try to find which side of the fence he was standing on. I asked him what he thought of Helen.

"She's an evil witch that can't be trusted as far as you can throw her. Stay away from that one."

"Well, what about Urstin and Ivan?"

"Same thing, my dear. They work for her. I'm caught in a net at this moment, but I have a plan to free myself. Maria gave me some great ideas."

"Really," I said. This was getting interesting. The fool didn't know what side I played for, yet freely told me stuff I could take to them and damage his chances.

All he was interested in right now was a piece of ass, and I had to provide that for him. I did, but I really wasn't into it. Being raped just hours before takes some of the wind out of your sails. I put on a performance for him and when he left, he thought he was the world's greatest lover. I sat in the room and tried to recover. Maria entered next.

She was very concerned for my welfare. Asked if I was alright. I told her I wasn't and cried on her shoulder. I was a tangle of emotions. She soothed me and acted like she was a true friend. How could I kill her now?

"The moment I saw you enter my living room to kill me, I knew what you needed. That is why I did what I did to you. There was no way you would ever admit you wanted this, so I had to show you against your will. The simple fact that you have made yourself so beautiful confirms what I say."

I had to think about it for a minute or two. Maybe she was right, I did want and need this. I felt so much better about myself now. Except for the rape part of it, I was enjoying every minute of it. I hugged her for the first time. Looked her in the eye and thanked her. Then I punched her in the eye.

She lay on the floor confused, but then started to laugh.

"I guess I deserved that one."

I helped her up and we hugged again.

"That was just to let you know that I didn't appreciate you not giving me a choice. The first month with Leon was absolute hell. Now we have got to work together and form a plan. These people can't get whatever they came here for."

She giggled, "Oh, they're going to get it alright. I saved a nice special drink just for Helen. If the rest of them get it, no big deal, but if Helen takes it, we plant her in a nice grave shortly thereafter. I'm not sure if you can take it. Might be best if you don't touch it."

"Why?" I asked her.

"It might kill you too. The formula is deadly to females. I'm not sure why. It might be our hormones, or it might be something else. I don't want to find out the hard way. Just don't drink it."

CHAPTER 29

Joey takes R.J. for a ride.

I had to kill someone on my first day back. Didn't even get five miles out of the terminal. A crazy guy and what I thought was a woman were on the tracks and I couldn't do a damn thing to stop the train. She looked like she was restrained. Rope around her legs. The guy was trying to get away when the lady reached up and grabbed him so that he couldn't get away and I killed them both. I found out later that it was just a sex toy, one of those blow-up dolls. I could have sworn it grabbed him. It was all too much for me. I resigned and packed my bags.

Scarlett was right. She could support me until I made enough money from my bit spots to get us by. The money Katrina was making was enough to support us, but I wanted her to have that money for when she got older. Hollywood was so fickle – one day you're hot, the next you're not. I figured it would get her by the tough times. I never knew she was going to be a megastar. Mr. B did. He saw a superstar when she was just a little baby.

I wanted to get back to LA, but my pilot was missing, and I couldn't fly. I decided I wanted to drive, but I didn't want to take a week to get there. I figured R.J. and I could share the driving and then I would fly him back. That was my plan. The news can be a help, it can also hinder you. My face was plastered all over the television and was seen by some unscrupulous people calling themselves the Zihile. They were of German heritage and weren't much nicer than the Nazis were. One of their members knew me from my time in the Navy and was sure I was close to sixty years old. This made me a person of interest to the group. The person they saw on the television appeared to be in his thirties.

They had long ago known that a formula that could keep you young and vital for many years existed. Apparently, I had discovered and used this formula and they wanted me to share it with them, whether I wanted to or not. I was about to get a visit from these people before I could get out of town. There was no time wasted getting to Richmond. They found me within hours of arriving.

"R.J., I'll pick you up in an hour. Thanks for doing this for me. Yes, I'll make sure you get first-class tickets back, I promise."

I hung up the phone. When I turned to grab the rest of my stuff, I was no longer in the room with just Samantha. She had a very nervous look on her face and a hand that was practically wrapped around her throat. The man holding her was armed and his gun was pointed directly at me. I knew from the look of this guy, that this was not a common robbery. Something more sinister was at hand.

"There is no need for your gun. Please put it away and we can talk civilly."

The man pondered my request and put his weapon away. Another man stood behind him. He remained standing with his weapon pointed at me. I offered the leader of the group a seat. The rest could stand. Another was standing by the door acting as a lookout.

"What brings you here today in such a way?"

I had to ask the question, so I would know just how I was going to play this.

"You are Joey Hopkins, correct?"

I told him I was.

"You serve in the Navy back in the eighties?"

I think I had an idea where this was heading now.

"Yes, I did, why do you ask?"

"You appear to be too young to have served so long ago."

I laughed. "I had work done when I was in Hollywood. I'm going to be a big star now, I needed to look younger. Believe me, I still feel like I'm creeping up on sixty."

"You sir are full of shit. You had no work done."

"You're calling me a liar? You come in my house uninvited and call me a liar!"

I was trying to act indignant. He stood, calmly looked over at his men, and asked if the van was in place. The man at the door nodded that it was.

"We are going for a ride now. You're coming with us along with the girl. Her health will depend on whether you choose to cooperate with us."

Samantha cried out as they grabbed her and covered her mouth with duct tape. Zip ties were next, and then her hands were secured behind her back.

"Do we need to do the same with you?"

I told them they didn't need to do it with her. I would cooperate.

"Why do we need to go somewhere else? Let's talk here."

"Can't do that, my friend. We need to be someplace where you can't hear the screams."

This was not looking good.

Jacob tapped me on the shoulder and asked me if I needed some help.

"Thank you, Captain Obvious. Yes, I could use some help."

"I'll see what I can do, but before I can do anything, you must be in danger."

I could have sworn I was in danger. I think I'm going to have to get my eyes checked. Nope, three guys with guns taking me away in a van along with Samantha. I'm not dreaming this, it is happening, yet dumbass thinks I'm not in danger yet. You just can't get good help these days.

I sat in the back seat while Samantha lay on the floor crying. I felt very bad about what was happening to this poor girl all because of me. I wish I could do something to make this situation better, but I was coming up empty in what I could do. We were headed west out into the more rural parts of the state. A place where it would be hard to hear our screams. LA was starting to look good about now. I couldn't wait to get back there. I closed my eyes and started to pray.

"What is your name, sir?" I called out to the leader of this group of four men.

"My name is not important, but you can call me Buddy. It's what you do when you can't remember a person's name." He laughed at his own bad joke.

"Well Buddy, when you came to my house, I had just made an appointment to meet with someone. When I don't show up, he'll come looking for me. The man is like a bloodhound. No matter where you take me, he will find us."

I was trying to blow some smoke up his ass and see if I could get him to change his plans.

"Give me an address to your friend and we'll invite him along for the ride."

"I don't think you want to do that."

He turned in his seat and shouted at me, "Give me a damn address and let me worry about the rest!"

"Okay, it's your funeral." I gave him the address.

Why did I have to involve R.J. in all of this? The man was going to kill me when we figured out a way to escape. He already was mad at me for more than one thing I had done to him. This was just piling on as far as I was concerned. I was more worried about him at this moment than my new friends.

The van pulled up in front of his place and the driver honked his horn. Two of the guys had gotten out around the corner and were lying in wait. This was not good. The leader of the group had his gun trained on me. He whispered to me, "Not a word or the first bullet is for your young female friend."

"You don't understand, Buddy. Your friends are in grave danger."

He snickered, "No, your friend is in grave danger. Mine are the hammer, yours is the nail."

R.J. came out carrying an overnight bag. He had turned to shout last-minute instructions to Desiree when the first shot rang out. If he hadn't stopped suddenly to do that, he would have been gunned down in cold blood. R.J. dove and took cover. Funny how much love for the man had come his way in such a short amount of time. In this town, the last person you wanted to take a shot at now was R.J. His program, Not in My Neighborhood, was a huge success and the people loved him for that. They were also armed to the teeth. The two gunmen never stood a chance. Buddy sat and watched his men get blown away right in front of him. He was dumbfounded.

R.J. never blinked or hesitated. He ran up to the van and lifted it up. The man was so strong I truly believed he could flip it over by himself. The driver hit the gas, and this made it worse for us in the van. We quickly lost control and ran over a fire hydrant. In his panic, he overcorrected and hit a parked car. The folks watching out for R.J. presumed that the van was a threat and started to pump lead into the engine compartment. I dove for cover and tried my best to shield Samantha. My new friend and his driver quickly abandoned us. I guess Buddy's first concern was saving his own ass.

R. J. threw the door open and found Samantha and yours truly on the floor of the van. He was on an adrenaline rush and it took me a few moments to calm him down. Well, maybe it took me to LA to finally calm him down when I put him on the plane and said goodbye.

He called out to the good Samaritans and told them the situation was under control. He turned toward me as I was removing the duct tape from Sam's mouth.

"What the hell is going on here, Peter?"

Instead of answering him, I asked him if he had a knife. I had to cut the zip ties. I don't know where the knife came from, it just appeared in his hands like magic. I knew I never wanted to get into a serious fight with this man. I would lose for sure.

"I hate to tell you this, but I'm not Peter. Take a closer look."

"Son of a bitch, is that you Joey?"

I nodded it was me.

"Maria and her potions. Now it seems I have new friends that want the recipe for the potion. The problem for me, I don't have a clue what she gave me to make me look like this. The only thing I do know is that I won't age for another fifteen years."

"That's a bitch, Joey. Now, why did you feel you had to involve me?"

I stared at him with my mouth open searching for an answer.

"Look around you R.J. If I hadn't included you, I might be dead by now."

He looked around and saw the two dead men. The wrecked van and the sirens wailing in the background.

"I can't stay here. Chief Mondale just had a heart-to-heart with me and I'm avoiding doing jail time by the skin of my teeth. If the cops get here and see I'm involved, I'm heading for jail for a long time."

I looked at him and said, "Won't the witnesses say you were involved?"

He laughed, "What witnesses?"

I knew he was right. Nobody was going to implicate him in anything that happened here today.

He ran around the corner and came back driving his truck.

"Get in, Joey. We got to go."

I helped Samantha inside the truck. It felt like you needed a ladder to get in, it was so jacked up. We sped off to find a rental car company. No way R.J. was leaving his baby in LA. We parked in his old church parking lot. He went inside and told them he was going to park his truck there for a short time. I walked down the road to the rental place and got us a car. All they had left that would fit R.J.'s huge frame was a Dodge Charger. It was yellow with black stripes. When I started it up, it rumbled, I could feel the ground shake below my feet. I knew it would get us there, but I worried about how many tickets R.J. would get along the way. I knew without a doubt he would make me pay for every one of them.

We had to make a quick stop at my place. Samantha insisted she wanted to come along. She didn't feel safe at my condo right now. I couldn't blame her. We grabbed our stuff and were off within minutes. R.J. stood guard in case our friends returned. I knew I would see this group again. Maria had made my life a nightmare now. If I was able to get this group of thugs contained, how long would it be before the next group figured things out and came searching for me?

We had been on the road for about fifteen hours, maybe a little longer. Samantha was complaining about wanting to sleep in a real bed and R.J. was just plain cranky. I wanted to get to LA as fast as possible, but I caved in to them and got us a motel. Twin beds, one for R.J. and one for Samantha. I had to choose if I wanted to sleep on the floor or on the uncomfortable desk chair. To the delight of Samantha, I made her scoot over and make room for me. She made room for me alright. I had her draped all over me all night. I had to keep slapping her hand away from my tool. A couple of hours of that had me walking the streets and trying to walk my hard-on off. If I stayed much longer, I would have succumbed to her efforts to make love to me.

R.J. found me in the morning asleep in the car. I couldn't go back into the room. The temptation was too much for me. This being younger thing had some disadvantages. First was, I was always ready to procreate. I think it was something built into the ancient formula. The world needed to be populated back in those times. Now it was working the same magic on me in modern times. If I wasn't careful, I might find myself raising a dozen kids before too long. Maybe I should get a vasectomy. That might keep me from impregnating too many women. I thought about Anna. I wondered if she was with child, like my sweet Scarlett. I was in so much trouble if she was. I had no control. Even the second time around I tried to stop it, but I couldn't do it.

"Well big guy, I want to thank you. You left me with a nymphomaniac. You're driving first today. Seems Samantha and I didn't get a whole lot of sleep last night thanks to you getting her all worked up."

"I need coffee. How about you?"

"None for me. I just told you I need to get some sleep, and Christ, don't give her any. That girl is already hyped up enough as it is."

As I was walking to check us out, I saw her come strolling out dressed in yoga pants and a tight-fitting blouse. I almost walked into a wall. Derek was missing out on a very fine woman. I almost wish the idiot hadn't made the choices he did and married the girl. That way she would be with him right now and not tempting me.

I grabbed an extra-large cup of coffee and paid the bill. I turned to head out and was greeted by my ghostly friend.

"Joey, we have a big day today, you and I."

If he said we had a big day, that meant I didn't get enough coffee.

"What is on the agenda that's going to keep me from getting to LA anytime soon?"

He laughed, only it was a little sinister kind of laugh.

"You're going to love this one. We need to get to this high school by 10:00 a.m."

I looked at my watch, it was 9:30.

"Where is this high school, and why do we need to get there by ten?"

"If we don't get there in time, a whole lot of young people are going to die today. The school is only twenty miles away. We have plenty of time."

If he said we had plenty of time, that meant we better move our asses or else. I sprinted for the car, jumped in, and had the tires squealing leaving the parking lot. R.J. was already snoring, and Samantha was gazing out the window deep in thought.

"The highway is that way." I saw her pointing behind us.

"We're taking a shortcut. Got some business to attend to in the next town over."

I had the Dodge close to a hundred and accelerated some more. She squealed with delight.

"I have a need for speed. Go Joey, go!"

It was nice to be able to give her a little adrenaline rush. I must keep my eye on the road and not the rearview mirror or I'll have us in a ditch. Damn, she was hot.

I pulled into the high school just before ten. I had about eight minutes to spare. I hit the brakes hard and slid to a stop in a cloud of dust. This woke R.J. and he wanted to know what was up. Samantha told him I had business at the school. R.J. jumped out of the car and chased me down. Before he jumped out of the car, he told Samantha not to get out. This scared her because he was checking his weapon when he was talking to her.

I got to the locked front door the same time he did. I was banging on the door hoping someone would come. I saw R.J. had his gun out.

"We'll never get inside with you having that thing out."

He quickly stowed it away in his pocket. A security guard painfully and slowly made his way to the door. I yelled at him that he had an active shooter in the school. We needed to stop him before he killed many students. He dismissed me.

"All is quiet here today, buddy. No problem here but you. Now you just mosey along."

Jacob told me the student's name. The guard knew him as one of the problem students here at the school.

"Can't be him. He has been suspended."

"I'm telling you, he's inside and ready to wreak havoc. We must stop him."

"How do you know this boy?"

I didn't have time for fifty questions and told him so. The guard wasn't sure what to do. I looked at my watch – I had less than two minutes to avoid tragedy.

"This goes down at ten. We're too late."

The guard reluctantly let us inside. Jacob led the way. The guard and R.J. chased me down the hall.

We found the young man. He was looking at his watch, just waiting for the ten o'clock bell and the hallways to fill up with students going to different classes. I yelled to the guard to put the school in lockdown. He did, with about ten seconds to spare. The student looked up at me. His eyes were full of tears.

"Why did you have to do that? This school needs to pay for what they did to us. The students here are awful and need to be enlightened to their evil ways."

The guard and R.J. both had their weapons drawn, ready if the student made a move to use his weapon.

Jacob was tapping me on the shoulder.

"I forgot one very important detail. The boy is not alone."

I should have known. I yelled to take cover at the same time shots rang out from down the hall. A young girl dressed in goth was aiming at us. Fortunately, she wasn't very good with the weapon. The young man on the other hand was very good. R.J. dove for the men's room. The guard was caught out in the open. The guard got off several shots that went wide. He took two to the chest and went down. I had nowhere to go and had flattened myself against the wall.

"I'm not armed Travis! I came to talk, not to kill you," I shouted to him.

His girlfriend yelled not to listen to me and waste the bastard. She was having trouble with her gun. I think it might have jammed. I didn't know if that was just my good fortune or if Jacob had something to do with it.

"We can work this out. No one needs to die today."

I looked at the security guard and made a note to myself. If I didn't get this under control in a hurry, one man for sure was going to die.

I heard R.J. yell from the restroom that he had my back. He would be out as soon as he finished up. I heard the toilet flush. I turned and sprinted back toward the girl. She swung her weapon at me, because she couldn't get it to fire. I grabbed it from her and used the butt of the gun to put her asleep for a few minutes. The sound of many police cars heading toward the school could now clearly be heard. The boy ran in the opposite direction from me. I quickly figured out what had jammed the gun and now I was armed. R.J. came bursting through the door and I had to take cover once again. He was looking to fire at anything that moved. I think he might have had his eyes closed when he fired several times in each direction down the hallway. I yelled at him to get himself under control. He apologized for his recklessness.

"You got me so amped up. I'm sorry."

"Try and save this man." I pointed to the guard. "He's in bad shape."

R.J. knelt beside him and started doing what any pastor would do with a dying man. He was giving him Last Rites.

"How about you stem the bleeding while you're saving his soul? It might just save his life."

"Oh, yeah, I got it boss. You go get the other kid."

I ran down the hall after the Travis.

He was waiting for me when I rounded the last corner and nearly took me out.

"What are you a cat or something? You must have nine lives."

No, I have a very obnoxious guardian angel that likes to place me in all kinds of deadly situations just so he can have a little excitement. I yelled to him from my place of cover.

THE TRUTH

"Just put down your weapon. We can talk, and you can walk out of here alive today."

"Not going to happen, buddy. I made my choice. Today is going to be my last."

This was not good. The kid planned on dying today and he wanted to take as many people with him as he could.

I tried to get a better vantage point, but that was greeted with another burst of lead from his automatic weapon. I used his girlfriend's weapon and fired a burst into the ceiling above him. To my surprise, the whole ceiling came tumbling down on top of him. A lazy and overpaid maintenance man had left a hammer in the ceiling when he had been doing work up there months before. The poor man had searched everywhere for that hammer. I found it for him. It hit Travis right in the head, knocking his lights out. I stood and checked to make sure I wasn't going to get fired on again before I went and kicked the gun away from him. I looked up to the sky and praised the Lord for once again being there for me. I was sure Jacob was trying to get me killed. He couldn't have had anything to do with any of this.

I knocked on a locked classroom door and told the teacher that the threat had been contained and to call the front desk to let them know the police could come in now and get the two students. She didn't seem to respond to me, either that or she was so afraid that she couldn't move. I picked Travis up and carried him to the front desk. I passed R.J. along the way. The girl was gone. I asked him if he knew where she went. He said, "What girl?" I just shook my head.

I got to the front desk and told them what was going on. We still had a possible armed student running around the school. I asked if I could open the doors and let the police in. They gave me permission. I handed Travis to an officer and two more came inside. I described the girl to them. They told me they had it under control. The officer that was holding Travis started to walk away to a waiting ambulance. I yelled to him.

"We have a guard inside that is badly injured! He needs that ambulance more than the kid does.

He turned to me and said, "Take two men with you and those paramedics. Get the guard out. Once you've done that, I want you out of there as well. We need to talk."

I showed the emergency personnel where the guard was located. They moved R.J. out of the way so they could treat the man on scene. The two policemen provided us with cover. They quickly got the guard on a gurney and wheeled him out. As we were leaving, I heard shots fired from down the opposite hallway. I started to head that way when one of the officers grabbed me.

"We've got this. You've done enough for today. I can't begin to imagine how many people you saved today."

They walked us outside. The two cops that had gone after the girl walked out slowly and told us they had to kill the girl. She had a pipe bomb that she was getting ready to use. They called for a bomb disposal team.

The high school was quickly evacuated. The students were safe. I had done my job. I wished no one had to die today, but that wasn't the case. Another ambulance was leaving out with Travis. No one had bothered to pat him down properly. Sometimes things get forgotten in all the excitement. He said he was going to die today, and he did. A pipe bomb was taped to his calf, hidden in such a way nobody noticed it. He exploded it and raced to the other side along with everyone in the ambulance. I felt so stupid. If she had a pipe bomb, I should have realized he would have one as well.

We had to spend hours explaining why we were at the school. How did we know the student's name that gained us entry into the school and past the security guard? So many questions that needed a good answer that R.J. and I had no answers for. R.J. tried to explain that we were men of God and were led here today to save as many souls as we could. They thought he was a nut, but he had them laughing so hard that they were having a hard time conducting a proper interview. I on the other hand, well after a few calls to Richmond and Police Chief Mondale, was not getting out of this so easy.

"We see you have a reputation in Richmond, Mr. Hopkins. Seems you're getting one in LA as well. I loved your movie by the way. I think you deserved that Oscar. Your girlfriend is hot. I loved it when she had that wardrobe malfunction on live TV."

I knew very well it wasn't any malfunction. Maria was very pissed off, she wanted revenge on Scarlett and tried to ruin her career. The stunt made Scarlett more popular than ever. It backfired on Maria. God only knows what she would do next, like make a potion that would make me younger for a very long time. Who else was going to benefit from this little harmless potion she had made? I only knew one thing for sure. The death toll was going to be in the thousands.

We had a nice chat, me and the detectives. Once they realized they had nothing to hold me on, I was released. R.J. and Samantha had been waiting at a nearby hotel for me. When I got there, I could hear them in the room. I had to wait several more hours before I dared to go in. The smell of sex was overpowering when I entered. R.J. had a big shit-eating grin on his face.

"The tension of the day's events was too much for us, we needed release."

Samantha was grinning as well.

"I like your friend. He is so big."

I looked at R.J. as he grabbed his crotch and pointed. I just shook my head. I made them leave while I grabbed some shut-eye. I had to spray the room with air freshener that I got from housekeeping. They had heard the noise. They knew exactly why I needed it.

I had wasted two days now and only gotten about six hundred miles. Just a little over two thousand miles to go. What would we encounter for the rest of the trip? I wondered as I tried to get some sleep. If I had known, would I have continued, or would I have just turned around? We would end up on a ranch in the desert in California. Today was nothing compared to what we were in for.

CHAPTER 30

Anna continues at the hearing.

I stood up and requested a break. My back was sore from sitting so long and I was very hungry. The story about how Joey had gotten to the ranch, and how Bob and all the others had all come to be at the ranch at the same time was just getting started. Beats, I still can't believe all the things he did in those few days. I rubbed my leg to confirm just what he had done. Not even a scar or any trace of damage could be found. I thought I might lose the leg. The damage had been so bad.

Walter granted me twenty minutes to grab a bite and bathroom break. The commotion from outside was getting worse by the minute. He warned me that time was growing short. Ivan was convinced this was my plan all along. He glared at me with his evil eyes. He was still pissed at me for saying he had raped Franny. He assured me it had been consensual. She assured me it was not.

I went to the kitchen and the staff made me a hotdog and gave me some chips to go along with it. I headed back to my seat and waited for the rest of them to return. It was hard for me to tell the story of how R.J. had got to the ranch with Joey. R.J. and Samantha sure did have a good time all along the way. I tried to put her out of my mind. She wasn't a bad girl. She just wasn't right for him. I was the right one for him. I couldn't have him until Sophia was out of the picture. I was going to get to that part of the story, might not be today, but I was going to get to it. My favorite part of the story. Her lying dead up on stage, my hero foiling their plot to kill the President.

Walter came back in with Bob. He looked nervous. I was about to get to the part where he shows up at the ranch. This is when things really got interesting. The day of the time warp. Billy had arrived with me at the ranch, delivered by the Queen Bees. It was going to be our safe place until time caught up with us. I wondered if it would be a continuous loop, with me showing up every month or so. It didn't happen that way, thank God.

The fire alarm went off. Somebody had just tossed a Molotov cocktail through the back section of the White House. We could hear automatic weapons fire from back there. Time indeed was running out. The fire was quickly extinguished, and we were given the all clear for now. When the time came, we would be flying out with the President. They were going to take us to a secret location. Presumptively in a very short time. Walter waved to me to get on with it.

"I think we have at least a few minutes left. Let's get as much in as we can before we have to depart.

CHAPTER 31

Beats takes the shot.

I had only one thing I could do to prevent the Queen Bees from getting slaughtered. I would have to shoot at them. They weren't going to like it. I knew they would shoot back, but I had no choice. I fired at the front wheel of the lead motorcycle and sent it crashing into a ditch. The other Queen Bees immediately took cover and spread out to find me hiding somewhere above them in the hills. I didn't want to hurt any of them. I had many easy shots. I could have thinned them out very quickly. I saw I was being flanked. I had to make a choice, retreat and run away, or fight. No way after I shot at them that they would believe I was trying to keep them safe.

My position was compromised. Shots rang out all around me. I was ducking for cover. Now I couldn't even make my retreat. I had waited too long. I put my hands over my head and tried to make myself as small of a target as I could. I prayed to God for a way out. More shots rang out, hitting the rocks around me. A piece of rock struck me just above my right eye. Head injuries bleed profusely, my injury was no different. I couldn't see with all the blood that was flowing into my eyes. I tried to wipe it away to no avail. I was counting down to my arrival in heaven, it seemed this battle was nearly over. God had other ideas for me.

The aftershocks had been coming steadily. Some were a lot bigger than others. This aftershock felt almost as large as the original earthquake. The ground below my body gave way and I was free-falling into its depths. The water caught me on the way down. Just like Anna, I was in the underground river. Unlike Anna, nobody was going to pull me out of this mess. I was pulled down under the water by a swift current as shots hit the water nearly hitting me. I felt the current pull me and then push me up when an air pocket was available. I was able to take a gulp of air and just as quickly pulled back under and down the quick flowing river. This felt like it went on for hours, but probably lasted less than five minutes. I floated out of an underground cave and to the surface where I floated face down for a minute or two. Two hungry coyotes spotted me and dragged me out of the water and to the edge of the river where they could finish this unexpected treat that had come their way.

I gasped for air and began to choke. The coyotes were startled, but just for a minute or two. Their lunch was still alive. Time to make this meal more edible. First, it needed to be dead. I jumped to my feet and yelled at them. I snarled and made myself seem fierce. They did the same, only they had bigger and sharper teeth. I found a piece of driftwood along the shoreline and picked it up. I tried to use this to protect myself, but the coyotes pulled it from my hands. I jumped back into the water and started to swim. They followed me. I made it to the opposite shore with them close on my heels. This shoreline was a short cliff face. When I climbed up and out, I grabbed a rock and tossed it at them. Finally, they figured out that this meal wasn't as easy as they thought it was going to be and swam back to the far shore. I sat there crying, trying to figure out how I had escaped death once again.

Jesus sat beside me and said, "Why do you doubt me? I told you I would always be there for you."

I looked at him and said I was sorry.

"I should have more faith in you, Lord. I was so scared I was going to die a horrible death."

He patted me on the shoulder and said, "The time has come for you to be my hammer. I have termites that need to be removed from my house and you are the one that will help me remove them."

I wasn't sure what he was getting at.

"I need you to make your way back to the ranch and help Anna. She will be needing all the help she can get. You see that little shack over there." He pointed to a rundown shack by the river. "In there you will find all the supplies you will need. I had a friend put those things there for you a week ago. Make sure you don't kill him. I need him for the days ahead."

After he said that, he waved goodbye and left me. I wondered who it was that he referred to as the friend, he never did say.

I made my way over to the shack to find a treasure trove of weapons. I found a sniper rifle. It was a Barrett M82. Two full ten-round cartridges of ammo. I thought I could do some serious damage with this thing. With this rifle, I could be a mile away and hit something. I also found some food that was in packages ready to eat. I ripped open one of them and feasted. I found two pistols and ammo for them. I wouldn't be able to carry all this stuff, so I hid some along the way just in case I needed to make a quick getaway and had to ditch the rifle. A backpack was included so I put some of the food in it and started to make my way back to the ranch. It was hunting season now, and the prey were bad guys.

I had made it all the way back to the hole I fell through. I found a few dead bodies. A couple of motorcycles were abandoned in a ditch. I found some more casualties. There would have been more if I hadn't interfered. All the dead bodies were Queen Bee gang members. If they got any of the bad guys, they had been taken back to the ranch. I had to assume that the ranch was still at full strength.

I set up to have a look. This rifle sure was badass. The scope took me right inside the ranch and I was able to observe without being noticed from this distance. What I saw concerned me. Peter was tied to the board now. They had taken it outside and stood it up against a wall. Instead of darts, now they had pistols. Peter was talking a mile a minute, but I could see they weren't buying anything he was saying. I knew why. The story he was telling was unbelievable. Nobody would believe a thing he had to say, even though it was the truth.

The game they were playing was closest without hitting the target. The first man fired. I fired next. There would be no third shot. It was game over. I lost. I had hit my target. The surviving coward had hightailed it back inside under cover. He never got his turn. I knew I would have hit him as well.

I packed up and moved my location. They would venture out to try and find who was taking shots at them. I would be ready. Their numbers had to be thinned out. It was me alone out here. I had to be stealth. I hated killing, even bad guys. I only did this to save my friends. They were in grave danger now. I was their only hope. I found a good hiding place that allowed me to keep watch and provided good cover with an easy escape route. I set up and began the long wait. My eyes grew heavy and my sight began to blur. This was not the time to be tired. I did all I could to stay awake. Some battles you just can't win.

CHAPTER 32

Deke goes after the boys.

I had driven around for hours trying to decide what I was going to do. When I discovered the doll had once again found its way back into my truck, I freaked out. I wasn't thinking clearly and decided to do something stupid. I had made a promise to myself that I would save Holcomb's boys from his brother-in-law. It was time to keep that promise. To do that I would have to enter the snake's pit. His boys were trapped in that pit, and I was going to be their only hope. If I didn't get to them, they would be indoctrinated into a life of crime, drugs, and despair. They would probably be dead before they reached the ripe old age of twenty.

I knew where they were located and without thinking or a plan, I entered the snake pit. I was quickly brought to my knees and taught a valuable lesson. What was that lesson? Pain makes you think a whole lot clearer. I had so messed up this time. The fog I was in had begun to clear the more pain that was inflicted upon my body. They dragged me inside where they could finish me off. It was bad for business to kill someone on your front porch. Drag them inside, it gives you a better excuse for why you killed them. Gee officer, he came in here trying to kill us – what were we to do but defend ourselves?

I lay on the floor in front of Ricky. He would be the head snake, and just the man I needed to speak with.

"I came for the boys. They need a good home."

I mumbled from my position on the floor. I wiped the blood from my eyes and felt my split lip. I still had all my teeth, but a couple were a little loose. Ricky stood above me and laughed.

"Who are you, choir boy? What do you want that you need to come into my house and demand from me? I don't think you know who I am, do you?"

I lay there on the floor, his boots inches from my face and waiting for the kick to the head I knew was coming.

"I don't believe you know who I am? I look a little different without all the tats."

One of his men recognized me from Crystal's place. I heard him cry out Diablo and run from the house. He was the smart one. The rest were about to find out they should have run out with him.

A couple more of his men came inside holding the blow-up doll. They were laughing and ribbing each other as to who was going to get this fine maiden first. Ricky saw what they brought in with them and burst out in more laughter.

"You brought your girlfriend along. How sweet of you."

The kick I had been anticipating was administered. I lay on the floor watching all the stars floating around my swollen skull. What happened next is a little fuzzy. It might not have happened at all.

The man that had Jezebel also had a knife. It hung on his side in a sheath. It looked more like a dagger. One minute he was laughing and dancing with Jezebel, the next he was lying on the floor with blood pooling from a stab wound to his midsection. He tossed Jezebel as he was going down and his buddy caught her. He joined the other man on the floor. His throat sliced open and gushing copious amounts of blood. The room was in a frenzy. I lay on the floor and could do nothing to stop her. I tried to yell, but the words were lost among the screams and shouts around the panic-stricken room. When she was done, she lay on the floor beside me. I swear I could see her blood-covered face smile at me. I looked up to see Ricky was still alive. The dagger was sticking in the wall through his collarbone holding him firmly against the wall. The room was quiet now. His men were making the journey to the other side. Ricky called out to me in a very pained voice.

"You are Diablo! I recognize you now. 10th Street Knights. Without the tattoos, you look like a normal person. How could I be so stupid? Please, the boys are downstairs in the basement. You'll have no problem finding them. I would take you myself, but I have a slight situation here."

I slowly rose to my feet. I thought about removing the dagger for him, but why bother. I knew he wouldn't do it for me. I found the door to the basement and went down. The place stunk of rotten food and sour milk. Other odors invaded my nostrils. It was very unpleasant. The boys were duct-taped to a post in the middle of the basement. I looked into sunken eye sockets and hopeless expressions. They were so heavily taped that I would need that dagger to cut them from their confines. I raced back upstairs to retrieve the dagger. Ricky was no longer pinned to the wall. He lay on top of Jezebel, the dagger sticking out of his eye socket. I closed my eyes and pulled it out, raced back downstairs, and cut the boys free.

When we reached the top of the stairs, Jezebel was gone. The bodies lay all about in a gore-filled room. Blood covered everything. I tried to shield their eyes, but they took it all in. One of the boys asked if I had done all this. I answered truthfully. The other boy thanked me. He said his uncle was evil and was glad he was dead. I put the boys in the truck and drove away. Jezebel was back in the bed of the truck. I saw her in my rearview mirror. I was scared and had no idea what I was going to do with her or the boys.

I knew why Roscoe wanted her dead now. She was pure evil. He said that she arrived the same day as Annabelle. He had called that his shipment hadn't arrived, so the company sent him another doll. They both arrived the same day. Identical in every way, except one. It was the yin and yang concept. If Annabelle was the good and she was gone, the evil was in control now. Jezebel was now completely out of balance. She had attached herself to him to replace Annabelle, so he must be what was keeping her in check now. He was now her balance, so was she his balance?

He had gone into the snake pit to do harm. Jezebel picked up on it and took it to another level. His goal was to save the children and she had helped him do just that. Without her, he would have died inside the snake pit. Of this, he had no doubt.

It was time to visit Crystal. He needed someone to watch the children. Who better than a stoned crack head? They drove to her place to find the surviving Snake had retreated to the sanctuary of her place. When Deke drove up, he was sure that Deke was there to finish the job. On his hands and knees, he begged for mercy. Deke gave him an option. If he found drugs anywhere near Crystal from this time forward, Deke would hold him responsible and would come looking for him. The man agreed he would make this a drug-free zone from this time forward. He ran away praising God that he had made it through this day.

He knocked on the door and Crystal greeted him in her usual way.

"What the hell do you want now? First, you run my friends away, now I can't get any of my shit. What's next?"

"These two boys need somebody to look after them for a little while. I thought you would be the perfect person for the job, seeing you lost your own children to CPS. Do a good job with these guys, and we'll see if your kids can come home."

"Are you out of your fucking mind? There was a good reason I lost my kids. I'm a drug addict, irresponsible and selfish. I can hardly take care of myself. Now you think I can take care of these two boys. Are you nuts?"

"Yes, I am. I can get you help, money, food, and clothing. All you got to do is stay clean. I can help with that as well. Now tell me you will do it."

"You know if I get money what I'm going to use it for, why are you wasting your time with me?"

"Every person deserves a second chance. I'm throwing you a rope so you can climb out of the hole you've dug for yourself. Either accept my offer or die in this self-destructive pit you're in. I can help others that want and need it. I'm offering my hand to you right at this moment. You probably won't get another chance."

She pondered what I said.

"You're going to be checking up on me, making sure I'm doing the right things and not self-destructing?"

"I will be watching you, yes. I won't hesitate to pull the boys if you slide back into your hole. I want them safe and protected until I can find them a good home."

"What if I do a good job and I bond with these boys? When you take them from me, I'll slide back into my hole for sure."

"I'll tell you what I'll do for you. If these boys tell me you're being a good mother and they want to stay with you, I'll make sure that happens. If they tell me it's not working out and want to leave, and I know you haven't kept up your end of the bargain, we're out of here."

The boys knew anything was better than what they had endured for the last few months. They promised me they would behave. I promised them I would be around to check on them as much as I could. I left them there with the hope that she would be focused on them and not her habit. She would be needing help in the next few weeks as the drugs slowly worked themselves out of her system. I knew she would have a very hard time getting anymore with what I had done to her network of suppliers. The detox is brutal, but worth it. I hope she survived it. I left my number with the oldest boy, told him if he needed me to call anytime day or night. I figured he would have to call me at least a couple of times in the first few weeks.

I got back in my truck and headed out. Jezebel had somehow found her way into the front seat. I had to keep pushing her off me as I drove home. Her head kept falling into my lap. When I got home, I left her in the truck and went to bed. I needed sleep, and I needed it bad. I woke with an arm draped over my shoulder. At first, I thought Ellen had come home. Elated, I turned and saw Jezebel had found her way into my bed. She was a sex doll, and she wanted to do what she was made for. I now knew what Roscoe was complaining about. She couldn't be satisfied, no matter what you did to her.

CHAPTER 33

Back inside the ranch.

Everyone was running for cover inside the ranch. Everyone except Maria. She stood in the kitchen preparing the items that were going to be used in the fountain of youth formula. The blender was whirling away as she made her concoction. She wasn't exactly sure of all the ingredients at the hotel where it worked the last time. Now all she had to do was remember everything that was consumed that night. Mr. B had provided another batch of Pharaoh Cicadas. He said that would be the last of them for quite some time.

"Dear, it will be another sixteen years before they come back. Put them to good use."

He raised his eyebrow and pointed to Helen. Nothing else needed to be said. The potion was being made to take her out.

As people were scrambling to take cover, Maria stood tall and kept working. Urstin would be back soon with Ivan. She really didn't want him to take the potion and become young like Joey. Her brain was working on a plan to make sure he didn't get the complete ingredients to make it work. If Joey was here, he would know what to do. The chill in the air made her grab a sweater that she always carried with her whether it was summer or winter.

"Jacob dear, could you bring Joey to the ranch, please? I need him. I know it will be dangerous and he might risk his life being here, but I think it would be best for all of us if he was here."

She removed the sweater as quickly as she had donned it. Her plan was working. Jacob would drag Joey here kicking and screaming if he had to. A big smile crossed her face.

"I think I wrote this scene in that last manuscript. Oh, Joey is going to have so much fun." She jumped with glee.

Mr. B had been watching her the whole time, just sitting back in the shadows, staying away from the windows. He knew the boy was out there somewhere and he also knew the kid was a damn good shot. No need to make a target of himself. The ice in his glass was all but melted and another cocktail was very much needed. He kept his head down and made his way over to replenish his glass.

"Do we have everything we're going to need, Maria?"

She nodded that she had everything.

The peppers were being cut up and just being near them made your eyes burn and took your breath away.

"We have to eat that stuff?"

"Oh yes, very important part of the formula. I hope you like spicy food."

The Carolina Reaper was aptly named. Some people felt they were going to die after they ate it, it was that hot. Mr. B felt like he might just pass on trying the formula. Save his tender intestines the torture of being burnt away from the inside.

Franny came strolling out and was pulled away from the windows by the President.

"Bad man outside right now. Not safe to be walking around."

He held her tight and close by his side. She in turn was forming a plan in her head. That plan was going to be put into operation right now. She clung to him and pretended to be afraid.

"Hold me, Stanley," she whispered in his ear. He was all too glad to oblige.

Peter was screaming for help from outside. Nobody dared stick their head outside to rescue him. Maria finally had enough. She took the knife she was using to cut the peppers with and walked to the door listening to all the protests from the folks hiding inside.

"I'll be right back," she yelled over her shoulder.

Peter was stark naked and sweating profusely. Maria studied his body and marveled at his manly muscles. She took the knife and poked at his genitals.

"I thought you would be happy to see me. I guess I'll go back inside."

Peter pleaded with her to cut him free and take him with her as he started to scream in pain.

"Make your soldier stand up for me and I'll take you inside."

She started to rub his chest and arms with her soft hands. He wasn't responding at all.

"What's the matter with you, Peter? I don't turn you on anymore?"

His balls were on fire and he thought she might be just a little bit crazy, but he also realized this might be the only way he got inside and out of danger.

"Maria, I would love to show you a good time, but not out here. Do you think we can take this inside and get comfortable in a nice soft bed?"

"Oh, you're so bad Peter. Wait 'til I tell Jenna what you just said."

Peter rolled his eyes.

"You'll say just about anything to get me to cut you free of your bindings, won't you?"

Peter hung his head in defeat. "You know me so well Maria."

He winced in pain as he thought his balls were about to ignite.

"That's right, Peter. I expect you to remain faithful to your girl, no matter what."

She cut him free and he scurried inside with her close behind him. He ran for the bathroom. He needed to wash whatever it was off his genitals and he had to do it fast – they were on fire! Once that was accomplished, he went into his room to find something to wear so he didn't have to walk around the ranch naked. Everyone just stared at Maria like she was plain crazy or something.

"What? I just gave him something to remember me by. Stop being so judgmental."

Besides, Elvis Presley said it best, "Burning Love." They sure are burning right now, she giggled to herself.

"The sniper is not looking to kill me. You guys are the target. Get used to it."

She walked back to the kitchen to finish up with what she had been doing. Helen slinked over to the kitchen and grabbed some strawberries. Maria slapped her hand.

"I need all that for the formula. You do want to be young and beautiful again, don't you?"

"I'm already beautiful. Age has only enhanced my beauty."

"If you say so. You might want to take a double dose. That double chin of yours is going to need all the help it can get."

Helen walked off in an insulted huff. Maria can be cruel at times.

The President's men along with what was left of Urstin's men formed a plan. They had lost a couple to the Queen Bees, but they still numbered seven men total. About half of what they started with. They would exit the ranch from both sides and hope they could get to cover quickly. Then they find and flank the shooter and snuff him out. The two groups bolted out the door and no shots were fired. It's hard to find something when it's not shooting or giving up its position. They lay outside and weren't sure what to do. They spread out and began to search. After a couple of hours, they returned defeated. No shooter could be found. He must have left the area.

A phone call was made and Urstin and Ivan were cleared to return. The SUV roared down the dirt road and screeched to a halt in front of the ranch house. Urstin and Ivan didn't take any chances, they quickly entered the house.

The first question out of Urstin was, "Where is she?"

He wanted to speak with his wife before he killed her. Ivan grabbed him by the shoulder.

"Maybe you might want to find out what she knows before you kill her. Might give us some insight on what we're dealing with out there."

Urstin grumbled. He really wanted to kill her this time. He felt like he was being denied his prize. They unlocked the door and found her sleeping on the bed. Urstin requested a little private time with his wife alone. Ivan was assured he wouldn't kill her just yet.

"Wake up, my sweetheart. I've come home."

He softly caressed her arm and treated her like before he knew she had betrayed him. He talked smoothly and gently like he still loved her. She rolled over and embraced her husband.

"It's so good to see you again, my love."

He pushed her away from him and slapped her in the face.

"Do you have any idea what you've done to me?! My heart is broken in two!" he cried. "I loved you with all my heart and this is what you do to me?!"

"Urstin, I was doing my job. I did have feelings for you, but I never loved you."

This really stung Urstin. His pride was damaged beyond repair.

"Soon Joey will arrive, and the fun is going to begin. I will take that formula and I will also become young. You will regret not keeping me as your own. I'll let you have what's left of Joey and his friend. He has some pastor with him. A very big guy. They'll make nice treats for the coyotes."

He got up and walked out, happy that he had made her worry about the big guy. He was going to take great pleasure in the killing of the good pastor, the man that had stolen the heart of his wife. He was going to make him pay dearly for that.

CHAPTER 34

Joey and R.J.

"What's wrong with you, Jacob? Stop! I can't see."

I was trying to drive but Jacob was blocking my view out of the front windshield. I tried to look around him, but he wasn't making it very easy to drive. Finally, I pulled over before he got us all killed.

Jacob was excited about something. Once again, my plan of getting us back quickly to LA was being shot down.

He said, "Big trouble, Maria is in big trouble."

I think he might have been hyperventilating. I would have given him a paper bag to breathe into if I had one. It was all plastic bags, or it was. Now they didn't want you to have plastic. Didn't want you to have paper. Bring your own bags now, save the environment. No plastic straws, we use paper. They don't work very well, but it's all we got now.

It made you crazy, sort of like Jacob does to me.

"Where is she, Jacob? What kind of trouble is she in?" I had to ask.

"She is at a ranch in California. We need to get there right away. Today is the day of the ripple in time. Very dangerous day for us."

I looked at him funny. "You do know that was close to a month ago, right?"

"Time is all out of whack. Some of it is still catching up to us. When we travel today, we go back in time, caught in the ripple. I can get us there, but we have to go now."

I looked over at R.J. snoring away. He would never know what I did. I looked in the back seat at Samantha. She was out like a light. She and R.J. didn't sleep much last night. Neither did I. They kept waking me up. All we could get was a king-sized bed, so we all slept together. It was a very bad idea, believe me. I kept waking up to someone's fanny in my face. Sometimes it wasn't one you wanted in your face, if you know what I mean.

"This is a bad idea, Jacob. If we go, won't there be another ripple in time? Then the three of us would have to catch up to where we are at today. It doesn't make sense. Bad idea. We don't need to do it."

Jacob whined. The love of his life was in trouble and I had just refused to help her. I wanted to kill her, but I didn't tell Jacob that.

"Anna is in trouble as well."

R.J. woke with a start. "What did you say?"

"Nothing, R.J. Go back to sleep."

He turned over and fell right back to sleep. Jacob smiled, the kind of smile that told me I didn't have a choice in what he was going to do.

"Don't you dare do it, Jacob! Don't –"

Too late. Another flash of light and bingo, not in Kansas anymore. I looked around after I could finally see again. We were now in the desert instead of lush farmland. This was going to be a disaster for sure. I could feel it. I shook R.J. awake. I pretended I had taken a wrong turn and was lost. The fact that the road was dirt and not a house or any sign of people at all was not lost on R.J. when he opened his eyes.

"I took a wrong turn. I think we're lost."

"Well turn around and head back in the other direction. Get us back to civilization."

"I wish I could do that, but I don't know how we got here."

R.J. got out of the car and looked around at his surroundings.

"How fast were you driving, Joey? Feels like we're in California already."

He went to look at his watch, tapped it a few times. I knew what he was going to say. I took my watch off and tossed it into the ditch.

"Yours not working either?"

I shook my head.

"Don't have a clue what time or day it is. I hate to tell you this, but we just jumped time and space."

R. J. paced around the car. I could see he was upset. He pounded his fist into the hood, making a large dent.

"Hey, don't do that. I didn't get the insurance."

"You should have, Joey. I'm going to flip this car over and set it on fire. Going to send smoke signals out to the Indians so they can come to our rescue."

He started to lift the car up. I had to grab him. He took me and threw me into the ditch.

"I told you not to mess with my life. We go to LA, you put me on a plane back to Richmond. That was the plan. I didn't sign up for this shit Joey, no – not at all. So far, you've nearly gotten me killed in a school shooting and now this! God only knows what shit you got us into this time asshole!"

He stomped and paced around for a few minutes. I let him vent and calm down.

"Hey guys, up here."

I heard his voice from a distance. I knew who it was.

"Beats, where are you?"

"Up here. Come quickly. I want to show you something."

I looked up the hill and saw a rock formation, saw his hand waving back and forth.

"Let's go see what the kid has planned for us, shall we?"

"You go. I want to bang some more dents into your rental."

I walked up the hill and cringed every couple of minutes. This was going to cost me a bundle. I didn't even want to look back at the damage he was doing. I told myself everything was going to be okay. That was until I looked through the scope and saw what was going on at the ranch. I ran down the hill as fast as I could. Time was not on our side. We had to go right now.

CHAPTER 35

Anna finally tells us what happened.

Maria had blended all the ingredients together to make this delicious-looking smoothie. It was the other ingredients that weren't all that inviting. A huge plate of nachos with the hottest sauce I had ever tasted. After one bite, my mouth was on fire. Sweat was pouring off my forehead and I could no longer feel my lip. That was after one bite. She wanted us to consume the whole plate. One of the President's men dove in and ate about five mouthfuls. He said he loved spicy food. He wasn't going to love it the next time he had a bowel movement.

She had bags of chips and fruits and an assortment of fresh vegetables.

"Eat up everyone," I heard her call.

The smoothies were only for a few select people here tonight. She handed one to Urstin, the President, even Helen Harrison got one. She went back and got one for Ivan and one for Mr. Bennett. I could smell a fresh pot of steamers cooking on the stove. They had been flown in from Iceland the night before.

"In order for this to work, you must eat from all the stuff I've prepared. If you don't, the potion will not work," I heard her instruct all that had attended.

I watched her closely go back into the kitchen and get the clams ready to serve. She put them out in individual servings with about four clams to a plate. These were brought out to the table and we were about to feast when the door burst open and he appeared.

Immediately guns were drawn, and Joey was thrown to the floor. R.J. walked in behind him and said, "I told you to knock. These people don't take kindly to folks just crashing their parties."

They had a harder time getting him on the ground. Three guys were draped all over him and he just shrugged them off.

"I'm not in the mood for this. I'll be over here getting some food when you guys are done playing around."

The secret service agents didn't know what to do. Should they just shoot him? I saw them glance to the President looking for his approval.

"Boys, he is harmless. Let him get something to eat. If you shoot him, it will just make him mad."

He looked over to Joey. Helen had stood and looked very concerned.

"Is that what the formula does to someone?"

She had known Joey all her life. He looks amazing. She turned and drank down the smoothie.

"I want to be young like that again."

All the rest of the players toasted to that and drank down their smoothies.

I watched the love of my life grab a bunch of celery and start munching. The bland taste made him make a face, so he dipped it in some of the extra salsa that Maria had made. He took a big bite and I literally saw smoke come out of his ears as he ran for the bathroom screaming.

"My mouth is on fire! My mouth is on fire!"

I think he was crying. I had to laugh, only he could make a painful situation hysterical.

Joey was protesting. He yelled at Maria, "You're going to destroy the world. God is going to end it if that formula gets out. Why did you have to give it to them, of all people?"

Urstin laughed at Joey as he whimpered on the floor.

"Once I'm young, I can control things for a very long time. This will be a very interesting country when I'm done with it. No longer will it be divided. I will unite all people and make them my slaves."

Another maniacal laugh followed that statement.

Helen followed with, "I will rule this country for years to come. I will make them love me whether they want to or not. I'm owed this due to our current President stealing the election from me. Right, Stanley?"

The President peered at her with disdain.

"I will do everything in my power to make sure that never happens."

This got a few cheers from his men.

"You don't understand, I have something very interesting that you might want to see."

She walked over to the television and put a CD in the Blu-ray player. We all got to watch him confess to a crime he never committed. I saw the color drain from his face. If that tape ever made it into the public's hands, he was finished.

Urstin whispered something in her ear and then she says to the President, "I need to divert some funds to Guadalajara for humanitarian reasons. Four hundred million dollars should be about enough for now. Urstin needs to take a little heat off himself for a small mishap. He accidentally shot down one of the cartel's planes carrying a shipment of coke. The warehouse in LA is still burning them up. They're working on stealing that shipment back as we speak. So, Stanley, what do you say? Do I have your approval?"

The woman wasn't playing fair. She knew he had no choice in the matter. He waved her off.

"Whatever you need. Just make it look legitimate."

He had already caved without a fight.

"Well, awesome! Let's get some more food and make ourselves young again." She was feeling very giddy.

Joey spoke up from the floor.

"Helen, if you take the whole formula, it will kill you."

I was shocked to hear him say that. I wanted her to take a double dose. What the hell was he doing? I spoke up.

"Don't listen to him, Helen. He is just trying to scare you."

Helen hesitated just for a second. Urstin grabbed her by the arm and led her to the table.

"Joey is full of shit. I'll have him locked up in the backroom so we can have our party. Afterward, we can tie him to the board and play our shooting game with him. Have you been practicing?"

"Well, not really. I'm still missing more than I'm hitting."

"Excellent! I'll let you have the first shot."

This was not good.

Maria started to raise a fit when they started to manhandle Joey. This got her thrown into the backroom as well. I stayed and observed. I would have to kill everyone in the room. We all had seen what went into the formula. I couldn't leave any loose ends. I didn't know when Beats would make his strike, but I sure hope it's soon.

Urstin and Ivan munched on the nachos. All they did was complain about how hot they were. Helen tried to eat some. I watched her vomit all over Ivan after the first bite. He stormed off in a huff as the President had a good belly laugh.

"You're never going to be young, Helen. You can't even eat the ingredients required. Wait 'til you get to sample these."

The President held up a freshly buttered clam and let it slide down his throat.

"They sure are delicious."

I think I saw Helen turn paler than her pale completion already was. Urstin grabbed a clam and downed it, grabbed another, and shoved it into Helen's mouth. She protested, but she managed to swallow. I heard her gag, and I scurried out of the way. I didn't want to end up like Ivan.

I watched the President eat some more nachos. The sick bastard seemed to be enjoying them. He washed them down with a couple more buttered clams. Ivan came out and rushed his portions down. He had all he could do with the nachos. Mr. B wasn't even going to try and attempt it.

"I can't do it. I guess I'm going to stay old."

Urstin screamed at him that he damn well was going to consume everything they ate in case this was a scam by Maria. If they were going to pay the price, so was he. I watched them force Mr. B into a chair and feed him like a baby. He struggled, but in the end, he had eaten all that was required.

Bob finally arrived after all the fun was over. He was young as well as Joey. The two of them were proof the formula worked. We waited, and then waited some more. Nothing was happening and the longer we waited, the more infuriated Urstin became. The President said his stomach hurt and was going to lay down in the other room. It was fine with us. Everyone was watching each other to see when this shit was going to take effect. Bob said he felt changes in a matter of hours, so we waited some more. It had now been more than six hours since they first drank the formula along with the food.

Bob was confused. He asked, "Has everyone drank the smoothie, eaten the nachos, and had a few of the clams?"

Everyone in the room confessed that they had done everything.

"Has anyone checked in on the President?"

Nobody had, so Bob went back to see if he was still alive. The next time I saw him, I almost fainted. The President looked twenty years younger than the last time I saw him. Everyone stared at him with an open mouth. He had eaten everything they had, yet he was the only one in the room the formula had any effect on. Urstin blew his top.

"Where's Maria? That bitch has tricked us again! She gave the President something she didn't give us. I must know what it is."

Mr. B. called over to him.

"Hey, Urstin. It's too late. You're going to have to wait another sixteen years to try again. We're all out of the cicada."

Urstin walked over and punched him right in the face.

"You knew this was going to happen, didn't you?" he was fuming.

"Actually, I didn't, but I find it funny as hell."

He kicked Mr. B in the stomach as the poor man lay on the floor.

"You find that funny as well?"

He was going to kick him again when I grabbed him. He tried to hit me, but I put him on his ass so fast he didn't know what hit him.

"You may be stronger than me Urstin, but I know a whole lot more moves than you ever will." I held him to the floor with my elbow choking off any air from reaching his lungs. "Next time you try to hit me, I'll kill you."

I let him up. He was choking and trying desperately to get his wind back. He pointed a finger at me.

"You'll be lucky to see the sun come up."

I screamed and ran toward him. I fully planned on kicking him right in the larynx, crushing it, and letting him choke to death on his own blood. Ivan tackled me before I could reach him.

I was restrained and put back into my room. Franny had been hiding out in there under the bed. Once they had left, she slid out and untied me.

"I have a plan," she said to me. "You okay to fight?"

I told her I was.

"Good. Get some rest. I'm still working out some of the bugs in the plan."

I rolled my eyes. She didn't have a solid plan. She was just trying to make me feel better.

A few hours later as I lay trying to get some rest, I felt her body slide into the bed beside me. She started to rub her hands over my body and rake her long nails across my skin. What in the world? I didn't take her for a lesbian. I jumped up out of the bed and scolded her.

"I'm not like that! I like men," I cried out to her.

She laughed at me. "I do too, but you are some hot stuff. I thought we could cuddle."

I had to get out of there, but I was locked in. I could see that the sun had come up. This was the day when everyone could finally go home.

I put my ear to the door and listened. Something was going on, and it didn't look like it was going well for the President's or Urstin's men. I heard a body hit the wall, then another. The doorknob to my room turned and slowly opened. I was going to smash whoever opened the door when I heard him call out for me. It was R.J. He had come for me. I was elated, but troubled. I heard Jesus in the back of my head tell me that I must keep my distance from him. I would ruin his future mission.

He puckered up for a kiss as I hurried by him. I turned and thanked him for rescuing me and told him we had to go.

"I figured I would at least have gotten a kiss."

THE TRUTH

"I'll give you one, honey." Franny planted a tongue-filled kiss on him. I didn't see what happened next, I was on the move. I had to step over two men that were in desperate need of medical attention. I ran out to see the President's helicopter taking off. I looked to see who was still present. There we several bodies with parts of their heads missing by the front window. That was obviously the work of Beats.

Mr. B sat on the sofa with a drink in his hands. He was very drunk and told me I had missed all the fun. It was the last thing he said before he passed out on the couch. Peter was in a corner roughed up badly, but he was still alive. I turned and saw Bob on the opposite side of the room. He didn't look much better than Peter. I went to run to him, slipped, and fell on my butt. I had stepped in brain matter and my foot came right out from under me. I recovered and crawled over to Bob.

"Maria is a crazy bitch. She was going to kill them all. They ran Anna, they ran."

He smiled at me with a very split lip and a few missing teeth.

"Who is the shooter? The guy was picking them off at will. Never seen anything like it." I held his hand and told him, "If I told you, you would never believe me."

I looked up and saw Joey limp into the house. He had been shot in the leg. He was being assisted by a young lady I had never seen before. They were followed inside by a crazed-looking Maria. She was covered in blood, I thought she might be injured severely. I jumped up to give her some assistance, but she batted my hand away.

"This isn't my blood. It's the blood of no good scumbags. They are so lucky they had that helicopter."

I looked over at Joey. He mouthed, "She scares the shit out of me."

I treated his leg. He was going to need to get to the hospital and soon. I could see he had lost a lot of blood.

"I'm not supposed to be able to get shot. My guardian angel wasn't doing his job."

I told him, "You're still alive. Maybe he was doing his job, you just don't realize it."

"He was too busy protecting her." He pointed at Maria. "He's her husband."

I knew he was talking about Jacob. I also knew he was probably right. Somehow, I didn't think she needed to be protected.

The other girl introduced herself to me and asked where R.J. was at. I pointed to the hallway behind me. I watched her go down the hall to find him. She was running. It didn't take long before the commotion erupted from the hallway. I saw her come running out bursting in tears. I could hear R.J. protesting his innocence. I had a pretty good idea what she saw when she went down that hallway. If Franny was as horny as I had left her, R.J. was probably fighting off her advances when she saw the two of them. Franny had just applied a fresh coat of lipstick, most of what she had on was all over R.J.'s face. It didn't take a rocket scientist to figure out what that poor girl saw going on.

Franny was smiling ear to ear. R.J. was pleading for Samantha to listen to him. It was complete chaos. I'm glad I wasn't involved in that love triangle. I had better things to do, like get the bleeding to stop so Joey didn't die on me. I held the compress to his leg and called out to Maria to get a car. We needed to get Joey medical attention this minute. She flew out the door and Beats flew in.

"I rid the house of the termite problem."

"Yes, you did young man. Mind if you tell me where you learned how to shoot?"

"I had a very good teacher. He was an army sniper."

I nodded my head.

"Where did you get the rifle?"

"Jesus showed me where it was hidden. He had a friend hide it there last week."

This story got better by the minute.

"The coyotes rescued me from the water, pulled me to safety. I then had to fight for my life. They wanted to eat me."

This boy has a very vivid imagination. I listened to his stories and nodded my head. Like I was ever going to believe anything he said. The story was way too wild.

CHAPTER 36

Anna back at the White House.

Walter stood and announced we were out of time. The amount of violence coming from above told us we might have stayed too long. I could hear rapid gunfire and explosions, screaming, orders being given. The place was in utter chaos. We all made our way to the back door and had a team of secret service agents cover us while we boarded the helicopter. The President was the last to join us. He just had to sit right beside me as close as he could get. I spent the whole trip slapping his hand off my leg as we headed to Fort Lee. The rumor had it that it was the safest place to be on the East Coast at this moment. We would soon find out why. The love of my life had a lot to do with it. Once the riots began in Richmond, he was at it again.

Walter grabbed me when we landed.

"We still need to finish this."

I looked at him confused.

"I told you how he came to be. What more do you need?"

"I need the truth. I want to know why he was the only one the formula worked on."

I laughed. "I already told you, I sure wish you had listened."

He scowled at me. "I'll set up another meeting room. We finish this now."

He stormed off in a huff. I can't help it if I hid it in the story of what happened. I wasn't going to come right out and tell him. Let him figure it out himself. If he did, I might have to kill him as well. This complete formula was deadly to the world as we knew it. The fewer people knew about it, the safer it was for all concerned.

An hour later, we were all in place once again. This time the President sat in on the hearing. Walter didn't have the balls to ask him to leave the room. I tried to hide the smile that was plastered all over my face. I had given everything I was going to give to Walter. All he was going to get now from me was the craziest story you've ever heard. Walter was mad that I had lied about Samantha and her role. He thought I was making her look bad because I was jealous of her. He might have a point. I felt a bit shameful about what I had done. The story he was about to get now was Maria and how she foiled Urstin's grand plan. Let me take you back to the house before everyone made their hasty getaway.

* * *

Maria and Joey, a scientific experiment gone amok.

Urstin had lost his patience with Maria. The two scientists he brought with him were tasked with getting the truth from Maria and Joey. The ranch has a large room they use for equine veterinary use. It was now a torture chamber. A very large and ugly woman had Joey strapped to a table. A scalpel in hand, she planned on slicing open Joey and having a closer look at his organs. She wanted to know if the insides were as young-looking as the outside. A very handsome, young, muscular-looking man had Maria pinned against a wall. He had his zipper open and had plans for Maria. If she didn't talk, she was going to get his full-sized equipment rammed into her waiting butt.

He had a knife placed against her throat so that she knew she had to be compliant. Problem with that is, Maria is never compliant. You do what she wants or you're going to pay a price. The bad doctor was going to find this out in a very short amount of time. He had his face close to hers and was telling her how much he was going to enjoy what he was about to do. Amazingly she was egging him on.

"I don't think your tiny dick is big enough. You sure you can keep it hard enough to even penetrate me?"

She went on and on insulting his male ego. The doctor exploded with anger and that is when she had him. In his hurry to shove his tool inside of her, he had brought the knife down to assist his other hand. Maria had brought her head forward enough that she had the perfect angle. The snap of her head backward caught the doctor by surprise and rang his bell. He fell to the floor, his nose gushing blood, knife in hand.

"You bitch, I'm going to kill you."

She knew he meant it and scurried to the center of the room. The female doctor looked up just before she could make the first cut on Joey. He was secured, so she decided to assist her colleague. Big mistake.

Maria, never one to leave the house with less than four-inch heels, removed her shoes. One in each hand, she used them like a weapon. These were fine leather stiletto heels made by Christian Louboutin. Nothing cheap about this pair of heels. She always wanted the best. Joey could do nothing but watch the action. That didn't mean he wasn't trying to get into it. He struggled mightily to free himself. He didn't want to be a frog on the dissecting table of some science lab.

The male doctor wiped the blood from his nose, but it kept coming. Dripping blood everywhere, he came at her. The fat ugly doctor lunged with the scalpel. Maria kicked the male doctor in the face and with the same motion, drove a stiletto heel into the female doctor's upper chest. The heel penetrated flesh and stuck there. The knife went flying and practically landed in Joey's hand. He quickly got to work cutting himself free.

Enraged, the female doctor once again attacked with the heel firmly embedded in her chest. The scalpel sliced through the air barely missing Maria and slicing through the arm of the male doctor who was attacking from the other side. He screamed out and gushed more blood all over the lab. He lashed out at her, "You fool! You cut me. Will you please help me with this bitch and stop trying to kill me!"

Joey was quickly cutting himself free while they were busy with Maria. Knife in hand and now free of his restraints, he joined in the fight. He picked up a large tray that held a lot of instruments and swung it at the female doctor's head. Stuff went flying everywhere, but the tray landed with a dull thud. When he put the tray down you could see the imprint of the doctor's head. She went down and played possum, Joey thought he had taken her out. He tried to assist Maria with this big dude.

While everyone was focused on the male doctor, big ugly was pulling her purse toward her and extracting a small pistol. Might not kill anyone, but it sure would slow you down. She yelled out to Joey. He turned just in time to get shot in the leg. Joey went down in a mass of pain and blood. Now the bitch was going to be next. Maria was too fast.

When you're young and bored and daddy is giving you all the money you want to live the good life, you find things that interest you. Mixed martial arts was something Maria tried for a few years until she got bored with it. It was just long enough to become a blackbelt. Very proficient in what she had been taught, she was using all these lessons in the heat of the moment. The male doctor was going to need a new set of teeth. First, the spinning elbow to the jaw, followed by a superman kick to the mouth was just about all the doctor could handle. He was down for the count. She raced across the room dodging bullets that big ugly was firing in her direction. Helped by the fact that her head was still spinning from the tray to the head, Maria finished the job and took her out. Big ugly found herself flat on her stomach with Maria's arm wrapped around her throat and trying desperately to take another breath that wasn't coming. Soon things started to grow dark for her until it all faded away into nothing. Maria held on to that choke for another couple of minutes. Once sure the ugly bitch was dead, she grabbed her gun and stepped over to the male doctor that was groaning on the floor.

"Would you like me to take all that pain away, pretty boy?"

He shook his head that he did, so she double-tapped him in the head. No more pain, just like she said.

Joey was shot. She was covered in blood, but uninjured. It was time to raise havoc outside this room now. She opened the door to find men were working over Bob and Peter. R.J. was in the most danger. Three men had him covered with guns questioning him on what he knew. He was telling them jokes that they were trying hard not to laugh at but were failing to. This was just enough distraction for her to sneak out of the room. The man that was kicking the crap out of Peter was her first victim. Knife in hand, the pistol was out of bullets, she pounced upon her unsuspecting prey. Two quick jabs to the back right where the kidneys were located were all it took to take this guy down. The commotion drew the attention of the man beating on Bob. He turned to confront her and lost his head. He literary lost it. The bullet that had come through the window took it off. The splatter covered Maria with more disgusting body fluids.

The man with the stab wounds was armed. He rose and aimed at her. Though he could barely stand, she knew she was a goner. Another shot from the outside world turned the tables once again. Now it was time for the men R.J. had to deal with. She looked and found three bodies strewn around the floor and in massive pain. R.J. was standing there with a massive smile on his face.

"I have no problem here, Maria. How about you?"

Maria told him Joey had been shot and she needed to tend to him. R.J. said he needed to tend to something as well and headed down the hall to where Anna and Franny were being held hostage.

The sound of the helicopter whirling to life could be heard from inside the house. She still hadn't found who she was really after yet, but Joey needed her right now. Maria had her priorities. She raced back in to find Joey had risen to his feet and was trying to hobble out of the lab.

"We have to get Urstin and Helen. They must pay for this."

"Yes, Joey. We will make them pay," she consoled him as they walked out of the lab. They found that only Mr. B was left behind. He walked over to the mantle of the fireplace and hit a hidden button. A secret door opened and out walked Ben. It was a panic room that Mr. B was able to sneak Ben into while all the commotion was going on outside.

The rest of the story you already know, but I still had to get Joey to the hospital. He was losing blood fast and I didn't know if I could get him there on time. All the vehicles had been vandalized. Not a single tire had any air in them. It wasn't looking good for Joey.

Beats said to bring him into the stable, he would see what he could do.

"Catch me one of those chickens. I'm hungry."

What was left of our group started to chase chickens around, hoping to catch one. Nobody was paying any attention to Beats and what he was doing. In moments someone had caught a chicken and brought it over to him. He took it from us and thanked us.

A very groggy Joey stood up and brushed the dirt from his pants. We all stared in amazement as Joey seemed to be none the worse for wear.

"Let's get that chicken cleaned up. I'm starved."

Beats was holding a bloody dead chicken. First time he got to use the thing that Jesus said it transferred to the best.

CHAPTER 37

Walter takes it all in.

"Nice going, Anna. You've avoided all the answers to the questions that I wanted you to give me. It's time you cooled your heels in the brig until you can finally give us the truth."

He slammed his gavel down only to be shouted down by the President.

"You want to know the truth, Walter? I'll tell you the truth," the President was foaming at the mouth.

"Everything this girl told you was the truth. You just can't see it. All your life you've been taught what was possible and what wasn't. Well, let me tell you something. There are many things in this world that nobody can explain. Things that would absolutely blow your mind. I have seen many of these miracles myself. Every morning I look in the mirror I see a miracle. My behavior isn't caused by this formula. It's caused by people like you that want to control the system for their own greed and power-filled selves. I'm going to make a difference from now on, I don't care if you don't like it, or any other corrupt politician. The dawn of a new era is upon us, Walter. Get used to it.

"Anna, come with me. You did a nice job. Let's go have some dinner. I want you to meet my new fiancé."

He led me out and across the base to a cafeteria. We could have eaten in the officer's mess hall, but he wanted to eat with the real men in uniform. He asked one of his men to fetch his future bride.

We sat down while his people went to grab us some food. I almost choked on my drink when I saw Franny sashay into the mess hall and give President Adams the biggest full-on-the-mouth kiss I ever saw. I urged him afterward to wipe his mouth and lips. They were covered in bright red lipstick.

This was the last person I expected him to hook up with. I was waiting for my marriage proposal. I was taken aback by this sudden surprise. I sat calmly and tried to regain my composure. Franny sat opposite me and gave me a wink. Was I missing something here? I had to wonder. You know how rumors fly around, and soon the rumors and gossip had gotten back to me. Leon had slipped up in something he had said when he finally returned to the ranch with my test kit. Something about how good Franny had turned out. I didn't know what it meant then, but the light was starting to come on. It was dim at this moment, but given time, I would figure it all out.

I asked the President what was going on to start all these riots. Why were the people so upset?

"My dear, I talked to Joey Hopkins. You were right, his plan did save my sorry ass. He knew all along of all my misdeeds. It doesn't matter if I get reelected. The one thing that matters is this – that I made a difference. This is what I have done. I secretly put together a team to go into ten cities at about the same time and find out where all the money these cities siphon off the American taxpayer are going. I also put together medical teams to vaccinate the poor and the immigrants. Most of the cities I targeted are sanctuary cities with large amounts of foreigners that have brought with them diseases that America had wiped out a long time ago. I don't have a problem with the people, I have a problem with their health. We have the power to prevent these diseases from regaining a foothold in this country. I made sure that happened."

"If you only wanted to help, why are they rioting?"

"The damn media, my dear. They spun it out as I wanted to deport all the illegal aliens. I just gave them a choice. Either vaccinate or get out. We are not going to tolerate them making our wonderful country sick."

I thought about it and argued with him.

"A lot of people, including American citizens, think all these vaccinations might have something to do with the increase in autism. Did you ever consider that?"

He sat and pondered what I said.

"It had been brought to my attention. I weighed the risks versus the benefits. I decided it was worth the risk. I must protect our country!"

He seemed determined on this point. Also, he was easily distracted by something Franny was doing to him below the table. I heard her giggle and he blushed. It was time for me to go. I excused myself and went to find a restroom.

I found it at the rear of the mess hall, off a long hallway that had plaques of former personnel. Many had given their lives in service of their country. I scanned the wall looking for one person I knew served here. I found her. Theresa Shrader, lost her life from complications during childbirth. The plaque listed her many accomplishments and deeds that she performed for the community and country. It even listed the fact that she had defused the bomb that threatened the cancer hospital. Cross off one story that Joey had told me that I thought was a myth. How many more of his unbelievable stories would I be able to confirm in the future?

My phone rang. I thought about ignoring it when I saw who was calling. I gave in and answered him.

"Yes R.J., what can I do for you?"

"I'm in the middle of something very big right now. I wanted to let you know just how much I love and miss you. Seeing you at the ranch brought back many feelings I had to suppress. After Sophia died, I thought I might never love again. As I get ready to go into battle, I just wanted you to know that if I die, I loved you the most. If you hadn't rejected me, I'm sure we would have been married with a bunch of children driving us crazy. I would've liked that very much."

He didn't even give me a chance to respond, just hung up on me. Maybe he feared what I would say and that was why he hung up so quickly, I wasn't sure. What I did know was, he was saying goodbye because he thought that whatever he was about to do might get him killed. I had to get to where he was at, right now.

Sophia was out of the picture, shot to death by a young woman who sacrificed her life doing what she thought was the right thing for her country. I could be with him now, no longer restrained from ruining whatever mission Jesus had for him. If he got killed before I got there, I would be devastated.

I sprinted for the door and ran into Walter. We both ended up on the floor. I had bit my lip and could taste blood. Walter on the other hand was groaning like he had just been knocked down by an NFL linebacker. I tried to help him up, but he brushed me away.

"What are you in such a big hurry about Anna?"

He struggled to his feet.

"I have got to get to Richmond. A friend of mine is in danger. I want to see if I can help him."

He shook his head trying to get the stars that were flying around him to slow down.

"Not going to be pretty in Richmond. We got a report of busloads of rioters having just arrived there. The streets are going to be in flames in a matter of hours. A very dangerous place to try to be going right now."

"What about the governor? Isn't he doing anything to stop the destruction of the city?"

"He told his troops to stand down. Doesn't want any of his people to get hurt. Counting on this blowing over without too much damage."

I now knew what R.J. was going to do. He wasn't going to let a bunch of people come into his city and destroy it. The Not in My Neighborhood program had grown to many other cities in the U.S. If what I thought he was going to do hit the media, the people watching in the other cities would do what he was about to do. Stand and fight. It was going to be a bloodbath.

"Sir, I need a way to get there right now. Do you have any pull here to get me a ride?"

He laughed. "Only a crazy person would take you into that war zone."

A voice of a man I didn't know was listening to the whole conversation butted in.

"I'll take her."

I looked up to see the man that had been in the SUV the day of the assassination attempt on the President. He had been promoted to head of the secret service detail watching over the President.

"I would like to get to know this woman a little better. We can talk along the way. I'll get you there and even help if I can. What do you say?"

I didn't know if I trusted him. The President did though, so I thought it might be alright.

"Go ask Adams if you can go. If he gives you the okay, then I'm fine with it."

I watched him run off and interrupt the President making a fool of himself in front of a lot of army personnel. I could tell by his body language that the President had other things on his mind and could care less what his topman did. I had my ride.

Within the next fifteen minutes, we were on our way. It wouldn't take us long to get there. The guy didn't have much time to pry information out of me. The trip wouldn't take us that long. He was silent for the first few moments of the trip and then just asked the question I knew was coming.

"How did you do it? One minute you're in the vehicle with us, and with a flash, you're gone – replaced with a despicable human being that the President killed with prejudice. He must have stabbed him at least a dozen times. I know it was you. Your eyes give you away. I have never seen a more beautiful color green."

The President knew it was me as well, and I gave his man the same answer I gave Adams.

"You must be mistaken. I was never in the vehicle that day. I never had a flash grenade to cause a distraction so I could switch with someone else while the car was in motion. Even the best magician would have trouble pulling that one off."

He smiled. I knew more details of the incident than the public had ever been given. I had just confessed that I was the one in the SUV.

"I can see I'm just going to get another wild story from you like you gave the senator the last two days, so let's try this. Why are we going to Richmond?"

I answered the best I could.

"The one person I love most in the world is about to fight the looters that are going to wreak havoc in Richmond. If he is going to die, I want to stand by his side. I know I'll never talk him out of it, so I want to fight to the death with him. Do you still want to help?"

He gave me a slightly nervous laugh.

"I'm in." He said it with some self-doubt in his voice, like he wasn't sure. I think he was wondering if this was way bigger than what he really wanted to get himself involved in.

"Are you positive? You can back out now and I won't judge you."

"I said I was in. I don't know why, but I feel the need to be in the middle of all of this. A sort of calling."

"Don't listen to him. He'll get you in trouble every time."

A confused look came across his face. "What do you mean?"

"I mean we are dealing with things we have no understanding of. I can't explain it, so don't make me try."

I had said more than I should have. I looked to the sky and thought about a song I heard a long time ago. "Spirit in The Sky" by Norman Greenbaum. This could be the day I died. I was ready.

"I have a question for you. What is your name and how did you become the President's top guy?"

He shrugged.

"My name is Frank Wells. I saved the President from an agent that was about to put a bullet in his head. Adams liked that, made me his guy. I thought I was just doing my job to protect the man. I didn't ask for any favors."

I liked the fact that this man was also humble. I looked up and saw the city on the horizon. The smoke was the first thing I saw. The battle had already begun. We were late.

CHAPTER 38

R.J. assembles an army.

The first thing I saw were the buses pulling in. I was out calming the flock while also garnering support if something went down. Okay, I lied. I was preparing everyone I knew for the fight that was coming our way. I had watched enough news reports to know it was just a matter of time before the protesters would show up in this city and rape it blind. I think these people they bus in are professional looters and protesters. I always wondered why they got bussed in. Shouldn't the people in this city protest if that was how they were feeling? We didn't need outsiders coming into our town and burning it down. If that is how it should happen, we wanted to be the ones to burn the damn place down.

I was a firm believer in the second amendment, so was my flock. We were armed to the teeth. As soon as I saw the first bus pull in, I put out the call. Meet by the park where we had the concerts. I called my buddies from Savage Storm. "Get your gear, be ready to play. I need to motivate a bunch of people." They were all in. I called Deke, even though the guy was a mental case right now, he still was the best cover guy we had. With him protecting us from above, we had a better shot of making it out of this thing alive.

I don't know the whole story with him and that sex doll of his, but when I entered his house and found all the bodies piled up, well I knew something was wrong. When I walked in, I stepped over two guys with their heads nearly sliced off. I took one look around the house, and all I could see was blood and gore. Somebody had gone berserk and turned his home into a slaughterhouse. I searched for his body among the many but couldn't find it. Out of the corner of my eye, I saw something coming for me. I turned and punched it as hard as I could and heard a popping sound. Then, I heard a sound very similar to air escaping from a deflating balloon. Deke's sex toy lay deflated on the floor, a very large butcher knife by its hand.

I found Deke in the bedroom talking to a man whose head was pinned to the wall by a bayonet. The blade protruded from his ear and went all the way through and into the wall. Miraculously, the man was still alive and was having a conversation with Deke. They didn't pay much attention to me, so I had a look around. I saw poor Ellen on the bed. Her body was riddled with bullets. I had a feeling this had been a hit on Deke that had gone badly for said hitmen and Ellen. She sure did have bad timing. Maybe if she had stayed away one more day, she might still be alive. Hopefully, Deke would fill me in on what took place here last night.

The man with his head pinned against the door called out to me.

"Deke here says you're a pastor. You think maybe you can give me Last Rites? Deke says that even people like me can be forgiven. I have a lot of regrets and desperately want God to forgive me for my sins. I think this is the reason I'm still alive."

I looked at his pleading face and pondered what I was going to do. I wanted so badly to just pull that damn bayonet out of his head and let him die. Ellen was a good person. I really liked her a lot. I knew I was going to miss her. I looked at Deke, his eyes were full of tears.

"What do you want me to do Deke? I'll let it be your call."

He grabbed me and cried like a baby. Never gave me an answer. Jesus Christ, the guy's going to die if I wait much longer for Deke to get his shit together. With much regret, I'm so going to hell, I administered Last Rites. As the man said his final amen, without giving it another thought, I pulled out the blade and watched him fall to the floor. He was dead within minutes.

That was weeks ago, maybe months, time kept getting away from me ever since that journey back in time with Joey. I keep losing track of what happened when. All I knew was that Deke had been a little on the looney side lately. He swears that the doll he called Jezebel, was the one that killed all those gangbangers that came to kill him. He says that she was enraged that his wife had returned and had planned to just kill the two of them. That was until the hit team entered the house.

"Nobody was going to get to kill me but her. She was determined that I remain with her forever."

Once everyone was dead, he says she spared him, or as he said, forgave him. I was just lucky I saw her coming and was able to defend myself from her onslaught. As much as I tried, I was having a hard time buying this story. It was a blow-up doll, damn it. Like I said, I had questions about his overall mental stability.

I grabbed the vest that I stole from Joey. Never knew when you would need something like this. The Velcro straps almost made it all the way around my body. I grabbed some duct tape. So many uses for this stuff. I just found another. Inside my cabinet, I grabbed a Colt .45 and a Smith and Wesson 9mm Shield which I easily concealed. And then I just had to have my tactical handgun. I always had fun at the range with that one. I thought I could use a few more, but that would have to do for now. I looked longingly at my AR-15. She would have to stay in the gun cabinet today. Didn't want her to fall into the wrong hands.

Deke showed up with his guitar case in hand. He was ready for some target practice.

"I want to sing a couple of songs to the crowd to motivate them before I take my place."

"Deke, the longer you wait, the better chance they see where you went and come and get you. I feel you should get into place now."

He was determined to sing. I lost that battle with my friend. I sure hope he doesn't regret his decision. I like his spirit, but he knows better.

The crowd gathered. I had to give my speech. After that, we would sing a song or two and go to battle. I took the microphone in hand and blessed the crowd and prayed for our safety.

"Remember, we don't fire on anyone that isn't firing on us. Our goal is to stop the violence and destruction to our personal property. We are not here today to start a war, but to defend our land. Does everyone understand?"

The cheers and alcohol-laden screams were all I needed to know that this was going to be a long day. I didn't tell them to get drunk, I told them to get armed.

Deke took the stage with Savage Storm. Jenna was going to be their new lead singer, so the old one left the band. He decided to start his own band. The guy didn't realize he was the reason the band was lacking the success they so deserved. With Deke out in front, Savage had an edge, the thing that was missing. They had a voice.

They opened with a song Sleeperstar performed called, "Apocalypse." This was followed by a Jeremy Camp tune called, "Same Power." Between these two songs the crowd was fired up and ready to go. The first Molotov cocktail had been tossed and a police car was already tipped over on its roof. It was time to show these people that the city of Richmond had a program called, Not in My Neighborhood. The crowd was called to arms and I led them screaming all the way. My eyes had been painted black with crosses under each eye. If people thought Deke was not stable, they should have got a load of me leading the troops to battle. Right now, Deke appeared to be the sane one.

The crowd went on. He grabbed his instrument and walked to a nearby apartment complex. It was a brand new five-story building with a pool about several floors up. He entered the building passing under an awning that had just been installed two days ago. The people that lived there had complained they needed someplace that had cover when it rained. The buses didn't always run on time.

He found a spot on the roof, set up, and began his watch. It took all of two minutes before he fired the first shot. A group of thugs were beating a harmless old lady. She lay helpless on the ground and was being kicked, punched, and jumped upon. Deke saw no choice. If he did nothing, she was going to die.

After the first guy lost his head, the others decided they might want to find a safer hobby. Deke made sure it wasn't here on earth. Only one of the three remaining hoodlums escaped him. Not happy with himself, he scanned for more targets. They were everywhere. A looter coming out of a building with a television in his arms. Another man robbing a pharmacy, stuffing drugs and money in his pockets as he exited the store. Let him try to stuff his brains back into his head. Now that was a nice shot.

His shots hadn't gone unnoticed. Before long, the enemy had formed a plan. Six men stormed the apartment complex and were heading for the roof. This guy was doing too much damage down below, it was time for him to go.

I lay on the ground. I was a bloody mess. Shot at least a half dozen times, I wasn't getting back into the fight very soon. I checked the damage. It could have been worse. The vest came in handy, probably saved my life. My arm had a nasty wound, my hip had another, and I had one in the leg. The vest had stopped the rest. I had put up one hell of a fight. Funny thing about drunks, when they sober up, they find that they're not as brave as they thought they were. The many people that I had led into battle turned out to be just a few. Badly outnumbered, the battle was lost.

The sight of Anna was a wonderful thing. The sight of many men going into the building Deke was in was not. As much as I wanted to hold Anna, she was going to have to save my friend. Now, who was this guy hanging onto her shirt sleeves? I felt the first few pangs of jealousy.

"Anna, I'm going to be fine. Deke on the other hand is going to die unless you get over to that building."

I pointed to where she needed to go.

"Quickly, there isn't much time." I could tell she was torn on what to do. "Take Romeo with you, maybe he can show you how much he loves you by taking a bullet for you."

Did I really say that? It must be the pain, yeah that's it.

"Sorry, I'm in a lot of pain. I don't know what I'm thinking."

She came to me and gave me a kiss on the forehead.

"I love you. Remember that if he doesn't take that bullet for me."

Did she just try to be sarcastic with me? I smiled. I could get used to that kind of banter.

I kept that smile on my face as I watched them run for the building. I still had it when I heard the gunfight erupt on the roof. I lost it when I saw Deke get thrown off the roof to his presumed death. Not a lot of people can survive a fall from that height.

I struggled to my feet. I dragged my bad leg back into the fight. I still had ammo, and a gun that hadn't been taken from me. The Shield is so small and hides so well they missed it. I dripped blood all the way to the entrance of the building. The folks that live here are going to be so pissed off. Deke had broken his fall with their brand new awning. It caught him like a baseball in a glove. The force was so strong that the awning gave way and tore, but Deke survived the fall. I was so happy I hugged him a little too tightly. If he wasn't sore from the fall, he would be now.

"I thought I lost you. I'm so happy you're alive."

I squeezed. He cried out in pain, not from his injuries from the fall, but the ones he was now sustaining. Sometimes I can get a little carried away.

CHAPTER 39

Anna and Frank.

"Slow down, Anna. We need to form a plan."

She didn't slow down and no plan was formed as they rushed inside the building and headed for the staircase. Frank knew she was headed for trouble, but he couldn't catch up to her. The first time she stopped, it was because she was almost shot. I ran past her body lying flat against the stairs and drew the gunman's fire. It was a stupid thing to do I know, but it worked. Anna took out the gunman. I stood in the stairwell as she ran past me. I was trying desperately to catch my breath. Resigned to the fact that she was determined, I followed her up the steps.

We could hear gunfire from the roof. Anna kicked open the door and immediately encountered two men. They never stood a chance. I quickly took up position and found another target. That man went down as well. Deke had taken out two of them, which meant we had one to go. Anna found him. He was hiding behind a ventilation hood crying like a baby. She took his gun and left him to go and check on Deke. If I hadn't been there, she would have died. The cry baby had another weapon and drew it. He planned on shooting her in the back. Instead, I shot him in the head. She never looked back, just ran over to Deke. He had run out of ammo and was doing the best he could to make as small of a target of himself as he could.

The first thing I noticed about the man was he looked like he was suffering from a very bad case of PTSD. He was shaking like a leaf and his eyes were darting back and forth between the two of us.

"Today was my day to die. Why did you have to save me?"

Anna tried to talk him down, but Deke fought her.

"I was supposed to die today for my sins. You've ruined everything."

I watched Anna do her thing and try to calm him. I stood up and looked around at the scene on the roof. Deke had survived one hell of an onslaught. Bullet holes pockmarked everywhere around him. I was very surprised he hadn't at least been shot once. Not a scratch on the man. Suddenly, I turned to the screams of Anna and watched Deke throw himself off the roof. I ran to the edge and peered over. I grabbed Anna so she couldn't see. I wasn't sure what were the results of the fall, but he had hit an awning on the way down. He might have survived, but I had no way to tell from my vantage point.

We sat down on the roof and talked. I wanted to draw her mind off the current situation.

"Remember back at the ranch when Joey and R.J. first got there. He had another girl with him."

"I guess so. I think she was Joey's neighbor."

"I want to tell you a story about her. She might just be an American hero nobody will ever know about."

Anna looked up at me, I could tell she was upset that we hadn't saved Deke. This story might make her feel somewhat better.

"Her name was Samantha. I guess she had been having a relationship with your boyfriend down there. When she found him making out with Franny, she kind of had a meltdown. It didn't help he kept looking at you with longing in his eyes. I could tell right away he loves you."

Anna grabbed my hand and gave it a squeeze.

"Well, Samantha came out and sat beside me, struck up a conversation. I'm afraid I fell for her charm and the next thing I knew we were tangled in the sheets in one of the bedrooms. When all hell broke out at the ranch, she went with us in the helicopter. We landed at this army base called Fort Irwin. A few of the top dogs at the base came out to meet us and I was shuffled back to another vehicle that picked up

Helen Harrison and Urstin. Samantha and I were stuffed in the back of this Humvee. Samantha was complaining about being very hungry, so the driver took us over to the mess hall to get a bite. Helen was complaining that she thought her taste buds would never recover from those God-awful hot nachos that Urstin had forced down her throat. He was bitching about a whole bunch of other problems. One of them was her damn attitude. He was sick and tired of all her complaining. Nothing was ever good enough for her. The other thing that had him upset was the fact that the formula had only worked on the President and no one else. He was trying to figure out what the President had done differently that the rest of them hadn't. He knew the formula worked. All he had to do was look at Joey, Bob, and now the President. He wanted it for himself. It had worked him up into a very foul mood.

"We got inside and Samantha had seen some blueberry muffins. She asked for one smothered in butter. Helen had ordered a bagel with cream cheese. Urstin only wanted a coffee. I on the other hand wanted breakfast, and ordered a stack of pancakes, bacon, and a couple of fried eggs. When the server was handing the bagel to Helen, a fly landed right in the cream cheese. The server waved it away like this was a common occurrence. Helen lost her temper and had one of her fits that endeared her so to the public. I heard a muffled argument from her and Urstin. He told her to sit her fat ass down and he would get her a muffin with butter, just like the one that Samantha had. I snickered to myself. I loved every minute that man was aggravated. I was hoping his blood pressure would explode and he would have a stroke right in front of me.

"The server brought my breakfast and Helen's muffin. She examined it carefully for any trace of fly prints. I almost choked on my pancakes when she put her glasses on to take a closer look. I thought Urstin was going to shove the whole muffin in her face, he was so mad. Finally, she relented and took a bite. She proceeded to complain that she couldn't taste a thing, her tongue was burnt to a crisp. Urstin's face was getting redder by the minute. I could tell he wanted to slap her silly. His fists were all curled up in a very tight ball. It was just a matter of minutes before he was going to knock her lights out. I tried to defuse the heat of the moment and make light of a few things that happened at the ranch. Nobody seemed to be in the mood for my humor, so I finished my breakfast in silence.

"It wasn't more than a minute after I had eaten the last bite of my breakfast that it began. I saw Helen struggle to get her wind. She was gagging on something, maybe it was her tongue, I'm not sure. Her eyes grew very large and wide as she realized she couldn't breathe. Urstin thought she was choking on something and got in position to do the Heimlich maneuver. I told him he was wasting his time, she's choking on her tongue, clear her airway. It was an obvious seizure. I reached into her mouth and pulled her tongue out of her throat. At this point, she had stopped breathing and Urstin started CPR. I wasn't putting my mouth anyway close to hers, so Urstin did that part while I did chest compressions. She was dead before the ambulance arrived.

"I remembered what Joey had said – Don't take the formula Helen, it will kill you. I didn't know then why he was trying to save her. I think I know why now. Over the last year, Urstin has grown out of control. I think she was what was keeping him in check. What do you think Anna?"

I looked over at her and she was staring out into space.

"Do you remember the Church Band concert and the speech that followed it?"

I said that I did.

"Well let me tell you about that day and the things that you might never have known about. All you know is the shooting on stage of Sophia, and the virus that was contained within the case she snuck inside. I know the whole story. I was there. I saw it all play out. Would you believe there is a manuscript that details everything that went on that day?"

I shook my head, "I find that hard to believe."

She laughed. "I did too. That was until he let me read it."

"Who let you read what?"

"The director. He let me view the script while we watched from the parking garage. Deke watched from his position outside the car, sniper rifle in hand just in case the scene got off script."

"Who is this man you call the director?"

"If I told you, I would have to kill you. It's classified. I will tell you one thing. He lives in the shadows. He lets other people do most of the dirty work. People like me," she answered.

She turned and looked away. I think I was beginning to understand all the crazy stories. If she revealed who she really worked for, it would be the death of her. Whoever it was, he was more powerful than the man I worked for, and I work for the President of the United States.

We got up and walked back down the stairwell. We found R.J. holding on to a very alive and well man whose name I now knew was Deke.

"Let's get you guys some medical attention."

I reached my hand down to help R.J. gain his feet. R.J. grabbed my hand and pulled himself up. He looked me in the eye and welcomed me to the team.

"What team?" I asked.

"We are on a mission to turn the tide of evil. We're all about bringing goodness and holiness back to the country. You're on the team now."

"What if I don't want to be on the team?"

"Take it up with the big guy." He pointed to the sky and smiled at me. "None of us had a choice in all of this. Don't fight it, accept it. Now get me to the damn hospital. I need drugs, high doses of pain meds," he groaned and then said, "This job is killing me."

I didn't think Deke would get up and walk away with us, but he did. I looked to the sky and wondered to myself if I had just been called into service by the Lord. I had never been a person you would see in a church much. Funerals and weddings were about all the time you would ever see me in one. So how was I to be a man to fight in the name of God? I was about to find out. They say he works in strange and mysterious ways. I would find this to be quite a true statement in the months and years to come.

CHAPTER 40

The story as Frank saw it.

I was starving and the breakfast at the mess hall was doing the trick. Samantha sitting beside me, my belly full. I was starting to enjoy life again. The last few days at the ranch had been nerve-wracking. Helen had been her usual self-important self and was driving the whole table nuts. Urstin was red in the face with frustration over her antics. I watched him come back with the same type of muffin I had just watched Samantha devour. She told me it was one of the best muffins she had ever had, said it loud enough to get Helen's attention. Helen sent Urstin to get her one as well. When he came back and practically threw it at her, I had all I could do to contain myself. I almost lost it when she took out her glasses to examine the muffin for any hint of a fly landing on it.

We had all finished and Urstin was on the phone making some arrangements for the rest of the day. I didn't know what the President had planned. Our normal to the minute schedule had gone out the window days ago. We were flying by the seat of our pants now. Nothing could have prepared us for the day's events. Helen choking on her food was just the start of things to come.

Urstin jumped up and was going to try to give her the Heimlich maneuver. I waved him off, could see right away she was having a seizure. I opened her mouth and pulled her tongue back from its spot lodged deep in her throat. We could tell she had stopped breathing and started CPR. Urstin was frantic. If he lost her, he would lose his meal ticket. I heard him mumble things in her ear I wish I had never heard. I looked at him, confused by the words he was saying to her, at the same time he was calling her a useless bitch. He was also telling her how much he loved her and that if she died, he would be lost. I shook my head at what I was hearing and continued chest compressions until I was relieved by a female army medic. At least I thought it was a female. It was hard to tell.

The two medics took over and I stood back to observe. Urstin could be a loose cannon. I had to be ready. He didn't disappoint. He was looking for anyone and everyone to blame when the female medic said Helen was gone. The President had shown up when the medics did, and he stood by with the commanding officer of the base. I watched them discuss something and then saw the President make a phone call. He had a huge smile on his face.

Urstin never missed a thing and shifted all his blame toward the President. His face was a bright red. Enraged and feeling like he had just lost it all, he pulled his weapon. I had to save the President, nothing else mattered. I pulled my weapon and fired at the same time Urstin did. We both hit something. I hit Urstin high in the chest just below his collarbone. He hit the commanding officer, most likely in the heart. He had jumped in front of the President and saved his life. That man was a true hero, now he was dead as well. Urstin fared much better. I scrambled over to where he lay on the floor and kicked the gun away from his outstretched hand. I didn't know what to expect from Ivan. I trained my gun on him and asked him to put his weapon on the table, very slowly. Ivan did something I never expected. He identified himself.

If Urstin wasn't already deranged, he took it up a level. He swore and cursed Ivan. Told him he had just signed his death warrant. What Ivan had just told us was he was undercover CIA investigating these two people we now had lying on the floor. One was dead, the other was severely injured. Urstin tried to get up. I put my foot on his chest and pushed him back down to the floor. It must have been very painful, for he cried out in a great deal of pain. Before he passed out, he swore he would have his vengeance.

The President checked out the commanding officer. He held onto his hand until he took his final breath and died. I could see he had tears in his eyes as he thanked the man for his selfless commitment to duty. I looked around for Samantha, but she was gone. Hightailed it for the exit as soon as the bullets started to fly, maybe sooner. Like she knew what was coming.

The President was back on the phone and I heard him thank someone named Adam and his son. I heard him say, "Your boy is a genius. His plan worked just like you said it would. I don't know how to thank you… I could do that, how about next week? I'll set it up and make it happen. Thanks again Adam, I owe you."

I sat down and tried to process it all. I felt like I had been set up. Somehow this whole event had been preplanned according to the phone call. I knew Helen was the biggest thorn in the President's side. Urstin was next. They both would be out of the picture for now. I should be elated, but I wasn't. Samantha knew something as well. Thinking back on it, the way she made sure Helen knew that the muffin was just what the doctor ordered. How she made such a show to how much she was enjoying it. Helen had been played. Joey was right when he said not to take the formula, that it would kill her.

Was it the blueberries in the muffin that was the final ingredient that she hadn't had last night? I tried to remember if I saw blueberries in that whole pile of food on the table. I couldn't remember. What did the President do differently from all the others? All these things were racing through my head when the President informed me that we were leaving. I looked for Samantha, didn't see her, and we left without her. I sat in my seat wracking my brain for the answers. All that got me was a very bad headache. The President was smiling ear to ear. He had just had the best day of his life. I, on the other hand, had just been a pawn in a game I didn't know how to play. I wondered to myself if this game was going to get me killed.

Now I'm told that I've joined the team. I have no choice. I felt the pull, made the commitment. R.J. said not to fight it, that it was the will of the Lord. I opened my eyes and saw the chaos in the halls of the hospital. Many new patients were coming in from the violence on the streets. The rumor in the hallway was that the looters had been defeated, the worst was over. Anna held my hand. I don't know why, but it felt soft and warm. I looked into those bright green eyes of hers and asked.

"Anna, why me?"

She replied, "I thought the same thing when R.J. came into my life. Joey is the leader, the one that holds us all together. Maria is the instigator, the one that makes all the bad folks crazy. They come out of their holes to kill her and Joey exterminates them with his Angel Armies. Together, we are a force to be dealt with against the evil in this world. R.J. said that when I have my doubts, I should listen to this song. Chris Tomlin does a song called 'Whom Shall I Fear.' I think you should listen to it."

She pointed to the sky.

"We do it all for Him. I hope you're a believer, because if you aren't, you're going to be very soon."

She giggled when she said that.

"Why did you just laugh when you said that?"

She smiled and flashed those gorgeous eyes at me.

"When I first was called into all of this, I can honestly say I didn't believe in God. Joey took me to a place where I not only met Jesus, but he gave me a mission. The world depends on me fulfilling this mission. We put a lid on it the night at the ranch. Very few people know the correct ingredients to the formula. My mission is to make sure it stays that way."

"What happens if the formula gets out?"

She calmly said, "We all die. God will end the world like He did in the time of Noah and the ark."

I sat back in my chair. I knew what was in the formula, but not all of it. I had made a mental list of everything that had been provided. The cicada, the clams, all the different fruits and vegetables. The nasty nachos that the President refused to eat. Was that the thing that was different in the formula? Helen and Urstin had eaten the nachos, the President had not. That must be it. The secret was not to burn your mouth off with those fire nachos.

Bennett said we wouldn't be able to get any more of the cicada for another sixteen years. I would be in my mid-fifties by then. I knew all the ingredients. Would I be tempted to make some up for myself when the time came?

As if reading my mind, Anna said, "Please don't be tempted when the time comes. This stuff was never meant for our time. It will do nothing but harm to all it touches."

Amazing how she knew just what I was thinking. It must have been written all over my face.

"I'm sorry. It's like knowing what the lottery numbers are going to be before the drawing. The temptation is overwhelming."

She patted me on the hand and said, "If you knew that winning the lottery would kill you, would you play?"

"I guess I might pass with you putting it that way."

"Trust me on this. It will kill you if you ever take it. The formula won't kill you. The people after it will do that for you after you're tortured and reveal to them what it is. The President is in danger every day now. Bob and Joey as well. Joey already has been attacked by some group trying to get the formula. If I were you, I would forget you ever knew what was in that mix of death. We are in the fight of our lives, and it only is going to get tougher from here. Do you understand what I'm saying?"

She stared into my eyes and held my hand.

"Yes, I think I do," I responded.

Ever since that day at the ranch, my life had changed. The President was doing things to make the country crazy. I think it was to take the focus off his change in appearance. With everyone going nuts with his new programs for change in America, they didn't have time to marvel at how young he had suddenly become. My job to shield him from all these nut jobs was even harder now. This last thing he had done was all formulated in a meeting with Joey and Anna months ago. I wasn't let inside to listen in on what was said. What I did learn was that I was to go to LA. and get two doctors. The President joked that their names were Mutt and Jeff. He needed them. I was the one who was going to go and get them. He couldn't send anyone else. I found out why when I got there.

CHAPTER 41

Mutt and Jeff.

Jeff sat in his chair, feeling like he was going to pass out any time soon. Scott, his roommate, had brought home some new stuff because there was a shortage of cocaine in the city for some reason. This crap made him feel like shit, whatever it was. The last time he had seen Scott, he was trying to crawl to the bathroom to take a leak. He hadn't seen him since then. Jeff reached down to take another swig of beer and knocked the bottle over, letting out the last few ounces to leak into the carpet that already stunk of stale beer. He just laid his head back and closed his eyes. Not going to do that shit anymore, he told himself. That was some nasty crap.

A while later, maybe just a few minutes, he didn't know for sure, an urgent knock on the door woke him from his stupor. He struggled to his feet to answer. The man standing on the other side of the door looked like a fed. He quickly closed it before he arrested him on some charge or another. Couldn't tell these days. After losing his job at the hospital for saving Helen Harrison's life, his and Scott's life had been made into a living hell. Banded from practicing medicine, they fell into a period of self-pity and loathing. This man at the door could only be more hell that Helen had sent their way. He was almost right.

The door was pushed open before he could lock it and now the man stood inside his house.

"You look like shit. Have you been using drugs?"

His bloodshot eyes and sunken cheeks might have given him away. "Where is your roommate?"

Jeff pointed to the bathroom and said, "I think he's still in there."

He watched the intruder head for the head, open the door and exclaim in a very excited voice, "Jesus Christ." The man entered and walked out with his friend in his arms.

"Help me get these filthy clothes off. We need to get the two of you sober and clean."

I watched him remove Scott's clothes. They were covered in piss and excrement. The smell even made my stoned eyes water. I tried to help, but things started to get a little fuzzy and I might have passed out.

We were both in the tub when the ice-cold water brought us back to the land of the living. It was quite a shock to the system. Trying to catch my breath, swearing and cussing up a storm, I was explained my options.

"Listen, punk. I was sent here to get the two of you. I hear you're doctors, but you could have fooled me. You look like stoners to me."

"We are in a low point in our lives. I'm trying to dig us out of the hole we're in."

"You'll never do it stoned and drunk, but it's your lucky day. You worked on a friend of the President and now he wants you for a special project he has."

I was confused, "The friend, or the President?"

He slapped me in the face, looked me in the eye, and said, "Does it matter? You and your friend have a paying job. Now get him dressed and be ready in two hours."

I watched him walk out. I was never so glad to see someone leave. I knew he would be back.

"Scott, wake up. We need to get the hell out of here. Grab some stuff. A lunatic is going to make us do some awful things and we need to be as far away from here as possible."

The way he was moving, we would be lucky to make it down the stairs to the lobby before he returned. Frantically, I packed a few things for him and me. Getting him dressed turned out to be harder than I thought it was going to be, but I finally managed to get something on him.

I put all our stuff in a suitcase that had a handle you could pull out and wheels so you could roll it. I pulled Scott's arm over my shoulder and made for the door. Who do you think was waiting on the other side?

"You forgetting something, Jeff? Where is my rent money?"

My landlord was standing outside my door preparing to knock and demand the two months I was already behind. I was broke. Scott wasn't doing much better financially. His parents were well off, but they had gotten sick of sending him money after a few months and cut him off. I don't even want to begin to tell you what we had to do to make any money just to survive.

We were saved by my friendly federal agent.

I smiled and told my landlord, "This nice man here is going to square up with you. We won't be needing the place anymore. We found a job in another state."

I turned to the fed and said, "Be a friend and take care of the man won't you? We'll be downstairs waiting for you."

I figured we might be able to wave down a taxi and make a getaway while he haggled with the landlord. I should have realized that this neighborhood didn't attract much taxi traffic.

We were still waiting for one when he came down. A pissed-off look on his face.

"You guys better be worth it. I called the President and told him he was making a mistake. Know what he said? I'll tell you. He said that Joey Hopkins recommended you guys and that was good enough for him."

I remembered the man. He was in rough shape when we first met him. I patched him up the best I could, and he went his way. Why would he recommend us? I had a feeling why. He couldn't go to a hospital because some very bad folks were after him. This must be something that must be kept hush-hush. A clandestine mission. I liked it. Scott was going to be so excited when he finally came to. He wasn't, but that's another story.

We were brought to an airport and put on a private jet. A wealthy man in a very expensive suit met us at the steps. He introduced himself, said his name was Tom. He told us we would be heading to the East Coast. We had to prepare for a mission. He didn't know when it would go down, but he knew when it did, there would be much danger and we could possibly die. I was all in, Scott still wasn't quite with it yet. I moved his head up and down and made it move like a ventriloquist. Without moving my lips, I said I was so excited and couldn't wait to get started. Tom laughed at my antics, bid us farewell, and left us at the steps to the jet. My federal friend pushed us inside. I knew we never really had a choice in the matter.

He made himself a drink, sat down in one of the leather seats, and closed his eyes.

"You think I can have one of those?"

"No, you've had enough."

He never opened his eyes.

"How long have you been having those headaches?"

This got him to open his eyes and stare at me.

"What makes you think I have a headache?"

"It's quite obvious to me. Just the way you move and how you want to sit with your eyes closed is a dead giveaway."

"Well, let me tell you something. If you had seen and been through all the shit that I have been through the last few weeks, you would have a headache too. Better get yourself some aspirin. You got some headaches coming your way," he snickered to himself, like he could picture just all the danger and pulse-quickening action we would be enduring in the very near future.

I swallowed hard, tried to wake Scott once again. He opened his eyes and looked around. I was in so much trouble. It was time to finally explain what I had gotten us into. Scott wasn't what you would call an action type of guy. Spoiled rich kid, yes. Street action, run-for-your-life type – not even close. He freaked out. Good thing we were on a plane. He had nowhere to run. I had to listen to him cry the rest of the flight. The fed guy gave me a look that could have killed. I shrugged. What could I do?

The weeks spent at the secret place turned into months. Scott and I trained every day with a bunch of Army guys. We were told that we had a better chance to survive if we were in shape for the action. The day finally came, we packed our gear. I noticed that we were supplied with a great deal of vaccination drugs. Measles, Mumps, and Rubella made up a large amount of what we were carrying. A large variety of other vaccinations most schools required were also packed. It looked to be one of our duties would be vaccinating children. All our equipment was packed into two military trucks. The order to move out was given. We were with a National Guard unit stationed out of Cumberland, Maryland. Our destination was Baltimore.

These guys were dressed like they were heading into a war zone. We weren't leaving the country. I could only imagine what was to come our way. Scott's leg was twitching a mile a minute. I put my hand on his leg to get it to stop.

"It's going to be alright. They just blew it all out of proportion to make it sound like it was going to be this dangerous affair. We're doctors, how dangerous can it get for us?"

I smiled my most reassuring smile.

"Jeff, we're going to die, I can feel it." He shook uncontrollably. "Look around you Jeff, open your eyes. These guys are dressed for battle. What are we heading for?"

I looked around and decided to play the judge's advocate.

"These guys are prepared, that's all."

Scott shook his head. "Yeah, prepared to kill and be killed – that's what they're prepared for."

I wish I had been prepared that day. I would have known what to do. Instead, I focused on my medical training and started to treat the many children that were brought to me. These kids were in desperate need of medical care. We were told that if medical care was refused, a bus waited outside for them. These folks would earn a one-way ticket home. Whatever country they came from would be their destination. I now knew that as soon as the people got a wind of what was going down, the chaos would soon erupt. It did, and with a vengeance.

I must have treated well over a hundred children that morning alone. Scott was handling the vaccinations while I treated the others for all sorts of problems. Many suffered from head lice to scabies, even a few cases of the crabs. I had my hands full. Just being around all this made me itch, even though I took precautions. The morning had come to an end. The afternoon would prove to be when the fun was about to begin. I walked up to Scott scratching another itch.

"How did things go for you today?"

He answered that he expected it to be worse than it was. It was going to be, we just hadn't waited long enough. The afternoon session, things started to heat up. The first couple of dozen buses had left for the airport. We had plenty more to fill up. The children kept pouring in, the disease kept getting worse. I found two children with measles, quickly got them away from the others. Several cases of chickenpox. If I wasn't already itchy, I was now. The stuff I was running into was easily preventable, but these children had never been given the vaccinations to prevent this outbreak. The immigrants that had come to our country from places that had little to no medical care had not sought out or been able to afford the proper medical care. The President had decreed that this was going to stop. Either get up to speed with vaccinations and free medical care or get out. He had done other things today. The media spun it all as he was doing a very bad thing. They said he was rounding up illegals and deporting them. They never mentioned what we were doing down in the trenches. The illegals he was rounding up were the worst of the worst. Criminals, drug dealers, rapists. The National Guard rapidly worked a list of addresses that contained information on where to find these people.

The auditors worked the books in the government offices. The President wanted to know where all the money was going. The school we were treating the children at was run down and badly in need of repair. Many thousands of dollars were allocated for this school, but it never made it here. More money was asked for and sent, still, it never made it here. Somebody had full pockets, and that was what the President wanted to find out. It was time to find out who the thieves were and put them behind bars. The problem with the plan, these

THE TRUTH

were very powerful and influential thieves. They took no prisoners and spread their lies. The media pounced on the lies and spread them nationwide. The riots began, the people worked into a frenzy. The smiles on the faces of the thieves grew. This President was no match for them. When they were done with him, he would be exiled from this country, driven away in disgrace.

Baltimore was only the first of ten cities hit that day. All timed almost exactly at the same time. The riots hit every city in the country that day. Peaceful protest would have been tolerated. The protests and riots were anything but peaceful. From coast to coast the mayhem had begun. Many people looked to profit from all the looting they would be able to do. The cops would not be able to control the masses and they knew they could get away with just about anything. That was until the people of this country stood up and said, "Enough is enough." It started in Richmond, Virginia with a pastor. The media mistakenly picked up on this story and aired it, motivating the whole country to follow in his footsteps.

I took a break and watched what was going on outside. The children stopped coming in and now we had no patients left to treat. Our armed detachment was overwhelmed. Told not to fire on anyone, just to be a deterrent, the people quickly made them run away, get in their vehicles, and leave us alone in the school. A janitor stood beside me.

He said, "I don't know about you, but I sure think they plan on burning this place down."

He pointed at the crowd. Several men were holding a couple of five-gallon gas cans. People were gathering around and filling empty bottles with gas.

"Damnedest thing I ever did see! Those folks are planning on cooking us alive."

The janitor hurried away. I stayed and stared out at the crowd. I opened the front door to speak and was quickly greeted by gunfire. The janitor was right. We weren't getting out of here alive. I ran back into the room where Scott had been cleaning up.

"We got big problems, my friend," I nervously proclaimed.

Scott looked up at me and said, "I told you we would die today. Now you get all worked up."

At least he was taking it well.

I ran around the building to see who else was still inside with us. I found a teacher grading some test papers that her class had taken earlier today.

"We have big trouble, miss."

"I know. These test scores are terrible. I don't think half these kids can read."

"Not that kind of trouble. The crowds outside are planning on burning this place down."

This got her attention. She smiled at me and said, "You must be overreacting. If they did that, they would have no school to send their children to."

I rolled my eyes as the first of many bottles filled with gas and a flaming rag stuffed into the top came pouring through the windows.

She screamed. I ran. We headed for the door. The crowd was waiting for us. More shots rang out and we were forced back inside. The teacher was an emotional wreck. The school was filling with smoke and flames. I had no idea how we were going to get out. Scott called out to me while lying on the floor down the hall.

"Make your way down this way! I have a plan."

I thought any plan was better than frying inside of here, so I made my way past the flames with the teacher holding onto my belt as we went. When I reached where Scott had been, I saw he had made his way to a door, just a short distance down the hall. He stood by it and waved for us to come to him.

The teacher was screaming. I turned to see that her dress had caught on fire. I did what I could to save it, but eventually, it just burned off. I had several burn holes in my pants as well, but at least I still had my pants. She couldn't say the same. Even her panties had some very revealing burn holes. I pulled my long sleeve shirt off and had her wrap it around her. It was the least I could do to help her save her dignity.

The door led to the basement. The janitor called to us.

"We just need to break this lock off. This tunnel leads to the building on the other side of the street."

The lock turned out to be a big and rusted-out padlock. The gate was made of solid steel bars —no way we were getting by them. I looked around for anything that we might be able to use to break the lock. I could find nothing. The smoke was starting to make its way down into the basement. We didn't have much time left before our air would be poisoned with what was most likely a school filled with asbestos.

We searched everywhere for something that could get us through that gate. To be so close and die because of a rusted old padlock was too much for my brain to handle. The teacher stood by and let us search. She reached into her hair and pulled out a bobby pin. While we scrambled in a frantic search, she worked the lock with her hairpin. I heard the gate squeal as it opened on rusted hinges, looked up, and thanked God. I had no idea at the time how the gate got open, just that it was open.

We all stared down the dark and narrow corridor. Overhead pipes ran the distance of the tunnel, which looked like it hadn't been used in years. We could make out the sound of rats scurrying away from the flames above us. They had the same idea as us. Get the hell out of this burning building. With no choice, I led the way. Within feet of the gate, my face was covered in spider webs. I turned and asked for something I could use to knock down the webs. Scott handed me a broken broom handle. It was better than nothing.

Inching my way down the dark tunnel, with little to no light, I sure hoped we didn't encounter another lock on the other side. I already heard things crashing through the ceiling into the abandoned cellar. There was no turning back now. The first rat fell from the pipes above my head. He landed on my shoulder and quickly took a bite out of me in his panic to get away. The others had the same problem. So many rats all trying to escape at the same time was becoming an issue. I swatted at them with the broken broom handle. They just raced past me on their way to a safer home. I finally reached the other side to find it was locked as well. The others had enough of the rats and raced toward me.

"The gate is locked! Stop!" I screamed as Scott plowed into me driving my body into the gate. It's amazing what a little adrenaline can do to make a human body much stronger than it would normally be. That gate didn't stand a chance and we all crashed through it onto the floor on top of one another.

Safe for now, I brushed the cobwebs from my hair. The teacher helped me once Scott found a light switch and gave us a little light. This building had been an old office building that had long ago been abandoned when the property taxes had been raised so high that businesses were forced to leave. As the businesses left, so did the jobs. Many people left the homes they had lived in for most of their lives, forced to go elsewhere to find work. The poor and the immigrants had taken over, living off the government with public assistance. Once a community that paid into the system, now it fed off the system.

"I guess we'll hide out here until the crowd disperses. I'll go upstairs and check on things. You guys just make yourselves comfortable."

I made my way up the stairs and peered out a dirty window. What I saw made me blink my eyes a few times. The crowd that had burned the school was in a battle with civilians. Many people were very angry that the only school they had in the area was now a flaming mess. The good people of this community far outnumbered the bad apples. They stood up for themselves and fought. I thought it was about time. I called for Scott to join me.

"Hey, guys. Check it out."

Scott came up and peered out.

"Amazing. I can't help but think about a song I heard yesterday. 'Great Are You Lord' by All Sons and Daughters. I never thought I would see such a thing. The Lord is surely great."

The teacher made her way up the stairs with a huge smile on her face.

"Let's sing and pray together. I want to give thanks," I said.

We all held hands and prayed. Not only did we give praise to the Lord, but we prayed for the many brave souls that were fighting outside.

"I don't have my medical kit, but we have got to do something for the many injured out there."

THE TRUTH

I looked at Scott in amazement. He was ready to go out into the heat of things.

"Okay, my friend. Let's do this."

The janitor stayed behind. He said he was good. The three of us ran out and joined the battle. It felt like the right thing to do. As I ran out, I saw a medical kit propped against a telephone pole. I grabbed it and checked the contents. It was a brand new kit that contained everything we would require.

It felt like hours later, with many injured treated, we were able to take a breath. It felt good to be able to help so many brave people. Most of the injuries were small, but we did find a couple that we were unable to save. I felt lucky to just be alive. I wanted to thank the janitor for his guidance and the teacher for her support. I couldn't find either of them. I asked Scott if he had seen them.

"Seen who?"

"The teacher and the janitor. You know, the two that were in the school with us."

"I think you might have hit your head or something, Jeff. We were the only two in the school."

I looked at him like he had two heads. I was confused. How could he forget?

"She burned her dress off. I gave her my shirt to cover her pretty ass."

"Jeff, your shirt caught on fire. You pulled it off and tossed it."

I stuttered out a reply, but I couldn't find an answer. Scott was sure I had lost it. I was sure I had help getting out of that building. The janitor had shown us the way out, the teacher had opened the gate. I sat down on the curb, covered my eyes, and wept. Scott put his arm around me, tried to settle me down.

"It's okay, Jeff. Sometimes we imagine things that aren't there in stressful situations. It happens."

I wanted to yell and scream at him. I held it in for another time. I had no doubt. We had help getting out of that building.

* * *

From inside the old office building, an old black man wearing a janitor's uniform and a pretty young blond by the name of Honey stood and observed.

"You did well today, Honey. I have more things for you in the future. Keep your phone on. I'll certainly be needing your help again. Seems your husband has a guardian angel that has a touch of ADD. He's very good at his job, just gets distracted from time to time. Now that Maria, with the help of Lucifer, has tricked him into taking the ancient formula, his life is going to be a full-time adventure. The man is going to need all the help we can give him. You up to the task?"

"Yes, Lord. I would love the challenge."

Honey felt very good. She was going to enjoy being around Joey once again. She had always hated his reckless ways when she was alive, but now that she was on the other side, her only fear was that Joey might get hurt. She would always love him, even if he did piss her off quite often.

CHAPTER 42

Mr. B at the ranch.

When Samantha had come down the hallway all upset that R.J. was smooching with Franny, I called her over. I had a job for her. I needed her to get cozy with the President's top man. The agent named Frank Wells. I told her what needed to be done in a great amount of detail. The girl was so excited to be in the game that she jumped at the chance to help. I never thought she would take the agent into the bedroom and rock his world. Well, whatever works, she got the job done. They took her with them, and she knew what to do from there. Get Helen to eat something smothered in butter.

Maria's manuscript told the whole story, right down to when Urstin shot the President dead when he blamed him for Helen's death. The phone call from the President made my knees weak. I had to sit down. Maria had gotten the story wrong, or maybe it was this damn ripple in time that has screwed everything up. I wasn't sure which one it was, but a perfect plan had just gone down the tubes. I reached into my bag and pulled out the latest manuscript that Tom had delivered to me. It needed to be reread. The story was in there. I had been confused the first time I read it. Now things were starting to make sense. It was off to plan B, also known as, save your ass and start over. I set up the meeting with the President to meet with Anna and Joey.

The President wasn't going to be able to hide the fact that he now appeared to be twenty years younger than the last time the public saw him. I had to solve this problem. I called Leon. If anyone could make the President appear older, it was Leon. Most people wanted to make themselves look younger, except for teenagers that wanted to look like they were older. I worked up a spin about a health guru and fitness training with seaweed drinks. Takes years off your appearance, we would tell the public. I would get Leon to gradually lessen his makeup until he could pass without it. The fitness plan was working wonders. Somebody would try to profit from the bullshit we would be presenting. I didn't care. I just wanted the President to survive what I knew would be coming. It was all written right here in this latest manuscript. I wondered how much of this insane story was going to come true.

When I reached the part about Scarlett, my heart sank. I could only hope that this was one of the parts she sometimes got wrong. It didn't matter what I did. If it was meant to be, it would happen. I filled my drink for the last time. I already had about twice the limit I allowed myself. The story had Billy in it, but he was dead outside feeding the coyotes. The Queen Bees would be here shortly. Before the ripple, this is the day that they brought Anna and Billy to the ranch. I had set this place up months ago to coincide with the manuscript. When they showed up a month before they were to die, I almost had a heart attack. I even checked on their whereabouts. The whole month they existed in two separate places. This was unexplainable, so I didn't try to explain it to myself.

I called for Beats.

"Son, I need you to heal someone for me. Have you ever brought a dead man back to life like Jesus did with Lazarus?"

He had a fearful look in his eye. I could figure out the answer.

"Jesus said I had the power to heal, but I wasn't able to do the things that he could do. He doesn't have to transfer the damage. He just releases it into the air. I have got to rely on transference. I'm scared one day it's not going to transfer. Please don't make me raise the dead. I'll have nightmares for weeks after if you do."

"I hope it doesn't come to that, but you might have to do this for me."

The boy walked away sniffling like he had caught a cold. I knew better.

I called Joey and Peter and sent them to retrieve Billy's body. An hour later, they brought what was left of him inside. His arms were gone, one leg was chewed off up to the knee, the other wasn't in much better shape. I don't even want to get into what his midsection looked like. They placed him inside the equine veterinarian office on the same table that Joey had been tied to hours earlier.

"If the Queen Bees bring him, we bury the body in the desert. If not, we must try to bring him back. If they bring Anna, I need a volunteer to kill her."

I couldn't have two of them. It would be like Maria and Scarlett all over again. I looked at Ben and slapped him in the head. He thought it was because he didn't volunteer. He should have known better.

"Okay, I'll do it myself."

I went outside to wait. I needed another drink, but I didn't dare get one. My nerves were all shot to hell. The sun was rising high in the sky when I heard the first of the motorcycles. My heart started to beat faster than an old man's heart should. I thought my wife might just get her wish. It was beating so fast. I let out a sigh of relief when I saw it was Leon and his crew. He had the test kit for Anna. God, I hope she wasn't pregnant. We had too much to do in a very short amount of time.

I told Leon what I needed him to do, took the kit from him, and went to find Anna.

"Dear, I think you have been asking for this? If you test positive, I would like you to stay here and have the child. I'll make sure you have plenty of protection and company."

"Thank you, Mr. B. That is very kind of you."

"Urstin survived this morning. He is in the hospital under police protection. If he finds a way to escape, we'll have to move you to a safer place."

"I understand. Thanks."

She took the test kit from me and headed for the bathroom.

"Joey, come here."

He strolled over to me with a big smile on his face.

"You can't leave here for another few weeks. Don't try to be a hero and fix something that you didn't quite fix the last time. It will be the biggest mistake of your life if you do. Understand?"

I knew he had plans to revisit that school. I couldn't let him do it.

"I have that film you need to be working on. Continue your trip to LA, get R.J. back home. Do the damn film. Scarlett hasn't told you yet, but she will be switching with Maria and doing the squirrel with the attitude. That girl is going to have a real attitude, it will come out in her voice and make her character seem real. Try to stay on script."

He told me he would try. I knew he would do it his own way, but why argue.

I watched Beats head into the surgical area where we had Billy on the table. Not yet, boy. We must wait. I chased him inside.

"This guy is a mess. Coyotes almost made a meal out of me. This could have been me looking like this."

"God was looking out for you. I won't make you do this. We'll find another way."

"Good, because I'm going to throw up."

He did. I had to go and find a change of clothes.

The second group showed up while I was finding something clean to wear. I came out and almost fainted when I saw Anna talking to Leon. In my drunken haze, I pulled my weapon and fired at her. Thankfully, I was so drunk I missed. The Queen Bees explained to me what happened after they let me get back up. Billy had seen what I was about to do and hit me from behind, knocking my shot astray. He pulled the gun away from me and tossed it. I felt awful.

Anna had taken the test and it came back positive. She had gone outside to talk to Leon and thank him for bringing the test kit to her. The next group showed up with Billy and had picked up Samantha as well. Billy had gone inside to take a leak, found me about to shoot somebody, and had tackled me from behind. I had fired at Anna, but I had hit someone else. Samantha was still twitching as she stared up at me with dead eyes. I was such a fool.

The Queen Bees had done as instructed. They could only rescue Billy. The female was hung up fried to a crisp in some power lines and the other male had been taken in by the cops. Billy was about twenty feet up in a spruce tree. The time they wasted getting him down was all the time they had. They did not realize it was Anna they were to save, only that they were to get two males and a female to safety.

I was brought inside and placed back in my chair. I was in great distress. We had Billy back in place, only one Anna, but had lost Samantha. I had big plans for her. I can see star material when I see it. This girl had that something I always look for. I wept, maybe I passed out. I'm not sure.

A familiar voice woke me. I thought I had died and gone to heaven. Samantha was holding my hand and telling me she forgave me. I could smell chicken cooking somewhere in the house. It was making my empty stomach growl.

I looked up and saw Beats.

He said, "The coyotes didn't eat her. I had something to work with." With a big smile on his face, he added, "I can raise the dead, who would have thought."

I hope you enjoyed another wild story. This was the third time I tried to write it. I felt like I had entered my own ripple in time. I was just about done the first time when I had a glitch and lost all my data except for the first nine pages of the story. I blamed Jacob. Started a second time and it blew up once again. I yelled and screamed, shook my fist at him, jumped up and down. The third time was the charm. I changed the whole story around. Same story but very different from the first two tries. The ripple in time was what did it. That's my story and I'm sticking to it. By the way, thanks Jacob! This version is much better.

It's time to stretch and get those cramps out. One last song before you go to bed. I always say you should praise the Lord. I give him praise for giving me the desire to bring you these stories of faith and hope. They may not be what you would find in a Christian bookstore, but believe me, not everyone was born to be a preacher. I have many flaws, as we all do. What we do with these flaws is what makes the person we are. Now, look up the song, "The Truth," performed by the Belonging Co, Lauren Strahm & Andrew Holt.

Get those hands up and give me a big stretch. Raise them up high and say, "Thank you, Lord. You reign."

CPSIA information can be obtained
at www.ICGtesting.com
Printed in the USA
LVHW090322031021
699315LV00003B/13